QUEEN TAKES KING

THEIR VAMPIRE QUEEN - BOOK 2

JOELY SUE BURKHART

Copyright © 2017 Joely Sue Burkhart

Cover Art by Cover Me Darling

Formatted by Tattered Quill Designs

All rights reserved. No part of this book may be reproduced, scanned, or distributed in print or electronic form without the express, written permission of the author.

This is a work of fiction. Names, characters, places and incidents are the product of the author's imagination and any resemblance to any organization, event, or person, living or dead, is purely coincidental.

Adult Reading Material

QUEEN TAKES KING

THEIR VAMPIRE QUEEN - Book 2

Published by
Joely Sue Burkhart

A Reverse Harem Vampire Romance

How many Blood will come to the vampire queen's call... and will they be able to protect her from the king?

For the first time in her adult life, Shara has plenty of money thanks to the Isador legacy--and she's not alone. Daire and Rik are devoted lovers, but they know other Blood are coming. Blood who may challenge Rik for the coveted alpha spot at her back.

As her power grows, so does her hunger. But without fangs, she fears she'll never be the queen her Blood expect. More Blood means power struggles and complications, and she has no idea how to keep everyone happy. Worse, her dreams are quickly becoming something to fear.

Moving to establish her permanent nest, she can't stop dreaming of the king. A massive monster. Chained in darkness. Lost to madness. He roars with fury in her dreams, demanding his release.

But is he the key to unraveling her own mysterious past--or the most dangerous threat of all?

For my Beloved Sis.

*Thank you to my beta readers, Sherri Meyer and Laura Walker,
and
Sherri's oldest minion for recommending
Eleanor of Aquitaine when I needed an historic figure!*

1

SHARA

Two gorgeous men asleep in my bed.

Merry fucking Christmas to me.

I stretched and felt a dull ache between my legs, and no wonder. I certainly wasn't used to having sex. Let alone with two men who were completely dedicated to blowing my mind as often as possible.

I could do without the miserable cramps though. It was so unfair that I was a vampire, but still had to deal with a period that came like clockwork.

I stared up at the ceiling, running through everything I'd learned.

Just four days ago, my life had turned upside down. I still couldn't believe it.

Mom was actually my aunt and the man I'd called Dad wasn't my biological father either.

I wasn't human. I wasn't even half human. But Dr. Borcht didn't know exactly what I was, either.

I had enough Aima blood—directly descended from the goddess, Isis—to be a vampire queen. Hence the two lovers, who called themselves my Blood, sworn to protect and please me, no matter what I ordered. (So they claimed.)

At some point when coming into my power the first time, I'd even died, though being a descendant of the goddess of resurrection had some major advantages.

Last night, I'd killed the man who murdered Mom. I'd burned him to death. With my blood.

It scared me how… okay… I was about that.

I didn't want to end up being a greater monster myself than the ones who'd killed my parents.

I'd never killed anything before, except the occasional spider. Greyson Isador was a murderer. He was directly responsible for both of my parents' deaths, and countless other humans he'd turned into his thralls, the gray lifeless demon-creatures who'd hunted me my entire life.

He deserved to die.

That didn't make me feel better. Because I was still glad he was dead. And I was glad I'd been the one to finish him.

What else would I end up being glad about?

I had no idea what time it was, but I didn't think I'd be able to fall back asleep. I tried to get up carefully without waking up the guys, but I lifted my head and Alrik's eyes popped open.

As my alpha Blood, he was the biggest, baddest man I'd ever seen. He looked like he'd walked off a superhero movie set.

"My queen?" He whispered, but my other Blood lifted his head too.

"Sorry, I didn't mean to wake you."

"We live to serve." Daire stretched as only a cat can do, like every muscle in his body had a kink in it. "Even if it's fucking six o'clock in the morning."

"It is? How do you know?"

He rolled over and faced me, smiling so his dimple showed in his cheek. "I have no idea what time it is. It just feels early. Are you well?"

"No," Alrik said before I could, a frown grooving his forehead. "You hurt. Is this normal when you menstruate?"

"Unfortunately, yes. Though that's a human thing. I have no idea why I'm so lucky to have cramps like this when I'm not even human."

I sat up, trying to think of a graceful way to escape to the bathroom when I'm sure I was bleeding heavily. "I really should have put a tampon in last night."

Alrik made a low, rumbly noise that was somewhere between the growl of a distant storm and the thunderous purr of some great beast. "There's no need, my queen. If you lie back, I'll be more than happy to clean you up."

Ew. Gross. It made me cringe. Human sensibilities, I guess.

Daire cocked an eyebrow at me. "It's our nature. Even more so for Rik. He'll be hard pressed to leave you alone for an hour when you smell so..." He inhaled deeply, running his nose along my arm. "Good."

As the alpha Blood, Alrik would evidently be the one to mate with me, if I ever decided to have a child. Aima women only menstruated when they were in heat, ready to breed. The better to attract the male vampire, my sweet. So me bleeding was going to drive the big guy nuts.

He rubbed his face across my shoulder to my back, one big arm coming around my waist. His fingers dipped lower, cupping my pussy, and he shuddered against me.

Power rose in me. The hairs on my arms prickled, the charge building in the air around me. Yesterday, I'd tried to tap that power to fix my hair, and about blew the top of my head off. And I'd only been flowing a trickle. This felt like a mess.

A mess to me, maybe, but not to him. He rubbed his hand over me, not stroking me, exactly, but just holding my pussy, treasuring me. Blood and all. Despite my hang ups, my head still fell back against his shoulder and I opened my legs wider. Need rose in me. His mouth pressed against my ear, his breath hot on my skin. His tongue dipped into my ear as his fingers slid deeper. One finger inside me, his thumb rubbing my clit. So slow and languorous, as if he was in no rush. I'd always thought foreplay involved the guy getting the girl off as quickly as possible so he could get on with his own business.

But not Rik. And not Daire either.

I opened my eyes, checking to see where Daire had gone.

"I asked him to start the coffee," Rik whispered against

my ear, twisting his finger deeper, making my hips arch into his hand.

"You asked him to leave?"

"Yes. I'm his alpha. He'll do as I tell him. Even when he doesn't want to."

"What if I wanted him here? With us?"

Rik's hand stilled. "With a thought, I'll call him back, my queen. But remember his nature. He won't be able to resist licking what I merely pet."

My stomach trembled, my brain quailed, but my body thought that was a brilliant idea. Through his bond, I could feel his hunger. He wanted to bury his head between my thighs too. More than anything. Need pounded like a jackhammer in his skull. He needed to mate. More, his queen needed him, evidenced by the blood, which to him meant breeding time. It was meant to drive him crazy, and it was.

Yet he only stroked me.

Just feeling his need was almost enough to convince me I should allow him to do as he wished. It would have been really easy for him to kiss and cajole me into going along with his need. In fact, I couldn't believe he wasn't, especially as badly as he felt. His urge to mate was just as urgent as his need to breathe after being submerged in water. He was drowning, driven to the point of madness by his own body's impulses. Yet without the bond, I wouldn't have even known.

"I would like nothing better than to feast on your blood, from whatever part of your body it came. But you would not enjoy it, and so I will not, either. If there comes a time you'd welcome me in that regard, know that I'm more than eager. Any of us will be. It would be a priceless gift to us. And yes, the power kick from a breeding queen is insane."

I was relieved—but a little disappointed and guilty too. I didn't like denying him when he'd do anything to please me. "But I'm not breeding. It's just my period."

"We don't know that you aren't breeding too. And by your scent…" he rubbed his face up the column of my throat and pressed his nose behind my ear, up under my hair, and breathed deeply. "You're breeding. That's what your scent and your body are telling me. Fuck. Would it upset you if I tasted your blood from my hand?"

Blood itself didn't bother me. It was just the whole period aspect that put a damper on sharing that particular blood. But I'd love to watch him do something that would bring him so much pleasure. I pulled away enough to turn and face him. "You can on one condition. I want you to come when you taste it."

His eyes smoldered, his mouth partly opened, his lips full like he'd been kissing me senseless for days. His fangs had descended too, making a surge of desire crest inside me. I knew the pleasure he could bring with those fangs. His vampire sensibilities knew exactly when to bite to maximize my pleasure. But this time he wouldn't have to bite to taste my blood.

Or to make me come. Because I had a feeling I was going to be able to climax just from watching him.

Reaching over with his clean left hand, he dragged his palm up my slit, hand cupped, catching everything he could get. He wrapped his bloody right hand around his dick and hissed. His nostrils flared, a muscle in his cheek ticking as he restrained himself. But he didn't pump his cock at all. He just smeared my blood over himself, running his hand up over the head and down the sides. His shoulders bunched, his neck corded, and I shuddered at the memory of having him on top of me. Inside me. All that power. All that force. Thrusting into me.

He lifted his left hand up to his mouth, closed his eyes, and tipped his palm, letting my blood slide into his mouth. I felt the rush of fire exploding through his veins. His muscles twitched like a live wire jumped inside him. He let out a guttural cry and arched his back, shaking as he came, hard. Every shudder pushing me closer to the edge as he licked his palm. Sucked his fingers. Making sure to get every drop.

And I couldn't help myself. I threw myself at him and locked my mouth to his throat. I bit him, willing my fangs to emerge. I wanted to have his blood filling my mouth. I wanted to hear him groan with the sweet pain as I penetrated him. I wanted to take him, possess him, as he had done to me.

He cupped my pussy again, sliding his fingers deep inside me, filling me, and climax rumbled through me. I came. But it wasn't what I wanted. At all.

I buried my face against his throat and fought not to cry.

"Let me—"

"No," I retorted, refusing to look up at him. "I don't want you to tear open a vein for me."

"If you hunger—"

"I want to be able to do it myself. Do other queens have this issue? Have you ever heard of a queen with no fangs?"

"You have fangs. You felt them. It's just not… time."

I pulled away, avoiding his gaze, and climbed out of bed. "I'm going to take a shower. A real shower."

"Shara…"

I paused but didn't look back at him. "I won't feed again until I can bite you myself."

"Don't say that." He got up too, coming to my side to wrap his arms around me, but I didn't soften. I didn't yield into his arms. He wanted to comfort me. Placate me. Distract me. "You need blood, now more than ever. You need to be strong."

"I'm Isis's last queen and I can't even take blood myself. Everyone keeps telling me that the other queens will want me dead, but they'll only laugh when they see what a sorry excuse for a vampire I am. I can't even bite my own Blood to feed myself."

He rested his chin on my head, his arms steady around me. "This Blood in particular will open every vein on his body for you before you can even ask."

Steel hardened inside me. "As Isis is my witness, I won't ask."

ALRIK

I stared at the bathroom door worriedly. She needed to feed. This was a crucial time in her ascension as the Isador queen. The more blood she took, the more powerful she'd be, and yeah, she was already fucking powerful. But it was raw and untapped. She needed time to hone her magic, and she wouldn't have that time if she wasn't strong enough to keep the other queens away based on sheer strength.

More troubling, though, was her adamancy. The ancient gods loved nothing more than one of their creations making such an oath, which opened the door for the deity to fuck with them. I didn't believe Isis hovered over this house listening to Her last queen's words, but that kind of refusal might have drawn the goddess's attention. And when a goddess wanted Her last queen strong...

She'd answer that prayer, that oath, but not necessarily in a way that Shara would approve.

I went back upstairs to the tower room and stripped the bed linens for her. It would upset her if she came back in and found Daire crouched on the mattress feeding on the soiled spots, and without a doubt, I knew he'd do exactly that. She could have called the blood to her and returned her energy somewhat, but she'd been too upset. Her emotions were volatile, and not just because of her period. Though that certainly didn't help.

Her whole world had changed in the span of a few days, and this was just the tip of the iceberg.

:Rik, you need to see this.: Daire said through our bond, alert, but not alarmed, so I didn't tromp downstairs like we were under attack.

I found him in the living room with the television on the local news station. As soon as I entered, he unpaused the show.

"A clothing store in the Power and Light District was vandalized overnight," the anchorwoman said. "They provided an exclusive to us of the security camera footage. Brace yourself, folks, because this is definitely something in the realm of 'we have no idea what this is.'"

A grainy black-and-white film played on the screen, displaying the front entrance. The glass exploded and two shapes appeared on screen.

I groaned. Thralls. Captured on human surveillance.

The news channel paused the security tape with a thrall prominently frozen on the screen. It was definitely human-shaped, though bent and lanky. Its eyes glowed oddly and teeth glistened.

"Police believe that two people dressed like monsters in order to break into the store. But what we find odd is that the store owner doesn't believe anything was stolen. One dressing room was ransacked but other than the front door, there was no other damage and nothing else was taken. I don't know, Bob. Does that look like two punks dressed up for Halloween—in December, no less—to you?"

The other anchorman, Bob, shuddered. "It sure doesn't, Helen."

We'd had thralls caught on television before. It wasn't ideal, but Shara was right. With modern technology, it was impossible to prevent detection. Most of the time, the human mind dismissed what it couldn't understand. Or came up with some other explanation, like kids dressed up in costumes. That was easier to believe than monsters roaming the countryside. "That's not too bad," I said to Daire, but he shook his head and let the show continue.

"Maybe it's a coincidence," a woman said into a male journalist's microphone. I recognized her as the sales woman who'd helped us yesterday. "But we had an unusual customer yesterday who used that changing room. A very beautiful woman, with two incredible men. They referred to her as queen."

"Queen?" The man asked. "Like 'Your Majesty?'"

"Yes. He called her that. He even went down on his knees at one point. And she spent..." The sales woman's eyes widened, catching herself before blurting out an amount. "A lot. We're supposed to deliver it today."

"The hell you are," I retorted.

"I gave her our address," Daire said.

"Fuck. The last thing we need right now is a bunch of curious reporters spreading tales about a queen in Kansas City."

"We'd better call Gina."

The doorbell rang. Daire checked through the peephole before opening the door to the very person we'd been talking about. She saw the television on and nodded. "Good. You've seen. Has she?"

"Not yet." My first reaction was to send Daire to knock on the door, but that was ridiculous when I had a bond with her. I just hesitated to intrude when she was obviously upset and needed some space, and Daire's lighter personality might be more welcome than mine. :*My queen.*:

:*Yes?*:

Her emotions felt calmer in the bond. She'd mentioned a bath before too. Evidently the hot water was definitely something I needed to be sure she indulged in when she was upset and stressed out. However, she was still worried she might never be the queen I expected her to be, which was nonsense. I had no expectations other than she take my blood whenever she wanted. I let her feel that shining in the bond, though I didn't say the words. :*We have a situation. Gina's here to discuss.*:

Mentally she sighed. :*I'll be right there.*:

2
———

SHARA

situation. Hmmm. That didn't bode well. Maybe somebody saw us driving off the monsters last night? Or me lighting up a person on fire?

Not a person, I reminded myself, though my conscience twinged.

I pulled on my tattered jeans, wincing at the stains. I really needed to do laundry. That was one benefit of working at hotels so often. I'd been able to get my things washed for free.

The washer and dryer were down in the basement. I hadn't been down there since I'd finally broken out of the safe room. I didn't really want to see it. I didn't want to remember.

Bracing myself, I carefully tapped my period blood. My

nerves lit on fire, my hair shooting up with energy, but I managed a quick power wash of my clothes and then let the energy go. Whew. Intense. My hair had instantly dried but looked like I'd crimped it in a waffle iron. Rather than try to do anything else with it, I pulled it back in a ponytail. I checked my pocket and then dug around in my messy bag until I could find my pocketknife. I just felt better when I had a weapon on me, even if it was a small one.

:*You have two formidable weapons at your disposal at all times.*:

I'd forgotten he was probably eavesdropping through the bond. At that thought, I felt a sense of withdrawing from me. He truly was trying his best to deal with my prickly pride and grumpy mood and he certainly didn't want to "eavesdrop." Which implied a violation of privacy.

Rather than say anything, I reached through the bond and pressed against him in a mental hug, picturing my arms around his neck, my face on his throat. Even though that instantly made my stomach knot with hunger. And started the cycle of emotional turmoil all over again.

Giving myself a mental shake, I went downstairs to see what was wrong. Daire handed me a cup of coffee and I curled up in the corner of one of the leather sofas. "Good morning, Gina. What's brought you over here so early?"

"Early?" She laughed as if I'd told a joke. "It's nearly noon."

I shot a glare at Daire. He'd told me it was six o'clock. He flashed that dimple and I instantly forgave him.

"Ever since you disappeared five years ago, I've had a team mining all local news stories that we could get our hands on that had anything to do with a 'monster' or unexplained and creepy events. I hoped we'd be able to find you that way, but you were always one step ahead."

"I had to be," I muttered, trying not to remember. Running, always running. Knowing where the closest bus stop was. Never unpacking. Never feeling safe.

Gina unfolded a large map and spread it out on the table, using the corner of the legacy box that I'd totally forgotten about to hold down one side. "Everything we felt was at least a seventy-five percent chance of being a thrall sighting, we plotted on the map. It's pretty interesting when you look at several years worth of data."

I leaned forward, cradling the warm cup in both hands. At first all I saw clumps of red dots, mostly centered around New York, New Orleans, and Dallas. The locations of the three other known American queens. "Wow, so the other queens are attacked regularly too? I guess I thought I was the only one, that it was a sign of my weakness."

Alrik sat down beside me. Too close, actually, but I wasn't about to complain. He felt too good pressed against me. "You were never weak. You just hadn't come into your power yet. And yes, thralls are drawn to the nearest queen, not necessarily the weakest. That's why I wanted to follow thralls, in the hope that we'd find a queen who was alone and in hiding."

The center of the map was scattered with red dots with no discernible pattern. Unless you knew I'd been on the run in mostly the Midwest. Of course there were many in Kansas City, but the stickers had faded a bit and were a slightly different dye lot. There hadn't been an attack in Kansas City in years.

Until I noticed a bright new sticker smack dab in the southern portion where Stuller should be.

"You're still plotting the sightings."

"Of course," Gina said. "And more importantly, I would be surprised if the other conciliari were not doing exactly the same thing. So they will be quick to note last night's events."

"We made the news?"

"Oh yeah." Daire hit play and allowed me to watch the tape. "I'm expecting the nice talkative saleslady to show up here anytime with the bill and hopefully no cameras and reporters."

"Well, I guess it's a good thing I saw where I want to move last night."

Gina's eyes lit up. "Excellent, I can't wait to assist you in procuring a nest, but you don't have to move if you don't want to."

"The last thing we want is to end up on the news. I mean, isn't there some Triune law against that sort of thing? If not there should be."

"The Triune definitely would not look favorably upon a major news story featuring the Aima, but some coverage is unavoidable in this day and age. It's not the end of the world and you certainly don't have to leave if you're not ready."

"What do you recommend?"

Gina tipped her head. "That depends on you. Will you

want to retain this home in the future and return occasionally? Or would you rather sell it outright and distance yourself from this location?"

My immediate thought was to sell it, but I didn't answer right away. I took several sips of my coffee, thinking. I had some good memories here, but I didn't have to keep the house to preserve those memories. There were painful ones, too. Every time I looked down at the back entrance to the park, I'd remember my parents' deaths.

And it was ridiculous to own more than one big house.

Daire made a low snarky sound, drawing my attention. "You already own more than one big house."

"I do?"

Gina's eyes widened. "Oh yes. We've invested in property all over the globe for generations. You'd be hard pressed to go to a major city in Europe or Asia and not have your own home ready and waiting."

"Ready? And waiting? Like this?"

"Of course. If the Triune calls, you would need to go immediately, and there won't be time to set up and open a house. They're all fully stocked with goods and perfectly maintained, ready for occupants at a moment's notice. Some are large enough that they're staffed all year around."

"You worry," Alrik whispered against my ear, his voice low and rumbling like thunder. "My queen does not worry. You should have all the houses you could ever desire."

His voice thrummed a chord inside me. My mouth ached, but that only pissed me off, because I wanted what I couldn't have. For whatever reason, my fangs hadn't come in. They may never come in. So the knife-thrust of hunger deep in my gut was torture, pure and simple.

I pushed away that longing, hardening my voice. "I guess I'll keep it, then."

"Very well," Gina replied. "My next question, then, is whether you care to be a bit of a celebrity, or if you'd rather hide in obscurity when you visit this house. Because we can let her think you're a minor royal princess from some obscure country… or you can lock the doors, draw the blinds, and post security to run her and anyone else off."

I didn't have to think about this one. "I've been hiding all my life. I'm sick to death of it."

She grinned. "Then let's have some fun with our nosy salesperson."

3

SHARA

Gina gave me her laptop to search for the house I'd dreamed about while she made a few calls. It didn't take me long to find the manor house in Eureka Springs, situated on a beautiful river with forty acres of Arkansas forest.

It was for sale, of course. Because when a goddess sends you a dream house…

You can damned well expect to find it available for purchase.

Though the price tag made me choke.

She looked over my shoulder. "Oh, excellent. Nice size, nice location. I'll have Angela look up the history on the place, see how long it's been on the market, and make the offer today."

"How long will it take? A few months?"

She laughed and patted me on the shoulder. "Oh honey, I see that I still have some impressing to do. Give me a few minutes and I'll let you know."

She walked over to the fireplace and started talking on her phone.

I turned my attention back to the real estate listing for my house.

My manor.

It was insane and awesome. Medieval towers rose above the trees and the main house had a Gothic castle feel. The pictures of the inside were just as cool. Rich, old wood paneling, hand-carved stair cases, huge stone fireplaces, and the master bedroom...

The ceiling soared two full stories above with exposed century-old rafters. I could already picture a huge bed beneath those rafters. Maybe two big beds pushed together... And candles. Lots of candles. And maybe something ridiculous like silk sheets and satin pillows and fur.

Nah. I had Daire's fur to stroke.

Alrik stood beside me and somehow managed to swing a leg around me, sliding in behind me so he could cradle me against him.

I shot a wary glance at Gina, unsure what she'd think of such intimate contact.

"She won't care," he murmured against my ear. "She's served queens before. She's served *breeding* queens before. She knows how hard it is for me to sense your need and not do anything about it."

"I don't need anything right now."

He didn't say anything. He didn't have to. We both knew I was lying through my very human teeth. Need crawled through me, a clawing, desperate hunger.

Lightly, he stroked my arms, but otherwise he didn't touch me, at least with his hands. His thighs pressed against me on either side, his dick hard against my buttocks, throbbing every once in a while to make sure I was paying attention. But he didn't rub it on me.

His scent made my mouth water. I wanted his skin and muscle in my mouth. A good solid grip. I wanted to sit back and look down at his gorgeous body stretched out in my bed and see toothmarks all over him.

Not rings of human teeth.

But punctures.

I swallowed the drool pooling in my mouth and concentrated on the pictures. A huge formal dining room held a heavy antique table that could probably seat twenty.

Twenty Blood. All like him and Daire.

I leaned back more fully against him, and he wrapped himself around me. Literally, it felt like I was wearing him, a heavy man-sized cloak of heat and muscle that enveloped me.

Gina hung up and stepped back, a huge smile on her face. He was right—she didn't bat an eye at him cradling me between his thighs. "Marissa's on her way to Arkansas this very moment. The house should be officially yours by five tonight."

My mouth fell open. "Today?"

"Money moves mountains. The seller was eager to accept our offer and the place was already vacated. Marissa will hire a general contractor as soon as she lands and take a crew out to make sure the house is in good condition. Evidently it's been empty for awhile, so it might need some repairs. Otherwise, you can take possession as soon as you're ready."

I didn't know what to say. I actually teared up a little. To have someone move those mountains for me was incredible. To have the money to do what I wanted on a whim…

"She'll need a full staff," Daire said. "Would the housekeeper here be willing to move with us? Because she fucking rocks."

"He, actually. Timothy Winston, a very British butler, who has told me countless times that he misses having people to serve, rather than just keeping the house in order. I'm sure he would love to formally take charge of your household. With a nest so large, you'll need an appropriate staff, and Winston has the experience to manage them for you. He doesn't have family of his own and has worked for the Isador house for the last forty years. "

I frowned. "Forty years? The poor man should retire!"

"The people who work for Isador do so for many reasons. Most of us have a touch of Aima blood that improves our longevity and health. As my grandmother attests, some of your staff will work right up to one hundred happily. They live to serve, and of course, they're very well compensated. More, though, most of us have a deep sense of loyalty to your family and house. Our families have worked for your family for generations. We take care of each other. We know things are... different. So thralls creeping around don't bother us."

As she talked, Daire came toward me. I thought he was going to sit on the couch beside us, but he dropped to the floor and wiggled around until he had his butt planted between my feet. He leaned back against my knees, worming his way deeper between my legs, which pushed me wider against Alrik. So in the end, he was between both of our legs.

And I was sandwiched between them.

Two glorious walls of muscle and heat.

Gina's lips quirked. "Neither do Blood hanging all over their queen."

"The newest Blood is close." Daire's voice rumbled with the deep purr of his warcat. "Just making sure he knows his place."

I closed my eyes, feeling for this new man's location. The deep glow of his red lit the tapestry, the thunder of hooves loud, like a heartbeat. "Where's that?"

Alrik tightened his thighs on me, which pressed me tighter to Daire. "A better way to phrase it would be to say so he knows where his place is *not*. His place is not at your back."

Daire let out a growling purr. "And not between your thighs."

4

DAIRE

I wanted to shift to my warcat, but I didn't want to appear defensive, rude and jealous, especially when Rik was taking a new Blood so well.

He didn't have as much to lose as I did. He already knew he was alpha.

I had no idea how far down the ladder I'd fall as our queen took more Blood. Fucking hell. I didn't even know if I'd be allowed to sleep with her and Rik once more Blood came to her call.

My throat tightened and I fought down the warcat. He'd only pace and claw and roar at this new Blood, and upset Shara. So instead, he paced and clawed inside me so hard I could barely breathe.

From the throaty roar of the engine, the man had the

pedal pressed to the floor as he drove up the street. Yeah, I'd flown to her side too. As soon as I'd felt her. I couldn't fault him for screeching to a halt outside. The iron gate wouldn't keep him from her, even if Gina had locked it shut behind her. He'd just vault over it. Easy.

"What do I say?" Shara whispered, her thighs trembling against my shoulders. "Is there a handbook for this?"

"Talk to him as you did us," Rik replied. "Gauge your interest in him, and his willingness to be loyal to you. You'll feel it. You'll know."

"And if you need to taste him first, I'll be happy to draw his blood for you." I regretted the words as soon as they were out of my mouth. I sounded too weak. Too eager. Too desperate. I hated it.

Gina moved to the door. "Should I let him in?"

"Hold on." Shara wrapped her arms around my neck, her chin on top of my head.

Then she stroked my bond.

Her mind reached into me, moonlight and rainbows, sweet jasmine on a gentle night's breeze. She touched my hissing, furious warcat and he rolled over on his back and purred, winding like fur through our bond.

The man thumped at the door hard enough it shook the entire wall.

"Not yet," Shara said absently, reaching deeper.

I knew she could see my fear. I didn't try to hide it. I couldn't hide anything from my queen, not if she was determined to find it. Her hand cupped my chin and she pulled my face around so she could look into my eyes.

"You're not going anywhere." She spoke softly, but her words rang with power, binding me to her. I saw us in bed with Rik, him at her back, me wrapped around her and him. Cat or not. She didn't care. She wanted me there. She made me feel it. She showed me the aching hole in her heart if I wasn't there with her.

"Let him in," she said to Gina, but then she leaned down and pressed her mouth to mine.

I sank into her, willing her to take me. Use me. Drain me. Whatever she needed. I would give it. Gladly. I would knock out my fangs and give them to her so she could feed.

Rik's bond flared to life in me too. While we'd had a bond for many years, we didn't constantly listen to one another's thoughts. It was exhausting and even Aima liked a little privacy in their own minds. Where she was magic and pearly rainbows, Rik was molten lava, streaming down the side of a massive volcano. Hot, but slow. Deep. Controlled. With enough strength to rock the entire world if he needed to.

But the volcano's fury was contained. He might show a crack here and there, but generally, he kept his feelings under lock and key, buried deep inside him.

I loved him too much to go mining in his private spaces. But this time, he let me in.

He wasn't as calm and confident and assured as I'd thought. He felt… young, green, and ill-prepared. We'd never served a queen before so we were bound to make mistakes. Shara would make mistakes, and we had to do our best to help her. He felt that pressure acutely, especially her lack of fangs and how she fed. It wasn't a problem for us—but he feared for her. He feared her pride and determination to do things her own way would offend the goddess. And when a goddess was offended...

How could we protect her against the mother of her own line?

Shara lifted her head, staring into my eyes. One corner of her lips quirked, but her eyes smoldered. Her hunger roared in our bond, and if she wouldn't have been ashamed before this new Blood, I would have torn my wrist open for her immediately. :Better?:

:I love you, my queen.:

:I love you, my furry warcat Blood.:

"I have a few ideas for our other human visitor," Gina said. "By your leave, Your Majesty, I'll make a few calls."

Heavy footsteps thumped into the room, drawing her attention. "Of course, thank you, Gina."

Since I was still fully connected to Rik, I felt his initial reaction as the man entered the room.

Overwhelming dread.

Not something I expected to feel from my alpha. Ever.

ALRIK

I recognized the new Blood.

Few of our kind carried the kind of scars or signs of age that he did because we healed and aged so well. Even though he wore jeans and a simple long-sleeved button-up shirt, I could almost hear the jingle of chain mail and the unmistakable sound of steel being drawn. He stepped into the living room, drawing Shara's attention, and I heard the ticking of the timer counting down to the end of my life much too quickly.

I pulled back from Daire, but it was too late. He felt my initial reaction and his eyes narrowed, claws unsheathing in his mind.

:Hold,: I ordered, willing him with every ounce of alpha drive I possessed to obey me. Claws sheathed, he turned to look at the new Blood.

:He doesn't look like much,: Daire said with a snort. :Your rock troll will smash him to bits.:

I didn't reply, but concentrated on locking down all my uneasiness. Control. No doubt. No hesitation. I'd tested the new Blood last night. I'd felt his response. He wouldn't challenge me for alpha. He wouldn't have to.

The man's step hesitated slightly when he saw us, especially Daire on the floor. He came a few steps closer, but kept his distance, his gaze locked on Shara. Daire and I were beneath his notice at this point, and I couldn't fault him for that. I'd have been hard pressed to look anywhere but her too when I first felt her call.

But he shocked the hell out of me when he knelt and then stretched out face first on the floor, arms spread wide, hands empty. "My queen, I come in peace in answer to your call."

"What are you doing? Get up. I don't require such..." Her words fell off, as if she only just realized that Daire sat on the floor at her feet. "Please, you don't have to do that. Who are you?"

He lifted his head and moved his hands in front of him, braced palm down on the floor, but he still didn't look into my eyes. He didn't want to antagonize the alpha. At least not yet. "Guillaume de Payne, Your Majesty."

Daire twitched so hard it jolted her body against mine so I felt his alarm without tapping his bond. He recognized the name at least. A low, rumbling growl started up from his chest and he raked claws on the floor in a warning screech.

"Daire." She only said his name, but it was enough to quiet him. "What's wrong?"

"I see my reputation proceeds me." Guillaume's mouth twisted in a wry smile. "As I said, Blood, I come in peace. I come to *her* call. No queen commands me."

"What reputation?" She asked, stroking her fingers through Daire's hair to calm him.

The little fucker started to purr, already relaxing against her. It wasn't his head on the line. "He has a reputation for wooing a queen long enough to kill her alpha."

Shara shot to her feet, digging in her pocket for her knife.

It amused and touched me at the same time. That she thought to defend me, albeit with a little pocketknife that would make a Blood laugh, let alone one with Payne's reputation. Especially when she had Isador magic at her disposal. I stood too, towering over her back and the Blood on the floor. But I held my tongue. If she wanted to take this Blood, I'd say nothing. Nothing at all. Exactly as the dozens of alphas before me who'd met their fate at Payne's sword. Alpha or not, no Blood commanded his queen. Not one.

She flicked the blade open, holding it out to her side, arm stiff. "Get. Out."

"My queen—"

"I'm not your queen," she retorted. "You won't have him. Do you hear me? You won't lay a finger on him. You'll turn around and march straight out my door."

I settled my hands on her shoulders, but I didn't draw her back against me. "You should hear him out."

She shook beneath my hands. "You want me to accept him? Even if he kills you?"

Payne stayed on his belly, but looked at her evenly. "I'll swear any oath you ask of me, my queen. I'll swear to never touch your alpha, any of your Blood, whatever you wish. If you only allow me to stay in your service."

"Fuck you and fuck your oaths. Why should I trust you, a man I don't know, just because you swear you won't hurt my Blood? Why?"

His nostrils flared, his eyes narrowing with intensity. "You question my honor?"

Before she could antagonize the last living Templar knight, I stepped around her and offered a hand to the man on the floor. "She doesn't know who or what you are, since she wasn't raised in a nest among us. I would not question your honor nor your word."

Guillaume took my hand and allowed me to draw him to his feet. We didn't shake hands exactly, but took each other's measure. I felt the immense weight of his age, century upon century stacked like slabs of granite across his shoulders. He'd lived a lifetime as a knight, was captured and tortured for years by King Philip's henchmen, and was nearly burned at the stake. That had only been the 1300s. And though I towered a good foot above him, I'd never felt so small and young in my entire life. This man was a living legend and he had come to serve my queen, and indirectly, me.

"Alrik Isador," I said quietly, not looking away from the dark burning intensity in his eyes.

"Guillaume de Payne, born of house Ashere."

Ashere, the line founded from the ancient mother goddess, Asherah. No wonder the man had managed to live for so long. I turned to Shara and held my hand out to her. She stepped around Daire and warily joined me, squeezing my hand like a lifeline, her knife gripped fiercely in her right hand. "My queen, Shara Isador."

"I thought all Blood took their queen's house name."

He inclined his head but didn't drop his gaze from her. "They do, unless they're me. I've never taken a queen's name, but I'm willing for you."

"Why?"

"Because no queen commands me to come to you. I come freely to your call. I'll accept your name. I'll accept your alpha."

"Why?" she repeated, her voice dropping lower. I felt the first prickle of her power, as if she only just remembered that she was a formidable queen with magic of her own.

Guillaume's nostrils flared again and he inhaled deeply.

He jerked his gaze to mine. "She's breeding. Young, yet laden with power, without a nest of her own, and only two inexperienced Blood to guard her. And you haven't killed me on sight? You're either a fool, or…"

He didn't finish the sentence. He didn't have to. Isis's blood only ran through my veins thanks to Her queen's willingness to share her blood and power with me, but I felt Her certainty. She had sent this man to be Her last queen's Blood. Who was I to object, even though his words stung? I was inexperienced. So was Daire. We'd never served a queen before. Let alone one with Shara's potential stature.

He lunged toward her so quickly she couldn't react. Eyes wide, she stared up at him, with her knife buried in his stomach.

"My queen. Take me. I'm yours."

5

SHARA

I stabbed him. Or rather, he stabbed himself on my knife. Hot blood poured over my hand.

I tried not to breathe. I didn't want to draw the scent of his blood into my body. Because I knew what would happen.

It already was. And it was already too late. It'd been too late the moment his red flame flared in my mind.

He smelled like horse. A big, steaming hot, pawing the ground, rearing up angry warhorse. With a hint of ash and sulfur swirling around him.

My mouth throbbed where my nonexistent fangs should be. My stomach knotted with hunger. My hair flared out, tearing free of the rubber band to float about my head. And yeah, my pussy clenched with need, aching so hard that my eyes fluttered closed a moment and a groan of pain escaped. Fuck these cramps. Fuck my stupid hormones. Fuck this need to bite and rend and tear when I had no fangs. And fuck this desperate urge to bury this stranger's dick inside me as quickly as possible.

I started to withdraw the blade, but his fingers wrapped around my hand, pulling the blade deeper into his body. A man I didn't know. Bleeding for me.

Making me ache like I hadn't had sex in years.

"Let go of me."

My voice sounded strange to my ears, fragile and breathy, so unlike me. At least he obeyed, his fingers leaving my wrist. I let go of the blade, leaving the knife in his body, and turned away. Found Daire, still on the floor, and I went to him. I dropped into his arms and buried my face against his throat. Seeking his scent, trying to get the other man out of my head.

"I apologize for any offense I gave in ignorance, my queen."

Daire cuddled around me. I could smell his fur even though he hadn't shifted. And I still wanted the other man.

"It's expected," he whispered into my ear, so softly. "You need him. You need Rik. You need me. We know it."

"I don't want to need anyone else," I whispered back.

But I couldn't stop myself from lifting my bloody hand to my mouth.

I heard a groan and a heavy thud, as if Rik had punched the new Blood in the gut, but I was afraid to look. Afraid I'd bury my face in the stranger's stomach like a lioness settling down over her kill, desperate to get more of his blood. Hunger swirled in me like a hurricane, tearing at my control, eroding my senses. It hurt so fucking bad.

But I didn't want them to pity me. I didn't want them to have to help me do something so... basic. How could I be a vampire queen if I couldn't even bite and feed myself?

"She's not feeding enough," the stranger said, his voice hoarse. "You must take better care of her, alpha."

"She refuses," Rik answered, his voice even. But I heard his worry and frustration aching in the bond. "She's not fully Aima and doesn't have fangs."

"The fuck she's not full Aima," he rasped. "You don't feel her power? No fucking way."

The new Blood sounded... rough. Like he was sick. Or hurt. Surely I hadn't wounded him that badly. We were Aima. We healed easily. Quickly. But he did have a lot of scars and with his gray hair, he must be old, even for Aima. What did that mean—a few centuries? More? One pale, jagged scar down his forehead, another around his neck, and his hands looked... misshapen, almost. Like too many bends in his fingers.

I dared a quick peek over my shoulder. Shocked, I turned around fully.

He lay on the floor, gasping, his face as gray as his hair. He clutched the wound in his stomach and blood pooled through his fingers and ran down his side. Rik had gone down to one knee and supported his upper body.

"What's wrong with him?"

"He hasn't fed in... awhile." Rik offered his forearm to the man. "Our queen needs you hale and strong."

"Thank you, but no," Guillaume said, his voice weak. "I can't drink from any but queens. It's my curse and my strength."

Blood. It called me. Sang a sweet melody. Crooning to my power, stroking my hunger to a fevered pitch. I didn't want to feed if I didn't have fangs. I'd sworn I wouldn't. But I found myself crawling across the floor toward them.

"When did you last feed?" Rik asked him. "Which queen did you serve?"

"I haven't served in over a hundred years."

I jerked to a halt, surprise shaking me out of stupor I'd fallen into. My cheeks flushed. I was on the floor. On my hands and knees. Leaning down to lap at a dying man's stomach. A man who'd only walked in five minutes ago.

But neither Blood looked at me with any accusation or condemnation. In fact, Rik looked downright relieved to see blood smeared on my face.

"Feed, my queen," Guillaume whispered, even though his head lolled to the side. "I offer my blood freely to you though I have little power remaining. Take what you need."

I tugged his shirt up enough to see the puncture wound. It wasn't an ugly or big cut, so I still didn't completely understand why such a small injury had literally floored him.

That crazy melody started in my head again. Like if I just listened hard enough, I'd hear the most beautiful song ever to be played on this earth. All I needed to do was to taste him.

I pressed my lips to the puncture and his blood filled my mouth. Sweeter than the other two men's, almost like a glass of dessert wine with a chocolate chaser. The symphony rose in me, a rising flurry of drums and strings and horns that made me lock my mouth hard to his side and drink my fill.

Even if it killed him.

It suddenly dawned on me that he was dying. Literally.

The flow from his side had slowed to a trickle and his skin was clammy against my mouth. I raised my head, alarmed to see how ill he looked. His cheeks were sunken and hollowed out, though his eyes still blazed with dark fire.

He would lie here and die if I did nothing to save him, and his only thought would be relief that I'd at least feasted once on his blood.

How could I not trust someone willing to make that kind of sacrifice?

I offered him my wrist. He lifted his hand to draw me close, but his arm flopped down weakly to the floor. I pressed my wrist to his mouth for him. Ever so gently, he pierced me. It was almost sweet the careful way he bit into my skin. With a few swallows of my blood, his color returned. He managed to sit up on his own, his fingers wrapping around my wrist.

In a vise. Harder. His eyes blazed and he gulped faster, his mouth like a hot branding iron on my arm.

"Shara..." Rik growled.

"It's all right," I said, waving him off. "He needs a lot. I can take it."

"Not when you're not feeding yourself."

Urgency rose in me. He needed my blood. A great deal of it. His hunger ravaged through our new fragile bond like a swarm of locusts devouring every scrap of greenery. He needed. He burned. He would die if I didn't save him, and the loss of the last Templar knight in this world would be too great a travesty to bear. I heard Her silent promise in my head. If Guillaume de Payne died, so would I.

I had to bring him back to full strength.

Sweat broke out on my forehead, my heart beating too quickly.

Rik jerked me into his arms and locked his own wrist to my mouth. Blood. I felt the torn skin against my lips and sent him a shot of accusation through our bond. He winced, but didn't relent. He had to protect me, take care of me, even if that meant feeding me when I'd sworn I wouldn't. Fat lot of good that did me. I'd tasted this new man too.

And still didn't have a fucking pair of fangs to show for it.

His blood steadied me, though. My heart slowed back down. A languorous pleasure flowed over me. I fed one, while my alpha fed me. I connected them. I was their source, their heart, three hearts beating as one. In that moment, we were fully connected.

Except one was left out. Watching. Hurt. But afraid to intrude.

I sent a mental call and Daire came to us. I wasn't sure

exactly what I wanted from him. I just wanted him to be a part of this. He needed to be touching me. Feeding. Connected.

His fingers settled on the fly of my jeans, a silent question. My hips arched up to him, so he unbuttoned them and tugged the denim down my thighs. My head was on Rik's lap, his arm around me, his wrist still in my mouth. Guillaume still fed from my wrist like a starving man had found a table laden with a fantastic feast. And Daire lapped just as eagerly between my thighs.

It should have horrified me. My pants were around my ankles and I was bleeding heavily. We were all on the floor in the living room in broad daylight. We were expecting an overly inquisitive human to arrive at any time. Goddess only knew when Gina would be back. But I couldn't find it in myself to care.

Not when the symphony rose ever higher, a sweet piercing crescendo that hurt to hear. It was too beautiful for this earth. Tears leaked from my eyes and I came so hard I blacked out, only it wasn't dark at all. The music exploded with color. Too many for my eyes to even acknowledge or make sense of. Magical music that pleased our goddess. Greatly.

Isis smiled, her eyes glowing like a million stars against black velvet and stroked my cheek.

"Well done, my daughter. Well done indeed."

6

SHARA

I didn't open my eyes right away. In fact, I didn't know if I was going to ever be able to look any of my Blood in the eye again. Or at least Daire.

Someone licked my wrist soothingly. Probably the new Blood. Gee something. What was his name? The stroke of his tongue didn't feel like Daire. Solemn, not playful. Tender, not teasing. Rik's arm banded around my front and I could still taste his blood, but I didn't feel his skin in my mouth. My lower body suddenly lifted and my eyes flew open.

Daire buttoned and zipped my jeans for me and dropped his chin on my pubic bone. "All clean."

Heat prickled my cheeks, but then I noticed his hair. I

reached out and stroked my fingers through strands that hung well past his shoulders now. "It's so long. Did I do that?"

He waggled his eyebrows suggestively. "You should see what else grew."

"A breeding queen has great power," the new man said to my left. "I like G. Though my queen can call me anything she desires."

His bond flowed inside me, tangled up in Rik and Daire. Touching his bond was like sliding into dark, cool water that had no end. So deep. So still. I had no sense of who he was from that small touch, and I didn't feel like I knew him well enough to go scrounging around in his head.

I turned my head to look at him and I gasped. The jagged scar across his forehead was almost completely gone. He looked so much younger now, his curly hair dark and full, his face still lined, especially between his eyes, but not haggard. I glanced at his fingers on my wrist, and they were no longer bent and twisted.

"My sincerest apologies for draining you so deeply, my queen. As you see, you wrought quite the miracle in me. When I can repay the favor and feed you deep and long, I'm eager and ready." He hesitated, his glance flickering to Rik and then back. "You need to be feeding as deeply and often as possible. It's crucial right now as you come into full power."

I sat up, avoiding everyone's gaze. "Yeah, well, there's a bit of a problem with that."

"What problem? You have three Blood with fangs, at least one with claws, and I'm always armed with blades. Direct me to which one you'd like to feed on first and I'll cut him open for you."

"I'm game," Daire purred, tipping his head to the side to show me his throat.

Someone knocked on the door. "It's me," Gina called. "I have an update for you, when you're ready."

I sighed, looking around at us. My jeans were disgusting. Again. The area rug looked like it'd been used to dispose of a body. Daire's shirt was smeared like he'd taken a roll between my thighs, and I'd stabbed the new guy. The only one relatively clean was Rik.

I gave G a warning look. "Brace yourself."

Then I closed my eyes and called the blood in the room to me.

Each drop hit me like an explosion that grew with intensity. I tried to hold it all in, but it was like trying to catch and contain a hurricane with a butterfly net. The power surged through our bonds and jumped into the Blood.

"Holy fuck," Daire panted, head hanging down.

Rik was squeezing me so hard I wheezed for breath. The new guy was face down on the floor. Groaning, he looked up at me. "The last time a queen was able to make me come so hard, without even touching me was when I spent Christmas at Angers with Eleanor of Aquitaine."

"Sorry."

He grinned, pushed up off the floor, and offered me a

hand. "A woman should never apologize for making a man come. Let alone a queen to her Blood."

I took his hand and allowed him to help me up. He didn't let me go, though he didn't pull me to him, either. He just looked at me with those dark, solemn eyes. I couldn't imagine all the things he'd seen. "Shara," I said firmly.

He inclined his head. "Shara. My queen."

I rolled my eyes. "You can come in, Gina."

He bent down and snagged my knife off the floor. He snapped it closed and offered it to me. "If you need more blades, I have plenty to spare."

At least he didn't ridicule my little blade. I shoved it in my pocket. This knife might be puny, but it'd saved me on more than one occasion.

Daire jerked his head toward the stairs. "Come with me, Guillaume. I'll show you where you can change."

"I need to grab a bag out of the car first." G lifted my hand toward his mouth. "By your leave, my queen."

I nodded and he kissed my knuckles before heading to the door. I ran my gaze over him. He looked good in jeans for being a centuries-old knight. And how many blades could he possibly have concealed on him? The jeans were tight enough I didn't think he'd have anything more than a pocket knife like mine stashed on him.

He opened the door for Gina and looked back over his shoulder at me, the first hint of lightness in his eyes and a bit of a smile easing the harsh lines of his face. "Ten, Shara, my queen."

Ten knives? Fuck, I was going to have to see it to believe it.

"I usually carry more but I was in a bit of a hurry last night when I left the hotel. My lady," he said to Gina as she stepped inside.

"Sir Guillaume, welcome." Waiting until he was outside, she stepped into the living room and lowered her voice. "Be careful, Shara. He's a fantastic catch to be sure, but I know you'd be devastated if anything happened to Alrik."

Rik grunted. "We know his reputation, but he's willing to give his oath that he won't harm any of her Blood."

"What do you mean by he's a fantastic catch?" I asked, sitting back down on the leather couch. I tried to do it gracefully, but my knees quivered and I sat a little too hard and fast.

:Bring something for Shara to eat and drink. She's weak.: Rik ordered Daire in our bond. Though he glared at me, because I knew he wanted to cut open a vein and give me more blood too.

"Oh, dear, we could gossip for days about the legend of Guillaume. First and foremost, Marne Ceresa has tried to lure him to her service for nearly a hundred years, ever since his former queen died, which is a whole other mysterious story. Once he was freed from those shackles, he swore he wouldn't be bound again. I'm definitely surprised you were able to call him to your side as Blood, and Marne will be downright pissed. She made it known long ago that no queen was to feed him, so he'd be forced to come to her, or die."

Great. The oldest living queen was going to be livid because I took the Blood she'd wanted for herself.

Guillaume came back in with a duffel bag, bowed deeply to me, and then joined Daire in the kitchen. "He hasn't had a queen for a hundred years? How is that even possible? I thought Blood became thralls when their queen died."

"As I understand it, Desideria meant to have all her Blood killed with her."

I gasped softly, and reached out to squeeze Rik's hand, pulling him closer to me.

"She would rather have all her Blood dead than serve another queen, especially Guillaume, whom she'd used for centuries as her own personal executioner to consolidate her power to lead the Triune. She ordered him to behead her own Blood one by one, until only he was left, and then she started to drink him to death."

I shivered, remembering how Daire had told me I wouldn't be able to hold enough blood in my stomach to hurt him. "That's possible?"

"It is, but it can take days depending on how strong the Blood is. She drank from him repeatedly but refused to allow him to feed. Refused him food or water. But somehow he survived and she didn't."

"You don't know how?"

"No one does, though there were rumors another queen must have helped him, though none were brave enough to admit to it. Marne was furious. With Desideria dead, she took over as the high queen of the Triune. Guillaume fled and has evaded her attempts to call him to her ever since.

And back to your original question, a Blood only becomes a thrall if they start feeding on humans. Guillaume only drank from queens."

She paused when Daire stepped back in with a gigantic sandwich and a glass of ice water for me. I couldn't focus on the food, though, because he was bleeding.

He knelt before me and looked up at me through ridiculous lashes and his longer hair that definitely emphasized his feline nature. "I had an accident with the knife."

"On your neck?" I tried to keep my tone light and teasing, but his blood called me. My hands started to tremble, my pulse jumping frantically, like I was an addict going through the shakes.

"Guillaume helped." He leaned closer, draping himself across my knees, tipping his head to bare the long, sexy line of his throat.

I. Could. Not. Resist.

I gripped the column of his throat with my teeth and drank him down, sucking on the slim, neat cut when it didn't flow quite as hard and fast as I needed. He tasted too good to resist and I wanted more.

His rumbling purr rattled against my thighs and he nestled against me, letting me take my fill. But I couldn't seem to get enough.

Rik cupped my chin, gently lifting me away. "Enough, my queen. Daire won't make it up the stairs if you drink much more."

I shuddered, my face flushing as I turned away. Gina had

just told me how Guillaume had been tortured by his queen, and I was trying to drain Daire to the point that he wouldn't be able to walk.

"Mmmm," he nuzzled my stomach, his purr still rattling my thighs. "I'm in no true danger. Rik's just being careful."

"As he should." I pushed on Daire, trying to get him off me. So I didn't lean back in and lick the trickle of blood still flowing from the cut. "Go help G. I still haven't gotten the update from Gina."

He lifted his head and kissed me softly, and then stood and padded back to the kitchen. Though he did send a flirtatious look over his shoulder.

Of course he caught me staring at his ass.

Gina coughed, probably to hide her laughter.

Through the bond, I felt Rik's readiness to give me more of his blood too, but I put a halt to that. "You already gave me blood today too, so don't even think about it."

"I'm far from weakened and you could use an alpha kick. Guillaume took more than he should have from a breeding queen, let alone one who's just come into her power. You need—"

"I'm fine." I interrupted and smiled brightly at Gina. "What update did you have?"

"I've hired a private security company to act as bodyguards." Rik started to growl and she raised her hand. "I know, I know, you're in absolute charge of her safety. The guards are for show. They're going to be outside only, at the gates and perimeter. If you drive anywhere, they'll either follow or lead the way in a separate vehicle, just to be safe. Anyone who gets too nosy will deal with them first, and that way we hopefully won't have to explain anything supernatural going on inside. These are good, solid, dependable people and if they meet your expectations, the firm is eager to take over external security in Eureka Springs as well."

My stomach rumbled and before I could move, Rik reached over and got the sandwich for me. I took it from him and started to eat—because he had that narrowed look in his eye that said he'd feed me each bite personally if I balked. It wasn't a grilled cheese sandwich, but Daire proved himself to be an impeccable sandwich king.

:*I try.*: If he was trying to sound humble, he failed miserably.

"Winston leaped at the chance to serve as your butler and is on the plane this very moment. He'll work with Marissa to ensure the house is ready for you, including hiring the staff."

"I had a few ideas of things to change, or fix..." *If that's not too much trouble,* I bit off, sure that Rik would growl about that too, and remind me again...

:*My queen does not worry. No want or wish you have is trouble.*:

"Of course. Marissa is going to take pictures of every room and angle this evening. I'll send you to the link once she's uploaded them to the cloud. She'll also include the contractor's recommendations for fixes, which right now are a new roof and central air and heating system."

I winced. A house that size...

Gina only smiled. "Which has allowed us to knock

another hundred grand off the price. The more things he identifies as needing repairs, the more money we'll save on the purchase price."

My phone buzzed on the coffee table. I'd forgotten to charge it last night so it was almost dead. I picked it up and read the text from a number I didn't know. "I guess the woman from the clothes store is here. It's the guard at the gate."

"I gave all of them the number to your phone, and they'll send updates to you if anyone tries to come inside. If you don't reply, no one will get in. I can add them to your contacts when you're ready so you can call any of them when you need to step out or want something delivered."

I passed the phone to her and she started typing rapidly. "So what's the plan with this woman?"

"I contacted the shop this morning and expressed a polite but firm request that they guard your privacy if they wanted your business. Since they want you to sign a several thousand dollar receipt, the manager agreed profusely."

My stomach did an odd little flip flop. Several thousand dollars. In clothes. I hadn't owned so many clothes in…

Rik dropped his arm around me and pulled me against him. Firmly. "I want to take her to Paris and New York for the best shopping, but maybe we should go to LA instead. I'd rather not deal with Keisha or Rosalind until we must." Through the bond, I read his intent to be sure I had at least ten or twenty Blood before we encountered either queen or entered her territory.

"Or London. No queen moved in after your mother left

and the shopping can be quite an experience. Or Abu Dhabi, I've been told, has some fantastic, one-of-a-kind shops."

"Where's Marne Ceresa located?"

"Rome."

Note to self—not going to Italy any time soon.

"The Isador jet can take you anywhere on the globe at a moment's notice, as long as we notify any queen in the city of your visit."

I'm pretty sure my mouth was hanging open. "We have a jet?"

"Two actually, though the oldest one is due for an overhaul." Gina stood and moved to the door. "Go ahead and let Frank know to send her up to the house. Just be polite, eccentric, and vague. If you need help, we're here."

I texted the new security guy and set the phone on the table so I could wipe my sweaty palms on my thighs. I'd never been too good with people. I certainly didn't know how to pretend to be some kind of celebrity.

Let alone a fucking vampire queen.

ALRIK

Shara thought so little of herself it made me a little bit crazy.

Okay, a lot crazy.

I wanted her to have everything in the world that she'd lived without. Every shopping trip. Fancy cars. Jets. Mansions. She deserved the best and the Isador legacy could easily fund it all.

Instead, she sat nervously gnawing on her lip, rubbing her palms on tattered denim that should have been thrown in the trash a year ago. In the days that we'd been with her, I hadn't seen her wear anything else other than the silver fairy dress we'd destroyed.

I was desperately afraid that she had nothing else. Literally.

And that made me want to shift to the rock troll and smash this entire house into kindling.

That she also was hungry and weak and bleeding at the same time only added to my heightened instincts. She needed. I provided. I was alpha. Her needs were my sole reason to be here with her. And I was failing.

Miserably.

I couldn't even get her to feed enough to bring her to full power.

Gina opened the door and stepped outside a moment. With some clanks and clatter, the two women dragged in a large clothes rack with items carefully wrapped in plastic.

"There's two more in the van," the woman said breathlessly.

I stood with my queen, but I wouldn't leave her side, even with two humans. :*Daire, Guillaume, we need you.*:

Both men stepped out of the kitchen. "Could you bring the other racks in from the van?"

Guillaume tipped his head at the ladies. "Of course, my pleasure."

"Oh my." The woman laughed, a hint of lasciviousness in her tone that set my teeth on edge. "So... polite."

I didn't bother with human interactions much, but I had a feeling that wasn't the word she really wanted to use.

She came to us and offered her hand to Shara. "Thank you, again, for your business, Ms. Isador."

"Thank you for delivering everything, Ms...?"

"Catherine Chambers, ma'am. We had everything cleaned and pressed, so you can wear right away. And if there's anything more I can do..."

"Actually, there is," Gina said. She gave a look at Shara that to me said sit, be comfortable, don't stand for this woman.

So I took her elbow and guided her back down to the couch. She sat more easily, so the food had helped bring some of her physical strength back.

"We'd like to know what else you told the reporters, so we can brace for any publicity that Ms. Isador may have to deal with. She's very shy and doesn't like to be in the public spotlight."

Catherine blushed and wrung her hands. "I'm so sorry. I just got caught up in the excitement and drama. I only said we'd had an unusual visitor, and I hinted that I thought you might be royalty. I never gave them your name or address. Definitely *none* of your personal information."

Shara's shoulders relaxed and she leaned against me more fully.

Gina smiled more kindly at the woman. "That's a relief. The last thing we want is a bunch of reporters hounding Ms. Isador, or she'll quite honestly go back home overseas and not return her patronage."

The threat was so gently done it took the woman a few moments to realize. "Of course. It was a blunder on my part that won't happen again. If I can do anything to be of service—"

The other Blood pushed in the carts as she said that and I gave Daire a warning nudge through the bond before he could growl at the woman.

"The silver dress I wore out of the store yesterday," Shara said, leaning forward. "Do you happen to know if you have another the same size?"

"I'm sure we do. Do you need it exchanged? Was something wrong with it?"

She floundered a moment, remembering how we'd damaged it. A beautiful soft pink flooded her cheeks and the woman's eyes flared and then she smiled.

"No worries, I'm sure we have another. I'll check when I get back to the store."

"Thank you. When you get a new shipment in, let me know. I'm sure the guys would love to drag me out shopping again."

Gina offered her business card and the woman dug in her purse to find the credit card receipt for Shara to sign. She gulped and looked up at Gina in a bit of a panic at the number.

:One dress in Paris could cost that much. It's truly nothing: I whispered through her bond.

:It's a year's worth of cleaning jobs for me.: Though she signed with a flourish and passed the receipt back. :And if all this needs to be dry cleaned...:

My rock troll took that moment to surge inside me. My spine popped and my muscled bulged with the effort of holding him in. :*You worry. About nothing. Dry cleaning is beneath my queen's notice.*:

:*Somehow I don't see Daire or the Templar knight dragging my clothes to the dry cleaners.*:

I didn't have to make an order. Guillaume already scanned the racks and quickly picked a fluffy cream-colored sweater and butter-soft glitzed out jeans that managed to look worn and comfortable while still being brand new and classy. Stripping off the plastic, he knelt on one knee before Shara and offered the clothes to her over his arm as grandly as if he'd drawn his family sword to display for her. "If these aren't acceptable, perhaps Daire has better taste."

His tone said he found that highly unlikely.

"Hey," Daire grumped. "I picked it all out in the first place. Rik's taste is all in his…"

"Daire." I didn't put much power behind his name, but the word still rumbled through the room.

"Are you really a queen?" The woman blurted out.

She stepped closer to Shara and I went on high alert. I flexed my left hand, ready to throttle her, but didn't remove my right arm from around my queen's shoulders, in case I needed to get her to safety in a hurry. Guillaume didn't stand, but shifted slightly so he was angled toward the threat, a glint of silver in his hand. Daire crouched, ready to pounce.

"Oh, no," Shara laughed uneasily, glancing at Gina. "Not really."

Another step. Her hand in her coat pocket. :*Weapon?*: I asked Guillaume, since he was slightly closer.

:*Doesn't smell like metal, gun or knife.*: He paused, breathing again. :*It smells like... Shara.*:

"Ms. Isador doesn't like to brag," Gina said. "Her family has a long, proud history."

"I was wondering if you left something in the dressing room." Catherine edged closer, slowly. Eyes locked on our queen, which told me more than anything that she was a threat. A woman would have been wary of approaching the two large men, but she didn't even glance at us. "I mean, don't you think it was odd that only your dressing room was attacked?"

Shara's embarrassment returned in the bond and that pissed me off. :*She left underwear stained with her blood behind as a lure. That's how she escaped the thralls alone for five years. Is that what you smell?*:

"I don't think so. But I suppose I could have, since I changed my clothes. Why? Did you find something?"

:*Hard to tell with our queen so close. I definitely smell her heat and her blood but I can't tell if any hint comes from the human.*:

"Just a scrap." The woman's eyes glowed oddly, like Daire's cat eyes in the night. She took another step and my instincts screamed with urgency. "That's all they left."

"They who?"

"Thralls."

:*Take her out.*:

Guillaume moved so smoothly and quickly that even I didn't see exactly what he did. Only that blood spurted from the woman's throat. He neatly caught her body and dumped it aside, far from our queen.

While her head rolled across the floor.

7

SHARA

I let out a soft cry and covered my mouth in shock. Blood sprayed me in the face and the saleswoman dropped to the floor. I blinked, frozen, staring at her head. I swear she looked right back at me, as surprised as I was.

Guillaume calmly wiped a knife on his jeans. A fucking six or seven inch-long knife. Where the fuck had he pulled that from? And to behead someone with it, so easily, so quickly...

Beheaded. A sound escaped my throat. More a whimper than anything. I dropped my gaze to my lap, avoiding the body. The blood. My new Blood who'd killed her.

Fresh blood stained the pretty sweater.

I started to laugh. I couldn't help it. But it wasn't a

healthy, good laugh. At all. "I guess I won't wear this after all."

Rik lifted me onto his lap. "I'm sorry that we shocked you, my queen. She meant you harm."

"What kind of harm? How did you know?"

I wiped my face, smearing blood. Human blood. My stomach knotted, the merciless hunger roaring back to life.

"No!" Guillaume seized my hand. I looked at him, surprised that I'd been lifting my bloody fingers to my mouth. "Not her blood, my queen. She's tainted." He looked at Rik. "Get this foul blood off her and don't let her taste it. It reeks of Marne."

My blood ran cold. Rik swept me up and raced for the stairs, Daire ahead of us. He started a bath while Rik helped me strip off the bloody clothes. Shivering, I tried to understand what was going on. "She was human. Right?"

"Yes."

"Then how could she reek of Marne Ceresa? The queen of Rome?"

"I don't know. We'll ask Guillaume for details once we get you clean."

I held onto his shoulders as he helped me out of my jeans. "He killed her. A human. In my living room. What are we going to tell the police?"

"Don't worry." Rik lifted me and gently set me into the water. Daire had made it nice and hot. "All will be taken care of."

"Do you honestly think we haven't had to hide a body

before?" Daire splashed me as he got in with me. "I'm sure Gina has things well in hand."

I still shivered, even with the hot water. "Why was I going to taste her blood? A human? I've never even looked at a human before. Not like that."

"It's your hunger." Rik said grimly as he climbed in too.

This hunger. It was quickly becoming maddening. I couldn't think about anything but Daire's throat. Rik's wrist. His blood. G's. I wanted them all and I'd just had Daire.

I couldn't keep drinking from him like this or he'd be sick and weak.

Daire snorted and gently washed my face. "Nothing you did could make me weak. I've had three sandwiches the size of the one I made for you already. You can take my blood whenever you want."

Rik eased me back so he could wash my hair, his arm underneath my shoulders.

"I used to swim laps in this tub when I was a kid. I never pictured it being too small because I had two men in with me."

G stepped inside and shut the door behind him. "Make that three."

He'd already stripped. I wanted to say to protect me from the tainted blood that must have gotten on his clothes, too, but I couldn't say for sure. Not when he had such a large erection. Very large. I didn't have a lot of experience comparing men's genitals yet but he seemed excessively big, even while I suspected Daire and Rik both had impressive cocks too.

"Gina and Frank are already resolving the issue with the body. It seems as though Catherine Chambers had a terrible car accident on the way back to the city."

He came to the edge of the tub but didn't climb inside. Instead, he knelt at the edge, watching me with those dark solemn eyes. "Why did you kill her?"

"Her manner was odd. She approached you too closely. As a human, she ought to have been wary of us, and if she wasn't human, she would have been downright terrified of three powerful Blood. But she wasn't. At all. She had only one thought and that was to get close to you."

"We suspected her but didn't react right away," Rik said, smoothing his hands through my hair. "Until she said thrall. No human would have thought to use that word. Even you called them monsters."

True. I just had the nagging guilt that we'd hurt, no killed, an innocent person. A human. Who had nothing to do with the monsters that hunted me.

"The item in her pocket." G laid a small tattered scrap of material on the edge of the tub.

Cotton. White, well, mostly. It looked like it'd been washed hundreds of times and taken on a slightly grayed tone. It took me a moment to recognize what it was.

A scrap of my very plain, very cheap underwear.

"Some humans have a natural interest in our kind. They're drawn to us. They're curious. Some say it's because they have a drop or two of Aima blood in their distant family tree that stirs when they're near us. It makes them easy prey as thralls, or for queens who use them for more nefarious purposes."

"Marne," I whispered, shivering again. I hoped that saying her name wouldn't bring her attention to me like some kind of demon.

"She has been known to..." He paused a moment, as if trying to think of the best word. Or perhaps, spin the story in a way that wouldn't scare the ever loving daylights out of me. "Booby trap humans such as this. She feeds on them, gives them a drop or two of her blood, and then looses them into the world with a simple command. Seek. Bait to reel her prey in."

I sat up, moving closer to the edge while Daire popped the drain to let the gross water out. I thought about getting out, but none of them seemed to be in a hurry, and then Rik turned the water back on to refill the tub with clean water. "I don't understand."

"A well-fed queen would usually not look upon a human and hunger," G said, his voice gentle and without censure. Yet I still felt heat rush across my face. "She does it on purpose, trying to catch the unsuspecting queens who might not know any better. Queens who were raised far from her court, in America, say, where there are so few known queens. Queens without enough Blood to satisfy their thirst. If you had tasted the human's blood, you would have indirectly taken Marne's blood too."

My eyes widened. If I'd taken the queen's blood... "That would make me her... sib? Is that the word?"

"Her pawn," Rik growled, his fury leaking through our bond like sparks from an blacksmith's forge. "She almost got away with it too. I had no idea she tainted humans like that."

"Don't blame yourself," G replied, shaking his head. "Only someone familiar with her court would know. Unfortunately, I'm all too familiar with her tricks. She's tried to snare me thusly for decades. Even a single drop of her blood would have given her a hold on you. Most likely, she would have been able to command you to come to her and offer throat to her formally. Though you are very strong, my queen."

"And stubborn," Rik muttered.

My cheeks flushed hotter. He was right. I knew that. Swearing some silly oath that I wouldn't ask them to help me out of pride was only going to get someone hurt or killed. Maybe it wouldn't be any big deal if I died, but could I live with myself if one of them was killed because I was too weak? Too stupid? If I died, what would become of them? And if I'd fed on that tainted human out of desperation…

Stupid. So stupid. When I had three magnificent men begging me to take their blood.

G stood, looking down at me. I ran my gaze over him, noting the many scars and puckered punctures that ran over his body. All faint now, rather than vivid on his skin like when he'd first come to me. I couldn't imagine how many times he'd been wounded, and so severely that they'd left scars when even Daire's and Rik's messiest, deepest bites hadn't left a single mark the next day. He was thicker and stockier than Rik, about the same height as Daire, but he carried himself so differently. He moved like a man who'd looked Death in the face a million times, only to spit in his eye and limp away to fight again another day. Over and over. For centuries.

I slid back against Rik, making room for G to step into the tub with us. "Bring a knife."

Flashing a small silver blade against his palm, he grinned and stepped into the tub. "Already ahead of you, my queen."

8

GUILLAUME

It had been my great misfortune to encounter many queens in my long, miserable lifetime, though I had only formally served one after leaving my lady mother's nest.

As Desideria's executioner, I'd bathed in queens' blood and wallowed in their Bloods'. I'd lived in their courts and been invited deep into their nests to the queen's own bed. I'd drank from their throats and yes, fucked plenty, both queen and Blood.

In service, always in service, waiting in dread for the order to begin the killing. The order always came, and yet the queens always allowed me in. Willing to play the game. Hoping to win. Or at least end up allied with the most powerful living queen in the world, if she was able to retain her head.

Once finally free of Desideria's yoke, I had sworn never to be captured again. To never again be forced to give my blood or wield knife and sword in service to another queen. For I had had my fill of queens and their twisted games. While not related by bloodline, Marne Ceresa was just as twisted as Desideria, and I would wither to a husk of what I used to be and damn my soul for all eternity before I would ever feed from that bitch's throat.

I had often wondered if all queens grew up deep in the game, dealing in blood and lives as easily as human children played checkers. Perhaps Aima queens were simply born cruel, their needs endless, their thirst unimaginable, both for power and blood.

Until I felt the call floating through the night. A queen in desperate need. A queen unlike any I'd ever felt or tasted before.

Shara Isador played a game, the same as any other queen. She played a dangerous game to keep her own life and her Blood's, but more, she played to keep her independence. Whether she knew it or not, she'd drawn a line in the sand and dared the Triune to do something about her very existence.

That was a game I was willing to play. Especially once I had a taste of her blood, her power, the likes of which I'd never tasted before.

She might be a young American queen without the

training of a formal court, but to me, that was a blessing straight from the goddess.

Her two prior Blood shifted closer to her, especially the big alpha, as much as the cramped tub would allow. He would not relinquish his place at her side, not that I'd fault him for that in the slightest. I felt her hunger burning in the bond, a wildfire threatening to consume us all, but she leaned back against the alpha and only looked at me.

I laid the thin blade on the side of the tub and waited for her first play.

Finally, she spoke. "There are things we need to iron out between us before we go any further." She paused, moving her arms gently in the water, thinking of exactly what she wanted to say. I appreciated the fact that she wasn't self conscious of her body—but neither did she flaunt her curves. We might as well have been sitting downstairs at the table sipping coffee than naked in a tub. "You said you would be willing to swear an oath."

"I am."

"I don't mean to insult you, but you take your word very seriously. More seriously than men of this age and country do."

"My honor is all I have left, my queen. Were I to give an oath and then break it, my honor would be destroyed." Just the thought made my stomach tighten with dread and I clenched my fingers around a nonexistent sword. I'd sworn hundreds of years ago never to dishonor my blades and I wouldn't begin now.

"Why were your fingers bent and twisted when you first came to me?"

I blinked, trying to follow her train of thought. "In the year of our lord thirteen hundred and seven, I was imprisoned by King Philip IV of France for being a heretic Templar knight. They tortured me. One of the things they did involved breaking every finger on my hands, numerous times."

I could only hope she wouldn't want *all* the gory details. I didn't want to remember those dark years. Because they couldn't kill me. They tried. Oh, how they'd tried. If I'd still been sane, perhaps I wouldn't have weakened enough to accept the service Desideria offered me.

Shara could have made me swear just about any oath under the sun when I came to her and lay down face first before her. I had been that ravenous. That close to death, which had not come easily to this unkillable knight.

"They're straight now and your scars are healed. Did I do that, or would any queen's blood have healed you?"

"Any queen's blood would have healed me to a point. Your power is great enough, and you allowed me to drink long enough, that I'm healed back to my former glory. Truth be told..." I took a deep breath and laid the truth out between us. "I have never been this strong, Your Majesty. You wrought that in me and you alone."

"I hear horse hooves when I look at your bond," she said softly, closing her eyes, her head tilting. "Why?"

"When I shift, I'm a hell horse. That's why in the old

days, when I served in Ireland, I was called the Dullahan, the headless rider."

"Gives hung like a horse all new meaning," Daire said. Rik punched him in the shoulder. "What? He is."

"What about that… um… test?" Her cheeks flushed and I suddenly identified the most beautiful color in the world.

I had no idea why Daire laughed and Rik looked disgruntled, as if he suddenly found himself the butt of a joke. "He accepted me as alpha."

"I did, and do," I said firmly, in case there had been any doubt. "I'm not a leader. I'm a killer."

"But why would they call you a *headless* rider?" she asked.

I winced, touching my throat. "I've been beheaded and lived to tell the tale."

Her mouth fell open and her gaze dropped to the jagged scar around my throat. "How is that possible?"

"It's my gift. My strength. I cannot be wounded and die, even if I'm separated from my head. That's why I was Desideria's executioner."

"And why queens were willing to allow you into their courts," the alpha whispered, his tone soft with respect. "They shared in that power while they fed on you."

"Yes."

"So you killed their Blood, but not the queen."

"I wouldn't have been able to kill the queen while my blood worked in her veins, but my gift doesn't transfer to secondary feedings, so the Blood were fair game. Desideria took great pleasure in running experiments to see how long it'd take for my gift to fade in a queen who'd fed on me. The record was two years and eighty-eight days."

"So when I feed on each of you, some of your individual powers transfers to me?"

"Usually, yes, though it depends on the gift. I doubt you would be able to transform into my hell horse, or whatever beast Daire is, but my imperviousness to injury and some of his hunting ability or predator senses might transfer to you."

She fell silent several moments. I didn't want to rush her, but on one hand, the water would chill, and on the other, her hunger was driving me mad. I hadn't been so hard in decades, though I had no idea if she'd care to use me that way as well as feed. But if all the years in unimaginable torture had taught me anything, it was patience. And I didn't mean when I'd been in prison.

"Here's the deal. Take it or leave it."

I nodded, focusing on her intently, both her face and her bond. She was inexperienced and green, but her core was true and strong. She reminded me of a master's blade, fresh and hot off the forge, beautifully unmarked and untried, but I had no doubts that her blade might fail in battle. Just looking at her edge made me bleed inside. She'd be a queen to reckon with for sure.

I didn't have the heart to tell her it was too late for us both. I couldn't leave. I had tasted her blood. I was hers until her death. Whatever oath she wanted from me, she'd get. Goddess let it be something I could actually live with.

"I swore earlier today that I wouldn't ask for help until I

had my own fangs." She sighed heavily, dropping her gaze down to a scar on my chest. The six-inch long ugly scar was left when they'd cut out my heart, but even then, it wouldn't stop beating. "I didn't mean it as a formal oath, but I felt a heavy sense of..." She shrugged uncomfortably. "I think my power took it more intently than I meant, if that's possible."

"It is," I said softly, my heart thudding with sympathy. "But you have no need to ask for help. A look is enough to tell me what you need, my queen. I feel your hunger. You never have to ask for permission. You're queen. You take what you need without fear or worry because we offer it gladly."

"But if I don't ask—"

I picked up the knife. "My queen doesn't ask. She takes."

In three quick flicks of my wrist, I made a small cut on each of us Blood. Me on the throat and the other two on the thigh, the body part closest to me without making her fear I'd lunge for her again with a blade and this time stab her.

I'd made the cut on my throat fairly deep, hoping to lure her to me first. She'd fed on the other two already today, though they were certainly hardy enough to feed her again.

With a low groan, she launched at me, bringing a wave of water with her. She locked her mouth over the cut and I closed my eyes, fighting down my need. Feeding her was the top priority, and she might not—

She threw her head back, blood running down her chin. Breathing hard, she finally looked into my eyes. "Will you swear to never kill any of my Blood?"

A fragile, delicate thing sprouted deep in the blackness that remained of my heart. That she would only ask for such a small thing, when she had my balls in a vise. "I will never kill any of Shara Isador's Blood, current or future, directly or indirectly with intent to harm, so I swear on my honor."

Climbing onto my lap, she took my dick inside her and locked her mouth back over the cut. :*I thought to ask permission first but you said I should take.*:

:*Without question, my answer is always yes.*:

9

SHARA

I fucked them all.

I fed from them all. Twice.

Chilled, bloody water filled the tub. Guillaume looked like he was asleep, his arm draped over the side of the tub to keep him from sliding in over his head. Daire tried to climb out of the tub to fetch some towels, and it took him two tries to get to his feet. He wavered like a drunk after a week-long binge.

And I still couldn't stop.

A sob tore from my throat, but Rik hugged me close, soothing me with his body, his big hands rubbing my back. "Shhh, my queen, all is well. You denied yourself too long is all. You're not hurting us."

"But Daire can't walk."

"The hell I can't," he growled, holding up a fluffy towel. "At least get out of the cold water and let us feed you again in bed."

G roused himself and took my other hand, helping me stand. I don't know why I was woozy too. I wasn't the one who'd been drained. "You're high on power, high on sex, high on blood. This is what helps your power come in fully. It's like filling up your cup until it overflows and cracks. Those cracks heal up and next time, you can hold even more. The harder you push us, the better. Though it will definitely be a good thing if half a dozen more Blood show up sooner than later."

I stepped out of the tub and held on to the vanity, waiting for the floor to steady beneath my feet. Half a dozen? Right now, I could definitely go for that. Which told me more than anything that I wasn't quite in my right mind.

Rik propped himself against the tiled wall and took some deep breaths as if he needed to build up the energy to do something as minor as get out of the tub. "If we're attacked by thralls right now, we're fucked."

"Guess it's a good thing Gina hired those security guards after all," Daire replied.

"Hey," Rik retorted. "Low blow."

Snickering under his breath, Daire padded down the hall, a little more steady on his feet. "I'm going to find a phone and order ten pizzas. What do you guys want?"

"What's pizza?" G asked. Rik and I stared at him with horror, and he laughed. "I'm kidding. Even this Medieval knight knows what pizza is and I could eat ten myself."

I hated to burst their bubble, but... "I don't know that they'll deliver this far out."

Daire snorted. "They will if I tip enough. Rik, where's your wallet?"

"Use your own wallet, dickhead."

Wheezing for breath, G leaned heavily against the door frame and laughed. "I have missed the banter of fellow soldiers. It's good to be Blood again."

Rik slapped him on the shoulder and scooped me up in his arms. "Good to have you."

"Put me down," I protested. "You can't get yourself up the stairs, let alone me."

"Watch me. Daire!" He yelled down the stairway to the first floor. "Put on some pants before you open the door, and let the security guard know we're expecting a delivery."

"Oh yeah. Thanks."

I'm pretty sure he was grateful for the reminder about pants.

Rik shifted me in his arms and headed up the second flight of stairs to my tower bedroom. He paused half way up and leaned a shoulder against a wall.

G came up behind us and paused. "Want me to take over?"

"No, I can make it. Just catching my breath."

"So do I pay you a salary?" I asked, watching his face for his reaction. "Because if not, I should. How else do you have money?"

"The queen's legacy funds everything," G answered.

"The nest, the food, the staff. We have no needs but yours, so we don't need funds."

"But you're paying for pizza, and there was that coat in Springfield..."

Rik started up the stairs again. "Nothing but small things to make you smile, my queen. We have a cut of our birth house's income to take as inheritances. Daire's better off than I am, but I could easily live as a wealthy human for fifty years and not worry about money."

"We're not here for money," G said softly. "We're here for blood, for power, and most especially, for you. Because without you, none of this would be possible."

Pausing inside the bedroom, Rik groaned. "I forgot. I stripped the bed earlier."

"Put me down. I've got some spare sheets stashed."

This time he cooperated and I reached under the bed for the storage container. "They may smell musty but they're clean. They'll be ruined by morning anyway so I guess it doesn't matter. Unless you'll let me put a tampon in."

"No," both Blood said immediately, along with Daire's emphatic, *:No.:*

I knew them all well enough now, even G, to realize that they weren't refusing me, or trying to order me. I was queen. I'd do what I wanted. It was their plea that I not deny them.

And after I'd drained them all to the point of barely being able to walk, they would need my blood to refuel them. *All* my blood.

We made the bed and G went downstairs to get drinks

and help Daire haul up all the pizzas they'd ordered. I sat on the bed, my back propped up with pillows, and Rik dozed lightly beside me. His hand on my stomach, his nose on my arm. As if even in exhaustion, he needed to touch and smell me to rest.

We ended up having a pizza party in my bed and I'd never had more fun in my life.

Sitting cross-legged on the mattress, drinking beer, gobbling cheap but cheesy hot pizza, laughing at Daire's antics. Even G laughed, his tired, worn face lightening as literally years of torture dropped from him.

This. This made everything worth it. The blood, the danger, the years of running from thralls. While the blood and sex were fantastic, they brought a whole new set of dangers. Desperate hunger, a thousand-year-old adversary, goddesses, political plots I couldn't begin to unravel, mysteries around my parentage.

But this laughter and camaraderie made up for it all.

This love.

And I knew, watching them, my heart straining to hold all the emotion inside me, that I would do anything to keep this love.

Anything at all.

10

GUILLAUME

I could not believe I had slept. Truly slept, resting, rather than the light doze I had adopted from necessity. Even crowded in a bed with three relative strangers. The big alpha took up the most room, but at least Daire was draped over him with Shara between us. The room was pitch dark and I had no sense of time, other than it was yet night outside. A soft rustle drew my attention to the foot of the bed, but I didn't smell an intruder. Only her.

"My queen?" I whispered, rising up on one elbow. "Are you well?"

"Shhh," she whispered back. :*Don't wake Rik or he'll lecture, 'my queen doesn't clean.' But I can't sleep with all this trash lying around.*:

My eyes adjusted enough to see that she'd stacked the

pizza boxes by the door. Now she made a quick circuit around the room, gathering beer cans in her arms. I started to sit up to help but she waved me off. :*Don't get up. I'm almost done.*:

She crept back to the bed, patting along the mattress. I reached out for her, thinking she couldn't see me, but then I heard the soft clink of another can. She set it with the others and then crawled up into my arms.

I closed my eyes, breathing in her scent. It had been so long since I'd held a woman like this. Let alone my queen.

I hadn't understood other Blood's willingness to die for their queen, because I'd begged for Desideria's death for centuries before the goddess heard my prayer. She'd used my honor to enslave me and I'd hated her every single day of my miserable existence. I'd certainly never made love to her, and she'd had plenty of others that fed her needs in that regard. No, her use for me only extended to my blades and how quickly I could behead her enemies. Or provide her with gruesome entertainment as she tortured the queens who'd dared feed on her executioner, when she herself had sent me to those nests for that sole purpose.

:*Can I ask you something?*:

I opened my eyes and she slid closer, her face just inches away. Her eyes were dark pools of liquid ink in the night, full of secrets and magic. :*Always.*:

:*Did you know my mother, Esetta?*:

I felt as though I ought to know the name, but when I searched my memories, I found only blank spots. Isador. I had to have known her. But I couldn't call up a face or any reference.

Shara sighed, feeling those blank spots in the bond. :*I figured as much. No one living can say her name or remember anything about her.*:

:*You remember her name.*:

:*The night I came into my power, I died in Rik's arms. Daire said he did CPR but they couldn't bring me back. I had to come back on my own.*:

Involuntarily, I shuddered. I could only imagine his acute agony, holding his first and beloved queen as she died, unable to save her.

:*What about Leviathan?*:

:*I've heard references to a Leviathan that might serve the Skolos Triune, though no specific name or queen.*:

:*Greyson told me he was my father.*:

Now I understood better why they'd told her she wasn't full Aima. :*I would not trust a thrall to be truthful. Even if he didn't deliberately try to mislead you, he might not know the truth himself.*:

:*Are the Skolos evil?*:

:*No more evil than Marne, who tries to lure unsuspecting queens with tainted humans, or Desideria who used me to slaughter hundreds of Blood and entrap their queens. Or me, for that matter. I have killed a great many people, my queen. The human today was the least of my sins.*:

Even though we used only the bond to communicate, I sensed a hushed confession trembling in her thoughts. :*I burned Greyson up with my blood.*:

I saw the torch she'd made of the monster who'd hunted her for years, and felt her underlying horror, not at the act, exactly, but her fierce gladness that she'd done such a thing. I deliberately sent her my enthusiastic approval. :*Good.*:

I tucked her closer and she nestled her face against my bare throat.

Something I'd refused to offer Marne Ceresa, or any queen who thought to wield me as Desideria had done. After she'd freed me from the prison cell, she'd had to order me to give throat and used her bond as a weapon inside me until I was forced to yield to her will. Feeding my queen had been punishment. Not enjoyment. Certainly not pleasure, tenderness, or dare I say, love.

In the end, she had even tried to kill me by draining me dry.

Shara didn't know how significant the gesture of a bared throat, offered willingly, could be, especially from someone who'd endured forced feedings. I'd seen Daire do it many times, and she'd gone to Rik for affection and comfort the same way. She didn't have fangs, yet, but even if she had crocodile teeth, I would have tucked her close the same way, silently offering my throat if she wanted it.

:*I suppose I could have burned up Catherine's body today so they wouldn't have to fake a car accident.*:

:*Don't waste your precious blood on any human, let alone one who's tainted.*:

She kissed my throat, her lips soft and tender on my skin. Butterfly touches. Angel wings. She sighed softly, a sound that had the alpha lifting his head, his eyes dark with slumberous heat.

:Do you hunger?: I asked her, sharing that thought with Rik at the same time.

:Not exactly.: She hesitated, her bond flowing inside us like a silver ribbon of moonlight. *:I need…:*

My intensity rose, as did Rik's. Nothing turned on a Blood more than when his queen needed. Whatever it was.

:I want… this.: She gave us an image of her smashed between us, that immediately had Rik rising to his knees and moving closer. *:If you're willing.:*

I met Rik's gaze over her shoulder, hoping my incredulity didn't offend her. *:Why would we not want this? Or want anything that you desired?:*

Aloud, she whispered, "I don't want to be like Desideria. Or Marne. Or any other queen who's hurt you. I never want to make you do something because I'm your queen and you have no choice."

"*Our* queen." I lifted her easily, holding her astride my hips, but I didn't enter her. "Does not hesitate to take what she desires, because she knows we want nothing more than to fulfill that need, whatever it is."

Rik moved behind her, straddling my knees, and rubbed his dick in the sweet dark blood pooling between her thighs.

Her desire slid through the bond, heating pearly moonlight to white-hot flame. "Bleed on me. Like you did Daire. Unless you've already lost too much blood tonight."

"Never." Rik bit his wrist and let blood spill on her back and buttocks.

I felt every drop on her skin, the delicious fire that

spread like wildfire through her body. She cried out, twisting in my grip, fighting to get my dick inside her.

But I waited. Rik was alpha. He might decide to fuck her on top of me before letting me have a turn. Or he might deny me entirely. She hadn't specified more than this, that we hold her between us.

He bent her lower, pressing her breasts against my chest. My arms trembled, but not from her weight, or from the effort of keeping her lifted above my hips. No, I fought myself. I fought to restrain the pawing, screaming warhorse from hell that pounded inside my body until the alpha had his fill. Or until he directed me otherwise.

Reaching around her, he cupped her pussy, stroking through the blood to make her quiver between us. "Tell us, my queen. Tell us exactly what you want so we may fulfill your desire."

I waited, my heart thudding heavily, aching to touch her again, but afraid to hope she would want to include me again. I had lived with a service I dreaded for so long that I'd given up on ever having something more. Something precious. And now that I had hope of something more…

I didn't want to lose that joy so quickly.

"I want you both inside me. And I want you both to feed on me while you fuck me."

RIK

Hovering over her back, I fought to keep my emotions from bleeding out as profusely as my wrist.

My queen needed.

Our queen.

She trusted me to see to that need. Even more importantly, her second Blood was waiting for my orders on how best to satisfy her.

Never being around Blood before, she might not understand the subtle power shifts among us. With only the three of us so far, we'd been able to avoid in-fighting, though she'd seen how Daire had been upset today with Guillaume's approach. I knew from experience that as the number of her Blood grew, so too would the difficulties in keeping each Blood feeling useful and needed. Let alone loved.

Guillaume de Payne could have easily toppled me from my position as alpha. He had the years, experience, power, and yeah, the bigger dick, though I'd seen alphas with smaller dicks that were still able to dominate the pack. As Daire had noted, Guillaume was hung like a stallion and could have fucked my rock troll senseless if he'd wanted.

If he'd wanted.

And that was the catch, because he didn't *want* to take my position. Even though both of us knew he could have.

Even if that meant I denied him access to our queen.

Which I wouldn't do, ever, because she needed him as much as she needed me.

I smeared blood across her buttocks, down her hips and over his hands. "Our queen needs." At least my voice didn't break, though my dick was hard enough to cut diamonds.

"Then we should fill her up." Guillaume sounded like my

rock troll had one fist around his throat and the other on his dick.

"Yes," she growled, fighting his grip.

"Let her take what she wants."

He loosened his fierce hold and she sank down over his cock with a blissful groan. We didn't rush her, though she didn't seem to have difficulty with his size. She worked him deep and let out another throaty cry that made him arch up beneath her. Her bond shimmered, my blood burning on her skin. "Rik…"

I pressed against her, nuzzling her ear. "I'm here, my queen."

"I want you too."

I drew my index finger down her spine, smearing blood between her cheeks. More blood. I needed her aroused to a fevered pitch. Guillaume rocked up into her, a slow, easy ride meant to stoke her need. I bled on her, waiting, lightly stroking her back and buttocks. Waiting for her breath to catch on a moan, her pleasuring rising toward climax. Waiting while I drew my dick down that crevasse, smearing blood, testing whether she would change her mind or have any last-minute qualms. Up until a handful of days ago, she'd been a virgin. Taking two men at once, especially one of Guillaume's size—

"If you don't get inside me I'm going to die."

11

SHARA

My skin was on fire. With G's big cock jammed inside me, it should have been enough, but I still burned.

I wanted Rik inside me too. I wanted to be between them, connecting them, the conduit that powered a detonation the likes of which none of us had ever felt before.

Rik pushed the head of his dick against me, and all I could think about was how he'd taken Daire. How hard he'd pounded him.

"Not yet," he growled against my ear. "I have to break you in gentle like first. I may not even get all the way inside you this first time before you come."

"I'll make it," I swore, even though my legs were quivering beneath me. I wasn't even doing any of the work, not with G doing that slow rub inside me, while Rik eased deeper, letting the natural rock and lift of my hips ease him in.

Hot chills raced down my arms. I groaned, a guttural, rough cry somewhere between a plea and agonized pleasure. So full. I burned all over. I clawed at G's shoulders and he cupped my face, pulling my mouth down to his.

I gave him my tongue, lightly touching the tips of his fangs. A pang rocked through me. :*I wish…*:

:*You will.*: They both said in unison.

Rik gave me inch by inch, more of his weight, until he was finally balls deep.

I twitched between them, though I could barely move. They didn't have to thrust; they breathed, and it shifted me, higher and lower, their dicks stirring inside me. Pressure built inside me. I couldn't breathe. I didn't have room in my body for air. Not when they filled every corner of me.

:*Ready?*: Rik asked. His bond glowed like the hottest forge.

My heart thudded. My thoughts had slowed. My brain incapable of words. All I could manage was a deep, "mmmm."

He sank his fangs into my shoulder, gripping the top of that muscle like a leopard taking his mate. G took my throat.

My blood erupted like a volcano. They both groaned against my skin, their hunger surging through our bonds. I fed them. I gave them power. Rik's rock troll swelled inside him, ever bigger, badder, a nightmare for anything or anyone who threatened me. G's stallion screamed a warning into the night, the thunder of his hooves rumbling the ground.

I soared in a night sky. Twirling, wings furled like black velvet to catch the soft sighing wind.

It took me awhile to find my way back to them.

G's face softened when I opened my eyes. "There you are, my queen."

Rik had shifted us so we all lay on our sides. He had my back, as always, his nose pressed to the hollow beneath my ear.

I yawned so hard my jaw ached. "Is Daire okay? I can't believe we didn't wake him up."

"He's still alive," Rik said, his voice tinged with amusement. "Though he'll be pissed when he realizes what he missed in the morning."

G tucked my face up beneath his chin. "I think perhaps you should skip feeding from him tomorrow, my queen."

I felt the ragged scar ringing his throat against my cheek, and it made me want to cry. I couldn't believe he'd endured that kind of horror. That someone had actually cut his head off. And he'd lived.

"I lived so I could be here with you."

12

DAIRE

"Why the fuck didn't one of you kick me in the head and wake me up?" I growled at Guillaume, pacing back and forth in the kitchen. "I can't believe you motherfuckers were menaging right there beside me and I didn't hear a thing."

"I'll kick you next time." He laughed. "Though it might not be in the head."

Fucking hell. I wasn't mad exactly. Or even jealous. I just wanted to be a part of everything she did. I wanted to wallow in her pleasure as much as her blood, even if she didn't touch me at all. I would have still felt everything she enjoyed.

Pain splintered through the bond so viciously I dropped

the coffee carafe in the sink. *Rik.* I raced for the stairs, Guillaume behind me. I hoped he had some blades on him because the fuck if I knew where my ketars were. *:What's wrong?:*

He didn't answer. When I threw open the bedroom door, I saw why.

A gigantic hooded black cobra had wound around him. Her coils were as big as Rik's thighs, and that was not something to sneeze at. She hissed and bared vicious knife-long fangs, making me flinch back against the wall.

"Well, I guess her fangs have come in,"Guillaume said mildly.

I would have given him a look like *dude, are you fucking crazy?* But I was afraid if I looked away, she'd drag me into her coils too. There were a lot of ways I'd willingly die for my queen, but squeezed to death or eaten by a cobra was surprisingly not too high on the motherfucking list.

"No," Rik gasped. "Stay back. It's all right."

"The fuck it's all right," I retorted. "I feel your pain."

"Pain. Okay." He took shallow breaths, because that's all her coils would allow. "Don't hurt her."

Guillaume raised his hands and softly crooned to her. "All is well, my queen. No one will take him from you."

She swayed, watching him a few moments. But as soon as he took a step toward her, her hood flared wide, revealing a ruby-red diamond against her black scales, and she scooted back against the wall, dragging Rik with her.

The snap of another bone was gruesomely loud. A rib. I felt it puncture his lung. Heard the blood starting to clog his breathing. But he didn't scream. He wouldn't. He didn't want to scare her, even if she was killing him.

Out of the corner of my eye, I saw one of my ketars against the wall. Slowly, I edged toward it, hoping Guillaume could keep her attention locked on him. But what could I do with my favorite weapon? Could I really cut her? My queen? I might as well cut out my heart instead.

Another pop, and this time Rik couldn't hold back the ragged gasp of pain.

"Daire," Guillaume said softly. "I wouldn't do that if I were you."

I looked back up at her head and the cobra's slitted eyes were locked onto me. Watching me. She knew damned well what I was doing. Now that she had my attention, she slowly tightened her lower coil on Rik's leg. Tighter. I felt the stretch of tendons in his knee, the joint close to tearing apart.

"Okay," I rasped out and backed away from the weapon. I couldn't fucking see because I was fucking crying. I hated feeling his pain. I hated feeling so helpless. But more, I hated that right now, I'd thought about slicing him free of her coils.

I was fully prepared to hurt her in order to protect Rik. Hurt my queen. It was unthinkable. Unconscionable for a Blood to even contemplate allowing his queen to be hurt, let alone doing it himself. Yet I couldn't let Rik suffer. I loved him too fucking much.

:She can heal me.: Even his mental voice was soft but anguished. :From anything. Remember. Who she is.:

Goddess. If I had to endure feeling him die, waiting on Shara to resurrect him, I was going to fucking lose my mind.

She struck hard and fast, sinking those long fangs into Rik's abdomen. It happened so fast he didn't even cry out. Maybe he couldn't. She lifted her head, and rather than blood, something black oozed from the punctures that were almost as big as my fist. I felt tears deep inside him. Nicked organs. Torn arteries. Blood dripped from his nose and leaked from his mouth. But he still managed to fucking smile.

"Worth it. Fangs."

His skin started to blacken, his body swelling. She hadn't used those fangs to feed on his blood—but to pump him full of venom.

"Fuck." I fell to my knees. "Rik."

Guillaume dropped a hand on my shoulder and I leaned against his legs. Rik turned his head to look at us, his face pale and clammy. "G. Take care. Of them."

Shaking his head, Guillaume replied, "I'm no alpha. And like you said, she can heal you of anything. Even death."

"You can." He gasped, his breath a horrible wheeze. "Just in case."

I could feel how hard it was for him to breathe. His heart labored to pump blood that was slowly thickening in his veins into a poisonous sludge.

"It's almost time," Guillaume whispered. "Hang in there. It's almost over."

"Time for what?" I was terrified he meant time for Rik to die. "You've seen this before?"

He hesitated a moment, his fingers digging into my shoulder. "I've lived it."

GUILLAUME

I remembered living through this nightmare, though blanks made it difficult for me to piece it all together.

Blanks—that might have involved Shara's mother who'd been wiped from living Aima memory. It made a dreadful kind of sense. She was a cobra now, and it had been a cobra queen that helped me kill Desideria despite my oath that I would never lift my hand in violence toward her in any way.

Daire made a choked cry and I squeezed his shoulder. "I lived through it. He'll pull through just fine."

"Right." Daire growled. "So says the knight who had his head chopped off."

A low rattling drew my attention back to the bed. It wasn't a purr, exactly, nor a hiss, but a deep guttural vibration that rolled from her sleek body. She struck again, but not with her fangs. She latched onto the puncture wounds and started to suck, her coils sliding over him in a sinuous feast.

"Her venom changes the blood," I whispered, watching in a sort of grisly fascination. "If you or I were to feed on him right now, we'd die. Even me."

"Why is she doing it, though?"

"She's using him to make herself, and him, and eventually us, indirectly, poisonous."

Daire shuddered. "Will she bite us too?"

"Undoubtedly," a man said to my right.

I whirled, blade sliding down my wrist to my hand. An Asian man about Daire's height stood beside us. I didn't wait to see who he was. I struck, hard, intending to behead the motherfucker who'd sneaked past the human guards at the gate and then three Blood to invade the queen's bedchamber.

The man just leaned aside and I missed him entirely.

"Is that how you greet all her Blood?"

Daire surged to his feet. "How the fuck did you get in?"

"I'm surprised it was so easy to approach her," the man drawled, making Daire's cat bristle. Claws shot out of his fingers and he snarled. "But I suppose you are a bit… distracted at the moment."

I opened my inner senses, using not just my eyes but my nose, ears, and mind to feel for this intruder. But I felt or sensed nothing from him. He didn't have a scent. I could hear the slowing, labored heartbeat of our alpha, but not this man standing next to me. He might as well have been a mirage.

"Good," Rik wheezed. "Welcome. Help. Them."

The man approached the bed despite our feeding cobra queen, and my estimation of the size of his balls went up considerably. He went down on his knees beside the bed and took Rik's hand. "I will help them and you in any way I can, alpha."

Rik looked rough. His skin white and oddly loose, like his body had dissolved underneath. The cobra was slowly transforming back into our queen, each swallow of his poisoned blood pushing the scales and coils back inside her. I feared that he wouldn't last long enough to see her fully transformed though.

I wished I could remember exactly what had happened when the cobra had come to me. I remembered so little. Maybe that was a blessing. Maybe Rik wouldn't remember his queen killing him, though I don't know that Daire would ever be able to get over it.

She threw her head back and licked her lips as the last of the scales sank into her skin. A small trickle of red dripped from the punctures on Rik's stomach, not black. So she'd sucked all the poison—and a great deal of his blood—back out. His heart stuttered. There wasn't anything left to pump.

Daire scrambled across the floor and grabbed Rik's hand from the new Blood, hugging his limp arm to his chest. "Shara, please. You have to save him. Shara!"

She blinked and stretched languorously, as if she'd only now started to awaken from a glorious dream. Her gaze fell on the new Blood and her eyes flickered with shock.

"Shara!"

She jerked attention down to Rik and her eyes flew wide.

We all felt her horror splintering through the bond, but she didn't hesitate. She slashed her wrist open on her new fangs without thinking and pressed her arm to Rik's mouth.

He was too far gone to feed. Her blood spilled from his mouth, his eyes glassy and unseeing.

She held her wrist over one of the punctures and allowed her blood to drip into the wound. Eyes closed, she sank into him. Our bond crackled with lightning, rippling with power. She surged through him like a bolt of pure energy, sealing the injuries she'd caused, casting sparks through his body. Cells refired that her venom had killed. Her blood raced through his veins, filling his heart. Pumping him full of antivenom and power at once.

He hauled in a deep breath and Daire buried his head in the crook of Rik's elbow. His eyes focused on her and he lurched up and sank his fangs into her throat. She held him, stroking his back, dripping tears and blood on him while he fed.

"I'm so sorry," she whispered, her voice breaking. "I thought it was a dream. I killed you. I can't believe..." She sucked in a ragged breath and squeezed her eyes shut, curling around him. "I fucking killed you."

He wrapped one arm around her back and hugged Daire to him with his other, but he didn't lift his mouth from her throat. :*And you fucking resurrected me too, my queen.*:

She shuddered against him, hiding her face from us. Shame and guilt thudded through her, tightening her throat.

I could not abide that feeling from my queen. I joined the new Blood on my knees beside her and dropped my forehead to her thigh. "Your power is great, my queen. The cost is high. But we willingly pay that cost to be here with you."

"Was it my stupid oath that did this? Because if Rik had to die to give me fangs, then I would have rather done without."

I lifted my head. "I don't think so, my queen. I've seen this happen before."

She finally turned to look at me, her eyes gleaming with tears. I'd seen eyes like hers before. Dark, but glittering with diamonds. Haunting, mesmerizing eyes. "When?"

"When your mother came to me."

"But you said you didn't know her name."

"I didn't. I still don't. Even though you gave me her name last night, I cannot pull it up in my mind. But when I saw your cobra, I remembered another cobra queen. I remember being envenomed like Rik. And that is how I was finally freed from Desideria. She drank from me and died of the poison my blood carried."

"Why didn't your blood kill me then?"

"Because Desideria drank me to the point of death. Luckily for me, she died before she could finish me off."

Rik finally licked his marks in her throat and sat back. For being dead a few minutes ago, he looked bigger and meaner than ever. His veins stood out in stark relief against ripped, tight muscles swollen with power. "So I'm poisonous now?"

"To anyone who doesn't carry our queen's blood, yes. Her blood has the anti-venom that will counteract the poison. If our new friend here tries to drink from you before our queen, he'll die and it won't be a pretty, easy death."

Rik leveled a hard stare on the man, and then both me and Daire. "I'm glad to have another Blood, but do either of you care to tell me how you allowed him so deeply into our queen's home?"

"It's not their fault," the man replied. "My gift is invisibility."

With that, he disappeared. I didn't feel any movement, hear any steps, no shift in air currents, nothing. The man was simply... gone.

"I can still see you," Shara said.

"Of course." The man revealed himself, still on his knees beside me. "You're my queen. I could never hide my presence from you."

"Who are you?"

He bowed his head. "Xin, my queen. Forgive me for not introducing myself sooner, but you were otherwise occupied."

Her mouth twisted in a grimace. "Such a nice way of saying that I was too busy killing my alpha to notice a new Blood." Her gaze fell on Daire, still curled into Rik, hiding his face. "I don't mean to be rude, Xin, G, but could we have some time alone?"

"Of course, my queen." I stood and held my hand out to the new Blood. "I'm Guillaume de Payne. Let's go make some breakfast."

Xin let out a low whistle and shook my hand. "I've heard of you, Payne."

I braced for the ubiquitous joke about keeping his head, or worse, our alpha keeping his head.

Instead, he said, "I usually go for the stab in the back myself."

And I decided Xin and I were going to be very good friends.

13

SHARA

I really was a monster. A terrible, poisonous monstrous snake that had killed my own Blood.

I didn't know how I would deal with this. I didn't know if he and Daire could forgive me.

"Forgive you?" Rik retorted, his voice low and hard. I'd never heard him speak that way before, let alone to me. "Daire is the one who needs to beg your forgiveness. You have nothing to apologize for."

My big, protective, tender caring alpha Blood. I might have only known him a few days, but he meant the world to me. I'd sworn to do anything to protect them and keep them safe, and the very next morning I killed him. My eyes filled up with tears and my throat closed off. I couldn't say the words but I knew he heard and felt my emotions through the bond.

He cupped my chin, squeezing hard enough I felt the imprint of his fingers on my jaws. I didn't want to look into his eyes and see condemnation. Or hatred. Or anger...

But he wouldn't let me go. He squeezed harder, making my face ache. Until I relented and looked him in the eye.

Leaning down so closely his nose almost touched mine, he whispered intently. "You. Are. Queen. My queen apologizes for nothing. Even if you hadn't resurrected me, I would say the same thing. Kill me. Use me. Drain me dry. I'm yours, body and heart and soul and blood. If you killed me and left me dead, then I would know that I had died in your service and your need had been great."

"No need would excuse your death. I would rather die myself."

"Never. We need you alive. Without you, we're nothing. You can find another alpha. You can find dozens of Blood. We cannot find another queen. We certainly can't find another Isador queen. The goddess blessed you for a reason. She needs you. We need you. We cannot lose you. No matter what. Our lives are nothing as long as you live and complete the goddess's plans for you in this world."

He touched his forehead to mine and released my chin, but turned that fierce gaze on Daire. He had his face pressed against the mattress, still clinging to Rik. I felt his agonizing fear still trembling in the bond. He couldn't bear to lose Rik. He loved him. He loved me. To have to choose between the two of us...

"There is no choice," Rik retorted, his voice harsh.

"There's never a choice. Her life above mine. Her life above all. Her needs above all."

"Rik—"

He jerked his gaze to me, eyes blazing. "No, my queen. I'll cut off my arm if you order it, but when it comes to Blood dealing with Blood, I'm his alpha. This is between him and me."

"I couldn't bear it," Daire whispered, finally lifting his head. His eyes were swollen and red and deep lines grooved his mouth and eyes. "I couldn't bear to feel you die and do nothing."

Rik stiffened against me, his shoulders squaring, his already impressive muscles hardening toward granite. "You failed me, but more importantly, you failed her." He leaned forward, his chin jutting out, his voice rumbling with thunder. "You. Failed. Her. You were going to hurt our queen. And for what? To save me? So what if I die? I'm nothing. You're nothing. We're Blood. Dying in service to our queen is the greatest honor of all. You would have dishonored my death by hurting the very person I'm willing to die for."

Daire pressed against him. "Rik—"

"No." He pulled back and used his foot to shove Daire backwards on his ass. "Love is no excuse for dishonoring yourself and me. What if you had succeeded in cutting into our queen? What if you had succeeded in keeping her from envenoming me? Who's to say that we wouldn't all die the next time a queen tries to overtake Shara's territory, because her greatest weapon was never made? Because *you* stopped her from doing what needed done? What if my blood was meant to poison Keisha, or Rosalind, or Marne herself, for daring to try and steal our queen's power, but you stopped Shara from accomplishing it? Then we're all dead. And for what? Because you love me? How does that serve any of us? We're fucking dead!"

Daire rolled over on his stomach, his face pressed to the floor. "I know. I'm sorry. My queen, please forgive me. Alpha, please forgive me. I failed you both."

"I banish you from our queen's bed," Rik said softly, though Daire's shoulders flinched. "You won't so much as sleep beside her until I'm satisfied that you understand the gravity of failing her again. Now get out of my sight before I shift to my rock troll and pound your furry ass into the ground."

Even as he said the words, he sent a surge of affection to Daire through the bond. He was angry, yes. He was punishing him, absolutely. But he understood, and yes, loved Daire too.

Daire slunk from the room and Rik sighed. "I love that bastard."

I threw my arms around him and pressed my face against his throat. "I'm so sorry. I don't know what I'd do without you. If I lost you…"

He squeezed me so tightly I couldn't breathe. "Never. You'll never lose me."

My stomach growled loudly, making him laugh. He loosened his fierce hug and started to pull away, but I touched the large punctures I'd left in his stomach. The skin was red and tender, though he had healed enough to close those marks. "I think this might scar."

"Good. I like wearing scars my queen has given me. It's an honor badge for all to see."

I narrowed my eyes and glared at him. "No one had better get close enough to see these honor badges, or see you without your shirt, but me."

"Possessive," he purred, taking my hand and kissing my knuckles like Guillaume had done. "I like it."

14

SHARA

I stared in the mirror and I didn't recognize myself.

What am I becoming?

It wasn't the clothes, though I couldn't remember wearing anything so nice in years. Brand-new one hundred dollar jeans, a sweater that probably cost twice as much, and a pair of cute ankle boots with a wedge heel that I'd never have selected before.

Wedge heels were a bitch to run in.

I ran my tongue along the back of my teeth on the top of my mouth and shivered. I had fangs. Big ones. I was both relieved…and terrified. Horrified. Every time I looked at Rik's stomach and saw those brutal scars, I'd remember that I'd killed him.

I'd been so concerned about hurting innocent people, or

enjoying killing monsters too much, that it had never occurred to me that I ought to be afraid of what I'd do to my own Blood.

What they'd *allow* me to do without saying a word.

That scared the shit out of me.

I tried to sneak quietly into the kitchen, but I took one step into the room and four sets of male eyes locked on me.

G and the new Blood pushed their chairs away from the table and stood. Rik and Daire were in the kitchen rattling around. Uncharacteristically shy, Daire approached with eyes downcast, carrying a cup of coffee. I wasn't even sure how or when he'd decided he was the one to handle my coffee, or how he knew how I liked it, but it was always perfect. No sugar, just a healthy dose of cream and strong, rich coffee.

"Thank you," I murmured and he flashed a dimple at me. Before the cobra incident, he would have slid in for a hug or kiss, or at least teased and flirted with me, but he quickly retreated to his chair and stood waiting with the other two men.

I looked at Rik as he brought our plates to the table, a bit worried. Maybe Daire was still mad at me, or worse, afraid of me?

:*He's trying very hard to be contrite. But I wouldn't suggest using your cobra persona to bite him anytime soon.*:

I shuddered. Yeah. I wouldn't want to be the cobra very often either. Even though I thought it'd been a dream, I still remembered how... detached I'd felt. Emotionless. I'd known I was hurting Rik, but at the same time, I didn't really care. I didn't want to feel like that again.

They all remained standing until I sat down. At least they'd chosen to stay in the breakfast nook rather than the formal dining room, though the small table was rather crowded. G and Xin had made scrambled eggs, sausage patties, and toast. It looked and smelled good, but my stomach still ached from cramps. Granted, I was physically hungry, but I didn't have much of a desire to actually eat. I sipped coffee and nibbled on toast, watching the rest of my men adjust to having a new Blood among us.

If he was Blood. I wasn't sure about him. I didn't feel anything from him. I certainly didn't feel like I needed to feed from him, or give him my blood.

"Tell us about yourself, Xin," Rik said in between bites. "Where are you from?"

"California. I served Wu Tien's court until she dissolved the nest fifty three years ago."

I forgot how long they—we—lived. He hadn't even served a queen for nearly twice as long as I'd been alive. I had no idea when he'd been born, even though he looked like a twenty-something year old man. Incredibly lean and tight, like an explosion of speed and power waiting to happen. "I was known as Eddie Xin in California, but I much prefer Xin."

"Wu Tien," Guillaume said. "Descended from Empress Wu?"

Xin nodded. "Wu Tien was her great-granddaughter, but none of Wu's daughters ever carried her level of power. She guarded her power too closely and never allowed her heirs to develop. When she died, that power died with her, rather than blooming in her few surviving daughters. Wu Tien's court was under constant attack and pressure, even before New York allied with Paris. She decided to dissolve the nest and return to her homeland, hoping to unite with any of her surviving sisters. Some went with her and others were drawn to New York, but many of us just… existed. Sibs remained sibs, for the most part, but our power waned without a queen."

He met my gaze. "If and when you're ready to enlarge your court, I have former sibs who would leap at the chance to return to a real court. Though they would never be able to serve as Blood."

"I guess I'm still confused about the difference."

"Think of a medieval castle, ruled by the lady of the manor," Rik said. "The lady has knights who serve her and guard the castle and land from their enemies. But there are also people who live around the castle and work the land. Craftsmen who work in the castle. People who tend the animals and the sick, or work in the kitchens. Blood are knights, protecting the manor, but sibs are the everyday workers who contribute their individual skills and lives to the betterment of all. Only the knights will ever feed from the queen directly, but most sibs prefer to live in a court where they're protected by a powerful queen, even if she never feeds them. They gain power by being close to her, and from occasionally feeding from one of her powerful knights. All power trickles down from the queen."

"So people like Gina?"

Rik didn't answer right away. "Maybe. I don't know that she's Aima enough to even have the desire to feed. She gains power by associating with you, absolutely. Status among the courts, money from managing your accounts. But that doesn't make her a sib. A sib will feed at least occasionally, but it varies greatly."

"But they won't feed from me. Only one of you."

"Yes."

I thought about it a moment. Maybe it was my human sensibilities, or maybe I was just a jealous queen. I didn't really like the idea of any of my Blood feeding someone else. If I was there, and we were all feeding each other, making love... Absolutely. I would love to see something like Rik taking care of one of the other guys, because that's exactly what it would be. Tender care. Like when Guillaume had first come to us, Rik had been willing to feed him, simply because I needed strong Blood.

But someone outside of my bedroom...

"Is that something you would want?" I finally asked.

Rik didn't hesitate. "I'm your alpha. My blood is yours, and indirectly, your Blood's. I'll feed anyone in your bed, if that will please you, my queen. But I'd rather not feed anyone else."

"I told you that I can only feed on queens, which is true." Across from me at the table, Guillaume gave me grave look. "What I did not tell you before is that I was often ordered to feed others against my will, especially my previous queen. So no, I will not wish to feed anyone outside your Blood, my queen."

My throat tightened. I could only imagine how terrible being forced to give blood would have been. Like a kind of rape. Forced to share your own blood against your will.

"I don't want to ever do anything like that," I whispered. "I don't want to force you to do something against your will, but I don't want to refuse you something that you'd want and enjoy too." I leaned forward slightly, daring to tap on my power just a little. His eyes and nostrils flared as he scented my rising power. "You must tell me. I order you all to tell me when you're not comfortable with something, or if you're feeling a lack that I'm unaware of."

He tipped his head. "I will abide by your order, my queen."

The other Blood followed suit, giving their oaths. I wasn't sure that was exactly what I'd had in mind. It seemed dumb to make them swear an oath not to obey me blindly.

They finished up breakfast and started to clear the table. Only Xin remained sitting with me, and I sensed through the bond that Rik had done that deliberately to give me some space to decide about this guy. Even though he was sitting right in front of me, Xin had a blankness about him that I didn't understand. "So, Xin, what's your specialty that you did for your queen in San Francisco?"

"A Blood of my skill has but one use, my queen. I was used to assassinate other queens."

XIN

I did not yet know what to make of my new queen. If she would become my queen at all. Her eyes flared with shock, and horror, I thought, at my talent. Instead of immediately planning on how she could wield me to further her territory.

Exactly what a Triune-worthy queen would do.

Doubts gnawed at me, though I don't think any of them could tell.

It took all my will to remain calm and blank, the skills that had kept me alive through one of the most tumultuous Aima courts. Empress Wu had been consolidating her power and widening her influence in both Imperial and Aima courts from the moment she was born over a thousand years ago. Even if that meant assassinating her own family members. A lesson that generations of surviving heirs had learned all too well.

House Wu was destroyed from the inside out, our own daughters slaughtered, blood and power wasted, until little of that great house remained, and I had played the knife in that destruction. I had been the silent shadow that eliminated competitors for my queen's power in her own house... until she found that no more power remained. She couldn't even sustain her own court any longer, and so dissolved the San Francisco nest and abandoned America—and her court—entirely. Leaving behind the knife she'd used to decimate the last of her competition.

I thought again of my alternatives. I could return to China and find a small Wu court that had survived. Or I could join one of the other American queens. Everyone talked about Keisha Skye's alliance with the Paris court, and how much stronger that made her, while ignoring the obvious.

Skye was weak enough that she needed an ally to hold her territory, and the Paris queen had been weak enough, despite her age and grand old city, to accept her offer.

I didn't even know why I was here, not really. I'd been waiting to feel a call for so long that I'd almost given up and settled on Skye. While Shara Isador certainly carried enough power to make the Triune queens tremble in their precious seats, I didn't sense the kind of drive and piercing savvy that would make her a threat. The cobra queen had been impressive, no doubt. But I was a killer, a silent assassin, and I didn't get the impression that she'd be willing to use me in that regard.

She seemed… soft. Another American queen who wouldn't be able to stand against the old queens. Too young. Too ignorant. Too… safe.

Standing, she gave me a lingering look, a bit of a frown on her lips. As if she had serious reservations about me, too. She refilled her coffee cup but didn't return to the table. "Do we have any plans today?"

The queen. Asking her Blood. What they were doing. I caught myself before I could shake my head.

"You should rest today, my queen," the big alpha said, his eyes narrowed with concern, even though he'd been the one killed—by her—this morning.

I stood and followed her to the next room with her other Blood, my mind whirling.

Shara picked up an old book on the table, but didn't sit down. She didn't say anything, but her alpha glanced at the other two and they disappeared a moment. He sat in the corner of the sofa with his leg up on the cushion, and she settled into his embrace, leaning back against him. The other young Blood tucked them in with a blanket and the knight brought a phone to her.

Guillaume de Payne. Even I had heard of him. That he served at her side definitely made me reconsider her potential stature. She'd managed to call him as Blood when he hadn't served a queen in a hundred years.

Scanning her messages, she jerked upright. "There's a man here asking to speak to the queen. At least he doesn't know my name."

"Is he Blood?" Alrik asked.

She closed her eyes, and goose bumps dotted my arms. I felt the brush of her mind sweeping through me like a ghostly phantom.

"No. Well, I don't think so." She looked at me, eyes narrowed. "I don't feel him, but I don't feel you, either Xin."

She didn't feel me. I didn't know what she meant.

My skin prickled harder and I scented her magic rising. I went down to my knees, submitting to whatever test she wanted to run me through. The more power she displayed, the more I'd be convinced I should be here, rather than finding the New Orleans queen to rate her power. Or perhaps I should have followed rumors of the other queen to Mexico...

A wave of energy slammed into me. I shuddered with bliss, my fangs aching. Sweet power. She had plenty of magic to spare. But power wasn't enough to hold court in America, let alone establish herself against the Triune. Power wouldn't be enough to hold me, either.

"Let me in," she whispered aloud. "Or I cannot allow you to stay."

I opened my eyes, meeting her gaze. "I don't know what you mean, my queen."

"Rik burns like Vesuvius, a volcano ready to erupt at a moment's notice. I can see him with my eyes closed. Daire prowls in my mind like his warcat, his fur winding around me even if I'm not touching him. All I have to do is think of G and I hear his horse hooves thundering in the night. I heard him before he swore his oaths and gave me his blood. But you..." She didn't rise or move, but I felt that brush again, as if she touched me. "I feel nothing. I can see you kneeling here, but I can't feel you at all. Did another queen send you to me?"

"No, my queen. Wu Tien dissolved her bond and returned to China."

"Are you a thrall?"

Taken aback, I fought to keep my face smooth, my tone normal. "Of course not. You would know."

"Would I?" She asked Rik over her shoulder.

"Yes. You felt Greyson, and he didn't feel like us."

She gave me another long look of consideration. "He's so

good at hiding, though. Maybe he's a thrall and is just trying to get close to me."

Now the big alpha gave me a suspicious look, his shoulders tensing. One gigantic arm curved around his queen, keeping her close to the protection of his body. "One or two human victims, maybe. Any more than that and he'd have a taint, a stench on him."

The gnawing hole in my midsection expanded. Urgency tightened inside me like a bow, but I didn't know why. "I'm not a thrall. If you wish to sample my blood first—"

"I won't taste someone I don't trust. I learned that lesson already."

I had no idea what she meant. If she wasn't willing to share her blood with me, then it was a waste of time for me to stay. I didn't want to be a sib, even if one of these Blood were willing to feed me. I tried to go to the door. I really did. I would just leave. New Orleans wasn't that far away. If that queen wasn't interested…

My body would not move. An inch. Panic welled within me, as if the walls were slowly moving in, trapping me. Was she holding me here? Or was it someone else? Her goddess? I'd never felt like this before. Like I would rip apart if I didn't stay here. Right here. With her.

The younger feline Blood suddenly jerked to attention like someone had stuck a knife in his back. "It's Kendall."

The big alpha growled and squeezed her so hard against him that she squirmed in his grip. "Fuck."

15

SHARA

Rik squeezed me so hard my ribs creaked. "Kendall who?"

He loosened his grip enough for me to breathe, but kept me tight against him. Even squeezing me harder between his thighs, as if he'd just enfold me with his entire body. "Skye."

His former queen. Daire had a guilty, panicked look on his face and he quivered as if he had fever chills. "He's asking. He wants. Fuck."

Alarm shrilled through me. I pulled free of Rik—actually he more moved with me, still pressed against me as I stood—and reached up to cup Daire's face in my palms. I closed my eyes and felt for his bond.

His fur bristled instead of flowed, his beast all teeth

and claws and terror. Instead of rumbling a purr of pleasure, the warcat hissed a warning and curled away from me.

Protecting me.

From what?

"Kendall was our sib," Rik said. "He's a lower Blood, but we both have a blood bond with him."

Have. Not had.

Sweat beaded on Daire's upper lip. I reached deeper inside him again, ignoring his warcat's snarl. I knew he wouldn't hurt me. I touched his bond again, looking for anything new or different. He felt the same to me, our bond strong and sure. But underneath it... There was a shadow. It was like walking into your dark bedroom as a kid, and feeling the certainty that something was watching you. Waiting for you to crawl into bed. In fact, it was *under* the bed. Creepy eyes staring out at you. A claw ready to snag your ankle as you ran and jumped for the bed.

"He's in you," I whispered.

Daire whimpered and gave a short, jerky nod.

The implications were staggering. After nearly contaminating myself with Marne's blood, I'd known it could be dangerous. I just hadn't realized that even sibs had blood bonds that connected back to the queen. That anyone who'd ever fed my Blood prior to them coming to me would still have a bond unless they were dead. I'd assumed my bond took over, or wiped them out.

We shared our thoughts and feelings through that bond. I could talk to them without anyone knowing. Like Xin, and my doubts about why he was here. I could give them orders...

My heart raced. "Can he command you?"

"He's trying," Rik said, his tone grim. "Or Keisha's trying through him."

"Can they get to you?"

"Never. I'm alpha. He can't touch me."

But he could touch Daire. I looked deeply into his eyes and hardened my bond inside him. I glistened like hard, cold steel. *"I'm* your queen, Daire. You're mine. You're stronger now, remember? My power is yours. They can't touch you."

"Yes," he whispered. "But he's still in me, and I don't want to fail you again."

"What does he want?"

"He wants to talk to you." His trembling settled a bit, his voice stronger. "He swears he means you no harm."

G snorted. "I would not take it as a solemn oath, my queen. From what I can sense, he's barely more than a pup, a bit older than our Daire. His honor won't mean much to him."

Our Daire. It made him stand taller, more assured, though his eyes still had a haunted look to them. He knew the monster was under the bed better than all of us. Even if we were all there with him.

"Okay. Here's our options as I see it." I paused a moment, letting every alternative light up in my mind, playing it out like a movie. "I'm pretty sure I could burn him out of Daire."

He nodded hard. "Yes, please. I want him out."

Xin took a step closer, making Rik rumble out a warning. "I don't believe that's possible, my queen."

I tipped my head to the side, running through exactly how I'd do it. I already had a bond with Daire. I'd give him more blood, watch the way my magic flowed into him, and then I'd light up that fucker that was hiding under my bond. I'd burn him out just like I'd done to Greyson.

G whistled softly. "That might just do it, my queen. Though it'll probably hurt like hell and you might have to do some serious healing for him when you're done."

"It'd be worth it," Daire said. "Even if I burn too. I know you can heal me."

Xin's shoulders were tight, his face drawn, looking from G to me and back again. "What? How?"

For the moment, I was very glad I didn't have a bond with him yet. He was acting so strange. Even when G had first come to me, and I'd been so worried that he might try and kill Rik, I had still felt him. I'd heard his hoofbeats. I'd seen him on the tapestry that rolled through my mind.

Xin was still a blank. Even with him standing so closely.

"I won't accept him as Blood, if that's what he's offering. Not happening. I refuse to give Keisha Skye eyes and ears into my nest once we move. So we can send him away now, without even talking to him. Or I can talk to him politely and send him away with some vague political correctness to ensure Keisha doesn't try for us yet until we're stronger. Or…" I hesitated, not quite sure what my Blood would think. "We can kill him outright."

Xin's head whipped around and he stared at me intently.

I definitely had his attention. Maybe he was thinking about whether I'd kill him too.

Rik's bond didn't waver in the slightest. Rock hard, steady, and sure. And yeah, pretty fucking proud of me. :*My fearless queen.*:

Aloud, he said, "There would be ramifications. He's not a high or close Blood, but Keisha would not take his loss lightly, especially when she sent him to you."

The fucking arrogance. To send a Blood to me as if I couldn't get my own. Or I'd be too stupid to know that she'd have a hook in me, then. Or maybe it was all a ruse and they intended to wipe us out now before I could gain enough power to stake my territory. That I'd allow them to waltz in without hesitation… or worse, be too scared to fight. No fucking way. "If she thinks that she can send someone into *my* house and hurt one of my Blood, then fuck the ramifications. I'll light him up before he can step foot in my door."

G moved slightly, like he was going to flick a piece of lint off his shoulder. And a knife gleamed in his hand. "I can chop off his head."

"Or I can use my gift and kill him before he even knows he's in danger," Xin said, his voice tight and sharp with… desperation. At least that's what it sounded like to me.

Was he so desperate to win a spot at my side? Or desperate that he prove himself so he could get closer… for some nefarious reason?

:*No way to know unless you taste his blood.*: Rik whispered in my head. :*Then he will have no secrets from you.*:

:Or I might give him, or some other queen, a foothold into my mind. Is that what Kendall wants?:

:Very likely.:

:Not fucking happening.:

I looked at each of my Blood, and then Xin. I had to decide about him. I didn't like that he was an unknown while we were facing an external threat.

He came closer and dropped to his knees before me, his palms on his thighs. On the surface, he looked relaxed and calm, but I sensed a sharpness around him, like the whisper-soft sound of a blade being drawn from one of G's hiding places.

"Burn me up if you must, my queen. Or poison me with your cobra. Whatever you must do to assure yourself that I'm worthy of becoming your Blood. I'll do it."

I didn't take his words lightly. He'd seen what I'd done to Rik this morning. Just the thought of doing it again nauseated me. I looked at Daire first, assessing how he was holding up. I didn't want to waste time with Xin if we had to get rid of Kendall sooner than later. "Can he hear or see what you do? Or can Keisha see through him?"

Daire's eyes widened and his head tipped slightly, as if he was listening. "No. I don't think so."

But we couldn't be sure. "G, I want you close, but out of sight. I'm going to assume they know about Daire and Rik, since they were in the Skye court. But I'd rather them not know how many Blood I have, or who they are."

G bowed low and headed for the kitchen. "If you need me, I'll come like the wind."

I looked at Xin, still not sure about him. I didn't feel anything when I looked at him. Would that change once we had a bond? Or was I just not attracted to him? I didn't think I could bear this distance with a Blood. Not after having Daire and Rik, and now G, so tightly interwoven with me. Their hunger, their desire. Did Xin feel anything at all when he looked at me? I couldn't tell.

But I didn't want to ask, either, for fear that would make me look weak and desperate in his eyes too.

He turned his head aside, offering me his throat.

I stared at him. My hunger definitely stirred. But I'd almost tasted that human's blood too. G had helped me understand the significance of offering throat. Xin was willing. He came of his own free will.

Rik slid his arm around me and turned me toward him. "I'll be the first to feel your new fangs, my queen. Then you can decide about him."

I didn't remind him that he'd already felt my cobra's fangs. Because I'd hurt him badly. Cupping the back of my head, he drew me close, cradling me against him. His skin like hot velvet against my face. His smoke and hot iron scent twisting like a knife through my stomach. My mouth ached and I felt the fangs descending. It made me shiver, goose bumps racing down my arms. My nerves screamed with sensation. I wanted my skin against his, every inch of me tight against him. Even better if his cock was deep inside me too.

He let out a low groan and tipped his hips more firmly against me, lifting me more fully against his erection.

I tried to be gentle. I wanted to be tender after hurting him this morning as the cobra. But once I opened my mouth and air hit those fangs, I couldn't wait. I slammed my fangs deep into his throat. The rush of hot, rich blood made me shudder against him, my heart exploding with adrenaline.

I was inside him. I'd finally claimed him. He was mine and mine alone. His blood poured into me, stirring my hunger. Power surged through me, coursing through our shared bonds. As alpha, he always had an extra kick that the other Blood didn't have, but this time...

Maybe it was the venom I'd pumped him with this morning, but I couldn't get enough. He tasted downright decadent, and the *power*...

It'd never been like this.

The floor rattled beneath my feet. The chandelier tinkled above us. And the power surged higher with no end in sight.

I stood in the center of a molten volcano. Lava pulsed and glowed all around me. Through me. Heavy, thick, sweet power. It stroked inside me, filling me impossibly full. And every swallow of Rik's blood brought me closer to climax.

Just from feeding.

I tried to pull back a little and contain the pleasure soaring through me, but my alpha would have none of that. My pleasure was in reach and he wanted it. Badly. He hauled me up harder against him, drawing my thighs around his waist.

With his dick pressed against my core, I couldn't hold back my pleasure. Climax poured through me, lighting up our bonds like a fireworks factory accident.

Rik groaned, his big hands kneading my ass.

If we didn't have an audience, both inside and outside waiting to talk to me, I probably would have pushed him down on the couch and had my wicked way with him.

Reluctantly, he let me slide back down to my feet. :*Anytime, my queen.*:

Daire bumped my thigh with his head, but didn't otherwise touch me. He'd gone to his knees beside Xin, who stared at me like he'd seen a ghost. At least that was my first thought. His face was pale and drawn, his hands gripping his thighs so fiercely the veins stood out in grim relief on his forearms and the backs of his hands.

Yet he said nothing.

With power flooding my system, I focused on him and cupped his face in my hands. I couldn't sink into him like Daire, not without a bond, but surely all this power had to be good for something. Touching him made my fangs ache. They were still distended and I didn't know how to hold my mouth without stabbing myself. Blood dripped down my sweater since I couldn't close my lips very well.

Closing my eyes, I focused my other senses on him. It took me a moment to block out the roaring volcano and the rumbling, purring warcat who were so near. Again, it was almost like searching for an absence, rather than his presence. A bit like Greyson, when he'd tried to hide from me, but Xin was different. He wasn't trying to hide. He was right here, his jaws working beneath my hand, his body shimmering with barely suppressed violence.

Holding my breath, I let my mind touch that silent

absence. It—he—resisted a moment, like a bubble that I had to push through. A shadowy fog that lingered at dawn, waiting for the sunlight to grow fierce enough to penetrate. He wasn't actively blocking me—he just needed... It was close...

Falling. Like I'd thrown myself off the Empire State Building. I clutched his face harder, holding on to that physical reference. Winds rushed through me, making my eyes water. My stomach felt like it'd slipped up into my throat with the sickening drop. He wasn't dark or tainted, though. Just so far removed from his exterior that it took leaping off the metaphorical skyscraper to find him.

Finding his emotions was like crashing through a glass ceiling. Splinters cut through me. I read his doubt. Whether I'd be able and willing to use his thirst for deadly strategy, the quiet slice of a blade, the whisper of steel. His gift made him invisible. Literally. He'd lived unseen and unknown for centuries, slipping through Blood and guards, human and Aima, always in search of his queen's quarry. He'd loved the hunt. He didn't want to lose that.

Losing the hunt and thrill of the kill would be worse than dying for him.

He'd been created for this purpose. He lived for this purpose.

And he could only be mine if I would use him. As the goddess intended.

I waited for Her sign, that tinkling of a pure, clear bell that I'd come to associate with the truth. But this time, I felt more of a choice in my head. The delicate balance of scales. I could take him, or not. He could be mine. Or I could allow him to leave and find another queen. I might never see him again.

Or he might be the one to end my life.

Even She didn't know exactly how the cards would unfold. Only that Wu Tien Xin would be at the heart of the deadliest Triune gambit.

It really came down to me. Did I want to make a play for the Triune? Did I want to play the deadliest game?

Or did I want to find my territory, carve out safety for me and my men, and bolt the doors?

Was I queen enough to use a blade like him?

16

SHARA

I didn't have to think for very long what my answer was.

I turned his face aside and sank my fangs into his throat. His blood was like iced vodka, somehow cold and slushy thick and burning pure, though hot from his body. A thick gray fog descended in my mind, cool and dark and comforting. I could hide in this fog. It wrapped me in silence, blocking out the world. All that remained were the four blood bonds winding through my mind.

They glowed in the fog, but didn't burn it away. Instead, the shadowy murk covered them too, enfolding us all in blessed quiet and peace.

I lifted my head, dribbling blood on us both. His eyes gleamed like polished ghostly silver. "My queen."

He didn't ask permission to feed himself. He just waited. Silent. Unknown. Invisible.

Except I could see him so perfectly now. Through the dense fog, he burned with need. His thirst for my blood was matched only by his eagerness to wield his gift against my enemies. He hadn't tasted royal blood in years. Decades. He'd been sustained by his sibs even while killing in his queen's name.

I had a feeling that my blood was going to do insane things for his power.

I drew him up to his feet and offered him my throat.

He had his fangs in me before I realized it. So fast, so silent, so deadly. Rik wrapped his arms around me, pulling me back against his chest, supporting my weight, while Xin fed.

And he fed. A long time. At least that's what it seemed like. His fog thickened in my mind. A ghostly, endless ancient forest. Trees whispering, words I could almost understand. The air thick and almost wet with moisture. Silence so heavy it was almost deafening. Something padded closer, barely heard, barely seen, only another whisper in the trees.

Until he brushed his muzzle against my cheek. A huge ghostly silver wolf with gleaming eyes like chips of ice. He whirled and disappeared into the trees.

Xin licked my throat, cleaning the blood and closing the wound. I opened my eyes, and for a moment, I saw his wolf flicker in his eyes. Then it was gone too, deep inside him.

Daire cleared his throat. "Kendall's getting impatient."

"He can go fuck himself." My words were slurred and slow, making the corner of Xin's mouth quirk ever so slightly. I was starting to understand and read his signals. For him, that was blatant amusement. "Rik, help me sit down. I'm probably going to need to eat something more substantial than toast now."

The sandwich king immediately headed for the kitchen as Rik picked me up and sat with me between his thighs again.

Xin only looked at me expectantly, waiting for my order.

"I want you to hide in plain sight while we talk to him and figure out what play they're trying."

He nodded, though the expression in his eyes was flat and empty. I read disappointment in his bond though he didn't protest or reveal any emotion on his face. He was eager to kill. Eager to slip behind his unwary target and slit his throat. It made me shiver a bit at how callously he regarded the death of another, but he would wait.

For my order.

"If I say your name," I whispered, waiting until he focused on me. "Then I want you to kill him."

An icy spark flared in his eyes. "And after he's dealt with?"

I didn't answer right away. Instead, I allowed my gaze to run over him. He was dressed simply in white cotton trousers and a loose gray T-shirt that only hinted at his physique. But the way he moved and held himself told me he was going to be just as magnificently powerful as Daire or G, though not as bulky and cut as Rik. Lean, wicked power, tightly coiled strength. I think I was going to have a very good time learning how to break his calm control. I might even find a way to burn through that cold fog that filled him.

His mouth actually fell open and his eyes blazed with burning coldfire. "You will use my body *and* share your blood?"

Um. Wasn't that the general idea? I hesitated, just as surprised as he was. "Unless you don't want to?"

Rik laughed behind me, hugging me closer. "I've never met a Blood who wouldn't leap at the chance to share the queen's bed."

"My queen," Xin said, his voice hoarse. "Let me kill this fucker quickly so you can use me any way you desire."

17

RIK

Normally, I wasn't the kind of man who enjoyed rubbing someone's nose in crap or beating a man for spite, but that's exactly what I wanted to do when Kendall Skye walked into my queen's living room. Or better yet, I'd say Xin's name myself and smile as the new Blood cut down this unwanted intruder. Though I had no idea exactly where Xin was in the room. He'd disappeared as soon as she'd told Daire to let Kendall in.

My queen. Mine. Don't touch. Don't even fucking think about it.

He was smaller than I remembered. Even Daire stood a few inches taller than him now. Or maybe we'd grown that much bigger with our queen's blood. He offered a hand to Daire first, but he only snarled. Kendall dropped his hand with a wry twist on his mouth. "I remember a time when you both begged me to feed you."

Daire's cheeks flushed and he stole quick look at me. Yeah, I remembered that night all too well. It'd been good. I'd fucked Daire while he'd sucked off Kendall and we'd all shared blood. That was as good as it was ever going to get for us in Skye's court.

Sucking off a Blood who never shared his own queen's bed.

Deliberately, I brought up my best memory with him and Shara, letting it play in my mind as I shared it with him. How I'd fucked him while he'd fucked Shara. Her blood burning in both of us. :*Don't let him get to you.*:

Her bond blazed hotter in both of us. :*We need to do that again. And soon.*:

Daire flashed a cheeky grin at Kendall and brought the massive sandwich to Shara. "Now I get to beg my queen to allow me to lick her pussy until she comes, but I don't have to beg her to feed me at all."

Kendall's jaw tightened and he met my gaze. Well, he tried to, at least. With my queen sprawled in my arms, sated on my blood, I was bursting with power, my muscles straining to stay inside my skin. I didn't have to scream alpha or growl or get into a pissing contest.

He couldn't look me in the fucking eyes.

He dropped his gaze to Shara as she tore into the sandwich. He noted the blood on her sweater. The fresh bite on her throat, though it wasn't mine. She didn't even look at him, as if he was beneath her notice.

Because he was. He wasn't her Blood and he never would be.

"Thank you, Daire." She paused a moment and ruffled his hair. He rumbled a purr and draped himself over my thigh so he could put his head in her lap. She looked up at Kendall as if surprised to see him there. "Who are you?"

"Kendall Skye, Your Majesty."

She ate another few bites, making him shift his weight from foot to foot. "What do you want?"

He flicked a quick glance up at my face, not quite meeting my gaze, as if he hoped I'd help him out. Not a snowball's chance in hell. "Well, to start, your name, please? Your Majesty?"

She tipped her head to the side. "You're here. Asking to speak to me. And you don't know who I am?"

She might not have been raised in a court, but she had an innate sense of how to make a worm wriggle on her hook. Casual royal arrogance. She played the part so well that I almost smiled.

Kendall actually looked a little pale. Maybe he'd thought he could come in here and throw his prior blood bond around, muscling us into letting him in. Or maybe Keisha was on the other end of his bond, squeezing hard for information. I didn't fucking care.

I could have reached for his bond and listened. But I refused. My queen's bond shone brightly in me and I wouldn't sully it by touching an old blood bond that I'd forged from necessity.

"I'm sorry, but I don't know your name. My queen felt

her sibs making a connection with a new queen and sent me as an offering to you."

"And who might your queen be?"

He looked at me and Daire with a dazed look in his eyes. "They didn't tell you?"

"I don't give a fuck about who they fed from in the past. They're mine now." Shara shrugged and handed the last bit of sandwich she hadn't eaten to Daire. He finished it with one huge bite and continued to rub on her, purring so loudly that he almost drowned out the other man. "I don't really care."

He blinked and swallowed a hard gulp. "You don't care about Keisha Skye, the queen of New York City?"

She sighed as if bored to death with this discussion. "What does she want?"

"Um. She wants her sibs back."

"That's what she sent you here to tell me?"

"Either she wants her sibs back, or she wants you to accept me as your third Blood."

I felt a moment of relief in Shara's bond. They had no idea how many Blood she'd managed to take already—so they couldn't hear and see everything through Daire. Then she felt for Xin, bringing my attention to her newest Blood. Through her bond, I could see him. He fucking hovered behind Kendall so close that I had no idea how the man couldn't sense death breathing on his nape.

Shara leveled a hard look on Kendall but she didn't call her power. "Or...?"

Kendall's eyes flickered and I could almost sense his

internal conversation with his queen. Sweat dripped down his forehead and his hands trembled. I almost felt sorry for him. Almost. "My queen says," he rasped out. He paused to clear his throat harshly. "You might be too… Um…" He looked up at me, daring to finally meet my gaze head on.

He was fucking terrified. He knew damned well if he said what his queen had told him, he was dead.

She knew it too.

And she didn't care.

He was only a pawn that she'd sent to judge how hard she'd have to play this game against a new, untried queen.

Shara sat up and gave Daire a gentle but firm push to get him off her. "Go on."

"You might be too ignorant," he said softly, his eyes locked on her face.

"Too ignorant to get my own Blood without her help? Too ignorant to know a spy when one's sent to me?" Her voice rose slightly, her power humming through our bonds. "Or too ignorant to know how to deal with another queen since I wasn't raised in a nest?"

Kendall's nostrils flared, breathing in her power. Though she held back the bulk of her strength. She didn't want them to sense how powerful she really was. Hopefully he wouldn't scent that she was breeding too.

"All the above."

She leaned forward, looking deeply into his eyes. "Can she see and hear me now?"

The pulse thumped so hard in his throat I could see it from feet away. Sweat poured dripped off him and his muscles quivered as if he would shift. I whispered to Xin. *:He shifts into a lion.:*

:Understood, alpha. He won't get a claw on her.:

"Yes," Kendall whispered.

"I'm Shara Isador and this is what happens to other queen's Blood who come into my territory." Through our shared bonds, she said, *:Xin.:*

Xin materialized against Kendall's back. One hand wrapped around his throat, the other shoved up into his back. The tip of the blade he used jutted through Kendall's ribcage. Xin held him, tucked against his back so that Kendall had no idea who'd killed him, so his queen would only know that Shara had a third Blood. Not who... or what... he was.

Blood trickled from Kendall's lips, his breathing a loud rasp. "You. Will. Pay."

Shara stood and took a step closer, staring fiercely into the dying Blood's eyes. "Don't fuck with my Blood again."

SHARA

Two days... two bodies to dispose of. "This is getting ridiculous."

Daire grinned and grabbed the dead man's feet. Guillaume took his shoulders. "At least Xin's kill didn't spray you this time."

I looked down at myself and grimaced at the blood I'd dribbled all over myself. Handling fangs were going to take some getting used to. "I'm still messy. What are you going to do with him?"

Guillaume replied as they carried him toward the door. "The easiest way to get rid of an Aima is to feed the thralls."

I shuddered at the thought. "We haven't seen any thralls since Greyson."

"They're out there." Rik settled me back against him. "You know that better than anyone."

Yeah. I did. Though I'd hoped that with Greyson dead, maybe they'd leave me alone. I hadn't felt anything out in the night—but we hadn't been anywhere, and I'd been a little too busy the last few nights to worry about any monsters roaming around outside.

I sat up enough to grab the ancient book that had been part of the legacy off the coffee table and then leaned back against him. Stroking my fingers over the leather, I imagined all the Isador queens before me. Who created it? How far back did it go? Would I be able to read it? Should I write in it... and what would I say?

Maybe I'd be the last Isador queen. No one else would ever read it.

"Do you need anything else, my queen?" Xin asked, startling me.

I'd actually forgotten he was standing there. Looking at me. Waiting for me to *see* him. On the surface, he was only being courteous to his queen and checking in to see what I wanted him to do next. When I reached deeper, though, and listened harder to his bond, he wanted so much more. My promise that I'd take him to bed too had stirred a different kind of hunger in him. He wanted closeness. Connection. And most of all, touch.

So many people never bothered to even look and see him. Let alone touch him.

"Yes," I said simply and drew my feet up. "You can come sit with us, if you like."

In the end, I had my feet on his lap and my head back against Rik's chest, using him like a body pillow so I could prop myself up enough to read. Xin cradled my feet in his hands like I'd given him a priceless artifact to hold.

I opened the book and my heart thudded painfully in my chest. *Esetta Isador* scrawled across the page, with a note. To me.

To my daughter I will never know,
   This book is for you. Your ancestors have recorded everything we know you will need for thousands of years.
   It all culminates in you.
   You are our most beloved.
   Our greatest hope.
   Our weapon.
   Long live the queen of Isador.

My hand trembled as I turned the page. Our most beloved. And she'd known she would never see me. That she'd be gone. Never raise me. Why?

Across the next two pages was a genealogy listing with every queen all the way back to Isis Herself. There weren't as many as you'd expect after thousands of years. Mostly because of the dates written beside each name. Dates that made my eyes bug out of my head.

The first queen of Isis, Baast, had lived for nearly two thousand years. She would have seen the rise and fall of the Egyptian kingdoms, Rome, and the birth of Jesus.

No queen after her lived so long. One poor woman, Isabella Isador, was only listed for twenty years.

Beside each woman's name, the father of her daughter was listed. I didn't recognize any of them, and though I eagerly traced down to the bottom right of the page, where Esetta and Selena Isador were listed…

No father was listed. His name was blank.

But I was definitely marked as descended from Esetta. Alan Dalton's name was listed by Selena, but they had no children.

The next few pages recorded the history of this translation. My mother documented each scroll, parchment, and personal journal that she'd transcribed into this single book. The last note said, "Every original source is locked in the Talbott safe if you need them for any reason."

I couldn't imagine holding a several-thousand-years-old parchment in my hand that had been written by my great-something grandmother.

I flipped through a few pages, but they were mostly sketches of the cannisters I'd seen in the legacy and other ancient Egyptian symbols. All of which were important, I'm sure, but I wanted to see what my mother might have contributed herself. I flipped forward to the very last page that wasn't blank.

So it ends. And begins with you. Start your own book now, daughter, and write our future.

Goose bumps prickled on my arms and I shivered. Daire suddenly appeared with a blanket. "I always knew you'd be the kind of reader who'd skip to the last chapter."

I held the book up so he could tuck the blanket up beneath my arms. "I always read the spoilers first. What time is it?"

"One in the afternoon," Guillaume answered. This time he brought my cup, rather than Daire. It was steaming hot, but smelled like tea instead of coffee. "Something new to try, if you'd like."

"Perfect, thank you. Where'd you put… him?"

"In the line of trees at the edge of the park," Daire said. "I'm sure he'll be gone by morning."

"What if someone finds the body? I don't know if Stuller has a police department of their own, or if they'd have to call the county sheriff. Or the state patrol…"

Guillaume shrugged as if I'd asked him opinion on the color of the drapes. "No one will find him."

"How can you be sure?"

He squatted down beside the sofa and laid his hand on my arm. "My queen—"

"Worries for nothing," Rik said in unison with him.

Making me roll my eyes, as they intended.

"No one comes down this road. No one comes to this town. And if a curious human like that woman turns at the park and approaches the house, you have two surprisingly sharp and dedicated security guards on duty who will firmly and politely get rid of them. They know about the body. Frank helped us put him there. They know that man meant you harm. And they're paid very, very well not to ask too many questions."

Looking at them, my sweet, protective, yet deadly men, my throat tightened up and my eyes burned. I'd never dreamed that even one man would care for me as much as they did. Let alone four.

Xin might be the newest, but I felt the same promise in his bond.

Nothing would ever get through him to hurt me. Never.

"Do you think this couch is big enough for you all to hold me?"

Evidently that was a silly question. Guillaume swept me up in his arms and turned to sit down. Daire squeezed in beside Rik. And then G sat back down with me so I was on top of them all.

It was interesting to say the least.

And not exactly comfortable. Not with four walls of muscle. Or erections.

But I wriggled around until I was comfortable. Tucked under a blanket on the laps of four men, their big hands a steady, gentle stroke on my body. Not to arouse, but to touch. Something they'd been denied even longer than me.

I tried to read more of the book but my eyes were too heavy. Lulled by their steady stroking, I drifted off to sleep.

18

SHARA

I heard whispers in the darkness. I had no idea where I was, but everything was gray and cold and still. I took a step so silently that I paused and looked at my body. I was Xin's silver wolf. No one would hear or see me.

I ghosted closer to the voices. Two women. One was angry, pacing back and forth, her voice rising with fury. The other woman occasionally murmured an answer, calm to her agitation. But the wolf smelled condescension in her polite and sympathetic tone.

"She killed my Blood. I want justice."

My stomach tightened, my ears tight to my head. They were talking about me. The angry one was Keisha Skye. Who was the other woman? She had to be another queen. Her Paris ally? Marne Ceresa herself?

"What did you expect?"

"I expected a civilized response."

The other woman laughed, a sweet tinkling sound of lightness that jarred with her wormwood scent. "She's as close to civilized as you are to the Triune."

Keisha gasped softly as if a blade had slipped between her ribs. "But you said... You promised..."

"You can't even plant your own eyes and ears in a fledging queen's nest. Oh, I'm sorry. She doesn't even have a nest yet. Why should I put forward your name for the third seat?"

Marne. It had to be.

I crept closer, using every bit of silence and stealth the ghostly wolf possessed. I wanted to see the greatest queen of the Triune. I wanted to have a picture of the woman who put a geas upon both my mothers: the one who birthed me, and her sister who raised me.

So close. I could hear their heartbeats. I pulled the fog tighter around me, making sure I was as hidden as possible, except for my eyes. I wanted to see. I needed to see her face.

The fog thinned before my focus, revealing two women, but they weren't together. Mist flowed between them and they didn't look at each other. So how were they communicating? Maybe a blood bond.

A staggering thought. A queen of Keisha's status... with a blood bond to Marne. Did all the queens have a bond with her? Were they her sibs? Her pawns?

What chance did I have of escaping her net if all the queens were hers to command?

I wasn't sure which one was Marne. They both reclined like an empress being carried on a litter. One was dark skinned, the other blonde, both classically beautiful with long model's legs and Grecian goddess faces carved from marble without any sign of age. Keisha was at least a couple of hundred years old to have gained control of New York City, and my first two Blood were nearly one hundred. In her court, they'd been young. Marne was much older, but neither woman looked like a thousand-year-old vampire.

"I'm the most powerful American queen," the darker woman retorted, giving me my answer. Keisha. "We have no representative on the Triune."

The blonde woman laughed. "You're like the evil stepmother queen in Snow White declaring yourself the most powerful of all, ignoring the message in the magic mirror."

"Are you saying she's more powerful than me?"

The amusement wiped from Marne's face, replaced with a grim tightness that sent a surge of glee through me. *Yes, be afraid of me. Maybe she'll leave me alone.* "I haven't felt her power directly, but Isador was always strong. Even her mother. Though why Selena ever loved that human I'll never understand."

My heart thudded painfully and my ribcage banded tight, making it difficult to breathe.

They didn't know that Selena wasn't my mother.

It didn't make sense.

Maybe I made some soft gasp. I wasn't sure. But Marne suddenly looked straight at me. I froze, sure that she couldn't see me, though she must have sensed someone watching.

"Even a half-human queen of Isador is a threat."

I closed my eyes and willed myself away. Cool, wet mist enveloped me and I drifted in silence, my mind racing.

If Marne hadn't put the geas upon everyone that prevented the living from saying my mother's name... Then the only person who could have done such a thing was Esetta herself. But why? It didn't make sense. Why would she want to be forgotten?

"To protect you. To hide you." The voice rolled through my head, a soft whisper carried to me on a ghostly breeze. A voice I knew deep inside. It rang like the tinkling chime of the goddess. My mother must have whispered to me often when I was a baby, though I didn't remember it. *"To lose you in the world so you would have time to grow and develop as you wished. Not in a court of Aima so unable to change and adapt that they die and do nothing to save themselves."*

I was afraid to say anything aloud, for fear that Marne might have followed me, or would hear. But I whispered the words in my head, sure that Esetta would hear. *"What am I supposed to do?"*

"Be true to who you are. That is all. You are controlled chaos. You are She, Goddess incarnate. Live, love, and make magic in the world. Embrace your nature your father and I died to create. Loose the wild hunt. Revel in the blood of your enemies. Some will worship you. Others will fear you. And no one will be able to stop you."

My father and she both died to create me? Guilt and dread settled in my stomach like cold lead. I shivered, hugging myself. The wolf was gone, leaving me alone huddled in the cold mist. *"Was he Leviathan?"*

"No. Your father was a dying god. I was his last love. And you are our only hope."

Then why had Greyson told me he was my father? My head ached and I was suddenly exhausted. Tired of trying to untangle half-truths and guess at political strategy that was alien to me. I was glad I wasn't raised in a nest, but on the other hand, it handicapped me. I didn't understand court politics.

"Take your king before it's too late. Soon he'll pass and be only a whisper on the wind like me."

Something howled in the distance, a faint sound of crazed agony. The snake-monster thing I'd dreamed before. I had no idea where he was. And honestly… I didn't know if I wanted to find him or not. All that rage, all that pain. How did you soothe someone who'd been tortured and trapped for so long that he didn't even remember who or what he was any longer?

"He's your destiny."

Something tugged on me deep inside, a razor wire that tightened and burned like molten steel. With a sigh, I stood in the fog. Xin's wolf flowed back over me. Nose tipped into the breeze, I took in all the smells of the world and filtered them out one by one until I found the scent I needed. Snake. Serpent. Dragon. Pain. Rage. *"I'm coming."*

19

RIK

Even alpha Blood occasionally needed a nap. I opened my eyes, surprised that I'd drifted off when I was so crowded. Daire's head was on my shoulder, his weight heavy on my arm, Shara's head on my thigh. Guillaume's head was tipped back against the sofa and he slept too. Only the new Blood, Xin, remained awake, giving me a slight nod of acknowledgment. Grateful at least one of us had been alert in case we came under threat, I nodded back. He closed his eyes and stroked his fingers lightly on her ankles. A look came over his face that made my chest ache, even the big, mean, alpha Blood.

Reverence.

Yeah. Me too, buddy. Me too.

I didn't want to move and disturb her rest, but she'd be hungry when she woke up. We needed to get the nest established, both for her safety and to have a staff take better care of her. I didn't want to feed my queen takeout pizza all the time, yet I didn't relish leaving her side a single moment.

Her phone buzzed on the coffee table. I carefully leaned forward, cradling her head so I didn't wake her, and snagged it, in case we had an issue that the security guards needed assistance with.

The text was from Gina. *I have an updated list of repairs for your house in ES. Thought I'd bring dinner and discuss what other changes you'd like made.*

Ah, now that was a consiliarius that was thinking ahead and trying to anticipate her queen's needs. I texted back. *This is Rik. She's sleeping, but that sounds great. What time?*

7 PM. How many?

I grinned. Definitely a good consiliarius—who knew her queen was calling Blood to her as quickly as possible. *4 plus her.*

Got it. Thanks.

That settled, I started to put the phone back down but Shara opened her eyes, suddenly wide awake. The sleeping Blood snapped alert with her, even Xin who'd only rested a few moments.

"My queen?"

"I know where he is. I have to find it on a map. And Marne doesn't know who my real mother is."

Uneasiness pitched through my stomach but I didn't

react outwardly. "Gina's coming tonight for dinner. I'm sure she can help you find the location."

She stared up at me, her mouth tensing. "Why are you upset? You're my alpha. Nothing will change that."

I drew her up into my lap, cradling her against my chest. "I'm not upset jealous. I'm worried for your safety."

Guillaume fingered a small blade like he'd start gutting the man. "Who's *he* who turns our alpha's stomach into a pit of acid?"

"Say her name and Ceresa is dead, my queen," Xin said right after.

I forgot that he and Xin had only just joined us. They didn't know all the tangled plots in which our queen was embroiled. "One of her gifts is dreaming, and she's been dreaming of a king."

"Fuck that shit," Guillaume muttered.

"Not you too." Shara sighed. "What's so bad about a king?"

"He won't be Blood," Guillaume replied, shaking his head. "That means he won't be dedicated to you, let alone obey you. The only king I ever heard of killed everyone in his mother's nest. Blood, queen, human, it didn't matter. He slaughtered them all."

"Why?"

"He was crazed. He shifted into his beast and couldn't control it. When he finally shifted back, he found himself sitting among the torn apart remains of his entire family. So he killed himself. He wasn't even twenty one yet."

"You two are older, right?" She turned to look at Xin and

Guillaume. "So do you know of a king who was some kind of serpent monster or dragon?"

Xin didn't have to think very long to reply. "Leviathan, a king born to the Skolos court."

"You asked me about Leviathan last night," Guillaume said. "But I didn't know he was a king. I thought you said he was your father?"

"I don't think so now. Not after that dream." She nibbled on her lip, staring at Xin. "How old are you? Or is that a rude thing to ask an Aima?"

The corner of his mouth twitched, as close to a smile as I'd ever seen the eerily-quiet Blood give. "I wouldn't ask a queen how old she is, but this Blood doesn't mind. I was born to Princess Taiping's court in the year 712."

Her mouth fell open and his smile widened. "Smart Blood—who are very good at killing—live longer than their queens."

"Okay, smarty pants. What can you tell me about Leviathan?"

"Not much, only that he was born to Skolos many years before me, so that he was a legend in my time. He inspired the sea monster stories, the monster from the depths. All the old religions and mythologies of the world reference a mighty serpent monster defeated by their god. Supposedly he was chained in the depths of hell to await his judgment."

"Judgment for what?"

"By the time I heard of him, no one remembered."

"I hate going into this blind." Frowning, she sighed heavily and reached over for the Isador book. "Maybe there's something in here. She said to hurry, that he was going to pass soon. If he was born before Xin's time, why would he die now?"

Embroiled in unraveling the mysteries of her dream, she didn't realize how hungry she was. I gave Daire a mental nudge and he reluctantly pulled away to rummage in the kitchen. *:Not a sandwich this time. She needs a variety. Preferably beef. She's bleeding. She needs plenty of iron. Gina's bringing dinner later, but she needs something now.:*

:I'll grill some steaks,: Daire replied.

Guillaume stood too, though I didn't ask him to. He caught my gaze a moment and tipped his head at Xin. *:In case she wants to break the new Blood in now rather than later. She might appreciate a smaller audience and I had my turn last night.:*

Flipping through the book, she certainly wasn't thinking about sex. Or blood. Or a new Blood starved for touch.

Though I didn't think it would take much to remind her.

SHARA

While I'm sure the ancient histories of my family line were very interesting, I went straight to the spoilers and skipped to the end of the book again. I'd work my way backwards and see if what I needed was in the final pages that my mother had written. I didn't have much to go with yet, so I hoped there would be something there.

What had she said? *A dying god. Their last hope.* Geez. Talk about the weight of the world on my shoulders.

The last page didn't have a date, but when I backed up a few pages, I found dated journal entries.

November 1, 1994

It is done. He's gone. I can't feel his presence any longer. The world seems somehow thin and gray without him yet life goes on around me. No one but me feels his loss. And that is why he was willing to die for me. For us. I feel her growing in my womb already. I know she'll be a queen to be reckoned with. My child.

I already know your birth will be the last thing I accomplish, but I won't fail you. I'll endure until I hear your first cry and know that you live. That you're strong. I'll hold you, so you know that you're loved. You're so loved that I'm giving my life to have you. Then I will join your father in the mists of time. It's been so long since he held me, though it was only days ago. It feels as though we've already endured lifetimes apart. My Blood are gone. Only the god's memory remains. And my daughter. I already have her name picked out.

Shara.

My throat ached but I didn't cry. I flipped back again, looking for the start of the previous entry.

October 30, 1994

The arrangements are all made. The nest is dissolved. The geas is laid. No one remembers me, even my sister and my own beloved Blood. Without their blood to sustain me, it took the last of my magic to accomplish, but it's necessary. I need to step out of Aima memory before I go to him. Or all is lost.

I dreamed of him again. He knows I'm coming. I'm sure She has told him and prepared the way. I heard on the news that Mount Vesuvius is stirring. I don't need to ask why. I hope it doesn't erupt when I rouse him from his long slumber.

Father of monsters—your bride is coming.

I slammed the book shut, my mind racing.

"What is it?" Rik stroked his fingers through my hair.

"Um, well…" I hesitated, not sure I wanted to find out what they knew about my father. Or if it would change anything between us. "I found a few clues to who my father was."

"Was? So you know he's dead?"

Nodding, I set the book back on the coffee table and drew my knees up, pressing into Rik's side. "So is my mother. They're both gone. They died to have me."

His arm came around me and he pulled me close, dropping his mouth to my shoulder. He didn't tug on my shirt or even try to find skin. He just put his mouth on my sweater and inhaled. Like he couldn't get enough air if my scent wasn't in his nostrils. Which made me want to smell him too. Only I wasn't quite so polite about it. I pulled his biceps up to my nose and pressed my face into the crook of his arm.

"Who?" He murmured, that low rock-troll rumble that vibrated through my bones.

It took me a moment to remember what we'd been talking about. "She never referred to him by name, but she called him a dying god, father of monsters."

Rik lifted his head. "Your father was a god that fathered monsters? Xin, ring any bells?"

His tone told me he knew, but he was looking for confirmation. I lifted my face from his arm and looked across the couch at Xin. He didn't move or say anything, but the intensity of his eyes seared me. Wolf eyes. Hungry. So hungry. The better to eat you with, my dear.

And yeah, I knew Rik had done this on purpose. He'd reminded me of the other Blood, who sat so silent and still that it was easy to forget him. Even me, his new queen. I only now realized the other two Blood had left the room too. Again, probably deliberately. Though I didn't know if I wanted to have sex on the couch.

Xin's eyes flickered a moment, a sheet of silver flashing through the darkness of his eyes like lightning.

"Xin?" I asked softly, my attention locked on him. "Do you know who my father is?"

He swallowed so hard I heard it. "Typhon. Father of monsters. Ancient god of Greece I believe. My queen."

Rik carefully pulled my hair to one side, baring the curve of my neck. He brushed his mouth against my skin, ever so softly. I trembled. My fangs distended so fast and hard that I made a sound of shocked discomfort. Blood dripped down my chin.

Staring at me, Xin didn't move other than a fine shimmy of his powerful, lean body. He wouldn't make a move toward me. None of them would while I was with my alpha. Not until invited.

His gaze followed the thin trail of blood that dripped

down my chin and splashed another stain on the sweater. I didn't have to use our bond to know that he was imagining what my blood would look like trailing down my breasts. If I'd allow him to lick it off my skin.

"Yes," I said simply.

And he was there, eager, his mouth on my chin. Rik tugged my sweater over my head. I hadn't bothered with a bra. My lip wasn't bleeding enough to drip that much, so I gouged myself again.

Xin didn't plant his mouth over the small wounds. He only licked my chin, my throat, following the thin trails of blood.

:*Give him more.*: I said to Rik through our bond.

He sank his fangs into the top of my shoulder. I felt his hunger, the surge of power that hit him at the first swallow. Then he lifted his mouth and allowed my blood to flow down my breast before closing his mouth back over the wound.

Xin lapped my breast in slow, sinuous strokes that melted my bones. His fangs scraped gently, and I shuddered at the thought of him sinking them deep. I didn't know how much blood he'd get if he bit me on the breast, but I was willing. His tongue slid under my nipple, lifting it into the heat of his mouth.

The tip of fang scratched across my nipple and I moaned. Such a small thing, but it sent chills down my spine. Good chills. Chills that made me think about the delicate sharpness biting elsewhere. He flashed his eyes up at me, all wolf. All predator.

I ran my hands through his short, choppy hair and stroked the planes of his face. I wanted to shake his silence. Find what made him crack open and bare his soul to me. I wanted to know him, inside and out. I wanted to hear him come. Not softly, quietly, but a loud roar of release.

I wanted him to come apart at the seams.

20

SHARA

I stood and unbuttoned my jeans. Xin made a low, strangled sound and I looked up at his face, surprised I'd already broken his silence. I hadn't even done anything to tease him yet.

His eyes were locked on my crotch even though my jeans were still very much up. Then I remembered my period. I must have fucking ruined another pair of jeans.

"You're breeding. So young. Alpha, forgive me, I had no idea."

"It's just my period. We're pretty sure I'm not breeding."

"There's nothing to forgive," Rik added. "I'm driven hard by my instincts, yes, but as she says, we don't know that she's breeding. She needs all her Blood now and she doesn't want just me. I wouldn't try and drive any of you away, even if she was fertile."

I appreciated that he said *try* to drive any of my Blood away. Because yeah, if he tried to send Xin or Guillaume or Daire away when I wanted them, he'd have a fight on his hands. I loved that he was alpha and the biggest, baddest Blood, but now that I'd had a taste of several men, at once and separately, I wanted them all. I wanted more.

"And you shall have more, my queen." His voice rumbled deeper. "All the Blood you can call. We're yours."

My stomach rumbled but I didn't want food. I wanted blood. I wanted *Blood*. "Does it bother you?" I asked Xin as I shoved my jeans down my thighs.

"Is a cherry blossom bothered when it blooms in the spring?"

I took that as a hell no, it didn't bother him, though he continued to sit there without moving. "You're not getting undressed."

He looked at Rik, as if asking permission, and that irritated me. "Don't look at him. Look at me. I decide who's putting their dick in me. Not him."

"Patience," Rik whispered, reaching up to snag my hand. "You're asking us to overcome millennia of Blood hierarchy in a moment. It's courteous for a Blood to confirm with the alpha before touching the queen, even if she's making the order."

My fangs throbbed. My pussy ached to be filled. I didn't have much patience remaining.

Xin stripped in record time, but remained standing,

waiting my next order. I pushed him down on the couch and planted my knees on either side of his hips so I straddled his lap, but I didn't take him yet. His manner... unnerved me. The hesitation, and sideways glances at Rik, even after I told him I was making the decisions, made me doubt myself. I'd feel like shit if I did something to him that he regretted later, because I was too fucking eager to taste him again and didn't make sure he was willing.

"I'm willing." His voice cracked like ice giving way beneath a heavy load. "More than willing. Though I've never put my dick in a queen."

I'm pretty sure I gaped at him. "Never? You've had sex before though, right?"

"Some. Not often. But my previous queen was not like you."

I wasn't sure if that was a good thing or not. I started to turn to Rik, doing myself what I'd just been irritated by with Xin, but I wanted my alpha's steady acceptance. Maybe even confirmation. I didn't want to be a terrible queen. I didn't want to mistreat them. Or force them. Or use them...

"Use me," Xin ground out. "Please."

I looked back into his eyes and touched his bond, but as before, his core was too deep. I could find him, sure, if I wanted to leap off the mental skyscraper again.

"My last queen was cold, calculating, and hungry for power. She didn't want bodies for pleasure. She wanted blood for power, and my blades to further her position. She had no other use for me. Forgive me if I seem shocked or dismayed by your passion, because I'm not, at all. I'm merely overwhelmed by my sudden good fortune to find myself here with you. That you hunger for my body and my blood is truly a miracle to me. One that I'm eager to embrace." His eyes crackled with ice and lightning and he finally touched me. He smoothed his palms down my back and shuddered like he'd never touched anything so exquisite before. "May I ask one boon, my queen?"

"Shara," I whispered, letting my eyes drift shut as he stroked me. "Yes."

"May I taste your blood, Shara, my queen?"

I opened my eyes, sliding back toward confused. He'd had my blood. He'd just licked blood from my breasts.

Standing behind me, Rik pressed against my back and reached around to cup my pussy. He stroked his fingers deep, making my head fall back on a moan. He pushed two fingers into me, but it wasn't enough. I wanted so much more. "He means this blood, my queen."

Oh. My cheeks heated. I still couldn't quite wrap my brain around their eagerness for all my blood. "Okay."

They lifted me up so quickly I squeaked out loud. I'd expected him to touch me like Rik, or even taste my blood from his fingers. Not hold me high in the air so Xin could bury his face between my thighs. But that's exactly what he did. Rik supported my weight and Xin drew my knees up on his shoulders so my thighs hugged his head.

He let out a rumbling growl, his shoulders bunching beneath me as if his wolf was trying to tear out of his skin. He clamped onto my clit and growled again, using that vibration to make me writhe in his grip. His fangs scraped tender flesh—not puncturing deep, but scratching, like he'd done to my nipple, and I twitched harder against his mouth. As if my body wanted his fangs. Even there. Climax roared through me and my fangs pulsed, making my whole face ache with need. I needed to bite. I needed his dick. Rik's. Someone's. I couldn't bear this emptiness tearing me apart.

Pushing into me from behind, Rik offered his wrist. I sank my fangs deep, not trying to find a vein. I needed him in my mouth, like I needed his dick. Pressure on my fangs, the taste of his skin and blood in my mouth. So good. Xin sucking my clit, feeding on my blood at the same time. I gripped a handful of his hair and dug into Rik's arm, holding on for dear life. He didn't fuck me that hard, not with fangs so near my most vulnerable flesh. In fact, he was already coming, and with his blood on my tongue and me under Xin's tongue, I couldn't stop coming either. Rik's bond sizzled with lava, and Xin's crackled with blistering frost. The two met in me and exploded into a fire and ice showdown of cataclysmic proportions.

My alpha roared with release and he bit my neck again. Xin turned his head and sank his fangs into my thigh. I bucked between them, unable to stop the surge of pleasure. I would have screamed but I still had Rik's wrist in my mouth and I wasn't letting him go. Not until I had Xin's throat close enough to trade for.

As if they'd worked together for years, Rik pulled out of me and let me drop down onto Xin's waiting cock. I took him deep and lunged for his throat as soon as Rik pulled his arm aside. Fresh power soared through me. A blizzard of soft white fur and crystalized ice. The heavy thud of thick wet snow and the deafening silence of the forest just after a storm had dumped a foot or two of snow. Xin's wolf turned at the edge of the forest, waiting for me to follow.

I ran after him on four swift, silent feet. Nose in the wind. Millions of scents on my tongue. But it was his blood I wanted, not any deer or rabbit. And I would hunt him… until I caught him in the dark shadows of the wood.

I came awake slowly. Aware of being carried. By someone not Rik. It took me a minute to feel skin against me rather than silvery white fur. "Xin? Where are we going?"

"Alpha suggested a bath before dinner."

I closed my eyes, feeling for Rik's presence. He was near, his bond immediately flooding my senses. :*My queen?*:

I didn't know what to say. Or what I wanted exactly. I was sated for the time being. My hunger satisfied. The blood of two fine men pumping through me. My nerves still singing with pleasure, my muscles pliant and liquid. My body felt like warm honey.

But I didn't feel like myself. Me.

It'd only been a handful of days and I didn't recognize myself. I wasn't alone. I wasn't scared. I sure as hell wasn't a virgin any longer. Nor human.

I'd done things in the last few days that would never have occurred to me in a million years. Like ordering the death of an enemy... without regret. Or having sex with two men at once. Riding one's face while another fucked me. Where had that come from? Had that wanton creature always been caged inside me and I hadn't known? Or was I changing at the very core of who I was? Was this me, now? Or had I lost myself?

Xin settled us into a hot bath. I lay against his chest and breathed his scent, wishing his wolf could provide some clarity. Or at least serenity. The wolf hunted. The wolf killed. It had no remorse. It didn't worry that it was becoming too wolf-like. It certainly didn't worry about the deer it'd just eaten.

It was hungry. It did what its nature drove it to do.

Carrying a plate of steak and potatoes, Rik came into the tub too and Xin shifted me so they could both hold me between them, our legs stretched out the length of the tub, while Rik fed me small bites of food. Xin still had blood on his face. My blood. Period blood. I waited for my cheeks to fire, my stomach to clench or pitch with disgust, but I only felt... satisfaction. That was my blood on my Blood and nothing could make me happier than seeing him pumped with power because of me.

He stroked my face, long sensitive fingers gliding like an artist chiseling a masterpiece from a chunk of marble. His eyes burned like quick silver. Hot, cold, bright, all at once. His bond a searingly cold yet eerily silent blizzard.

"She liked it that way," he whispered, keeping his touch light on my face. "My old queen. She didn't want to hear us. She didn't want to feel us. We were taught early to lock our bonds down tightly. She wanted blades. Not emotions. Not men. Not lovers. Not even protectors. She didn't want touch or conversation or service of any kind. She had servants for that. We were only in her presence long enough to receive her orders verbally. Never in the bond, unless it came from her alpha, because she didn't touch any part of us."

"Even when she fed?" I asked, reaching out to stroke his face as gently as he touched mine.

"Even then. She used a small blade and we offered blood into a cup from which she drank."

In some ways, that had been my existence alone, on the run from thralls. I'd had no one. I'd talked to no one. I certainly never touched anyone or fed, because I had no idea what that was. In a matter of days, Rik and Daire had managed to make me forget those lean, lonely years.

No wonder his bond was so far away. So silent. He'd walled himself off hundreds of years ago.

Staring into Xin's eyes, I wondered how long it would take me to help him forget. To fill up all those long, lean years of emptiness.

He leaned closer and brushed his mouth ever so softly against mine. "You already have, Shara, my queen. Thank you."

21

DAIRE

Shara turned the laptop around for everyone to see. "This is where we need to go." A huge plateau rose into the clouds with sheer rocky sides dotted with waterfalls. "Roraima, Venezuela."

"Why there, I wonder?" Gina said. "It's certainly out of the way and will be difficult to get to the top."

Shara shook her head. "He's not at the top. He's inside the mountain, like it's holding him down."

"Let me make a few calls, including a courtesy call to the queen in Mexico City. We won't stop over there unless you want to, but it'd be nice to let her know you'll be in her region, even briefly. Why don't you start going through the pictures Marissa uploaded and make notes of any repairs or modifications you're wanting?"

At least Gina had brought help along with dinner tonight, so we Blood could simply sit and look at our queen rather than clear the table. The food had been fantastic, but I didn't remember what I ate. I'd been too busy watching my queen eat and talk with her consiliarius. And I'd lying if I said I wasn't worried about the sleeping arrangements tonight.

Rik would be true to his word. He'd refuse to allow me inside her bed. I'd be damned lucky if I was allowed to step foot in her room, even to sleep.

I'd already learned my lesson, but that didn't matter. The alpha's word was law, second only to our queen's. I couldn't possibly ask her to overrule him, when I'd been willing to hurt her to protect him.

I'd scoped out the other bedrooms and found a full-sized bed I thought might have been hers, or at least set up for her. She'd said she rarely slept alone, even as a baby, until she'd grown up enough to take the tower room. That room still angered me… but I'd give my right arm to be there with her tonight, rather than the pink fluffy girl's room that didn't fit her personality at all.

"Marissa and Winston have already made notes about changes they recommend, especially the kitchens and bathrooms," Gina added. Then on the phone, "Angela, let's get the jet fueled and ready to go in the next few days."

Shara's eyes widened. "I've never flown before. Now I'm flying on my own jet. Insane."

Rik squeezed her hand. "Wait until we go shopping. Would you rather go to Abu Dhabi or LA first?"

"Let's start with LA. I've always wanted to see the ocean."

Fuck. There were so many things that she'd never done. Never seen. It was a good thing we Aima lived a very long time, so we could ensure she had all the opportunities she'd missed out on.

"How many more days will you bleed, my queen?" Guillaume asked on her other side.

"Probably two more. Three at the most."

Gina caught that bit and said, "Her Majesty will need the jet ready to fly to Venezuela in three or four days' time. Also look up Mayte Zaniyah and text me her consiliarius's phone number, please."

"This is really going to happen," Shara whispered, looking at each of us.

Rik's eyes flared with surprise. "Of course. You need to find him. We'll get you there."

"I guess…" She blew out a sigh. "I thought you'd try to prevent me from going, or try to talk me out of it."

"I'd love nothing better than to keep you from all harm, but a queen goes where the queen goes."

"We just keep you safe as you go," Guillaume said.

"And what about *him?*" She bit her lip and I'd give my left nut if every man at the table didn't go rock hard. "I don't know how that's all going to work out. Only that I must free him."

"Then we free him," Rik said firmly, giving her hand another squeeze. "But he will not harm you, Shara. I'll have

Xin or Guillaume kill him before I let this king harm one hair on your head."

Xin sat on my left, and I swear the temperature dropped a good ten degrees on our side of the table. "Leviathan was chained for a reason. Best we all remember that."

"I wish we knew why. Why he was chained—and why I in particular have to free him before he dies. Or even why he's dying now rather than the hundreds of years before. Who's been feeding him this whole time?"

"No one," Guillaume said with a grim slant to his lips. "Which makes this doubly risky."

"Then how is he still alive, if no one's fed him since before Xin was born?"

"There's a theory the old ones believe," Xin said, drawing her attention to him.

"Old ones even older than you?"

His eyes flashed a moment as if lightning crackled across a midnight sky. "I'm young for Aima, thank you very much. Our alpha is a mere babe and you… barely a twinkle in your mother's eye. The first and second generation Aima carried so much of the goddesses' blood that they were the same as immortal. The theory is that they fed on each other, and further fueled their longevity. They were slow to mix with humans, too. So their blood was pure magic."

"The first time Rik fed, I died."

Just remembering made both him and I shudder. I'd tried to revive her, but she was definitely dead. Her skin chilled. No heart beat. I could only imagine how horrible it'd been for Rik because he'd been making love to her.

"I went to Isis's pyramid and she gave me her blood. I lost track of time, but it seemed like She gave me a lot. *A lot.*"

"Good," Xin replied. "Then you'll live a very long time, perhaps as long as the old queens. According to legend, the original queens never really died. They just went to sleep and never woke up again. They were weary of the world, or heartbroken from losing their loves, or all the humans they'd known were dead and gone and it took too much effort to continually set up a new life somewhere else. It's very possible that Leviathan is old enough that he's basically immortal. That he's been sleeping for thousands of years. And now, something has woken him."

"And he's pissed."

I caught Rik's gaze and we didn't have to use the bond to know we were thinking the same thing. We knew exactly what had awoken him.

Our queen. Shara. Her very presence in the world would be enough to awaken a long-dead monster.

I'd fucking wake up after half a million years of sleep to have her touch me. Feed me. Love me.

Not sleeping with her tonight was going to feel like a half a million years.

Which was exactly why Rik had chosen to punish me this way. I'd rather he take me outside and beat me within an inch of my life than refuse me access to our queen and him, because I hadn't been apart from him in thirty or forty years. He would certainly not leave her side.

The help cleared off the table and Gina spread out blue

prints and pictures with notes and sketches. Shara's eyes were as big as a kid enjoying her first Christmas. A state-of-the-art kitchen that still managed to embrace the old world charm of a hundred-year-old stone fireplace that dominated one wall. A series of brand new decks from the master bedroom tower down to the other levels, ending at the pool. It was in good shape according to the contractor, other than needing a new pump. The hot tub was big enough for at least ten people and only needed a new heater. Then she could use it all year around. They'd sketched out some additions to the backyard, including a large fire pit and outdoor kitchen in the pool area.

The biggest project, though, was the master suite that dominated the large tower overlooking the river. The bottom level was a massive library and office with a private elevator to the next floor. The next two levels were open to each other with exposed century-old rafters and stone walls. It was plenty big enough for two king-sized beds placed together in the center of the circular room, with a massive skylight shining down from above. The bathroom was going to be redone in marble tile, with a massive circular tub that made the one we'd shared upstairs look like a kiddie wading pool.

Shara blushed at the double king sized beds pushed together, but that was exactly what she wanted. Gina and her staff didn't bat an eye, and evidently the contractor was more than happy to do whatever she wanted because I'm sure his bill was astronomical. If he did a good job, the

Isador legacy would give him a blank check as long as the queen was happy.

"Anything else you'd like to modify?" Gina asked. "Of course we can do projects at any time, but if there's something pressing, we ought to do it now while we have the crew in place to get it done as quickly as possible."

"No, I don't think so. This is... incredible. Tell Marissa and Winston thank you, please. I can't believe they've accomplished so much. And you too, Gina. I don't know how I ever survived without you." She looked at each of us, a tremulous smile on her lips. "Without any of you."

That fucking smile wrecked me. I wanted to die because I'd fucked up. It was my fault. I deserved to be banished forever. But fucking hell I wanted to bury my face against her and breathe her scent and make her smile like that every minute of every day.

"It's our pleasure, Shara. Truly. And that leads to the next question. Which of your staff would you like to employ in Eureka Springs?"

"You mean ask them to move with us?" Gina nodded. "Anyone who wants to go."

"Well everyone will want to go. It's an honor to live and work closely with the queen. I don't think you quite realize how many people are on your staff."

"I've heard you mention Marissa and Angela. Winston. Frank and his staff. Who else?"

"Marissa and Angela are my personal assistants. Talbott Agency is an international firm with offices in London,

Sydney, Tokyo, Rome, Paris, Hong Kong, Mexico City, New York, and Kansas City of all places. Plus smaller satellite offices and staff throughout the world. Basically we have someone in every city where there's a queen. Some are known to that consiliarius and some..." She shrugged with a smug curve on her lips. "Let's just say Talbott Agency is very very good at hiding when we want to be in plain sight. All together, we employ well over five hundred staff worldwide."

"You have five hundred people working for you?"

"No. They work for you. They report to me, some directly, some indirectly. Goddess, we probably have over two hundred CPAs and another hundred lawyers keeping the property and investments straight. That number doesn't include the people who worked for the last Isador queen most of their lives and retired. If you add them in..." She thought a moment, tapping the table. "You've probably got close to fifteen hundred people, then."

Shara thumped back against her chair. "Wow. I had no idea. I thought you ran a small office here in Kansas City."

"I do. That's the beauty of hiding in plain sight. When I call another consiliarius, like Bianca Zaniyah, I don't tell them Gina Talbott."

"You tell them Gina Isador."

"Of course. Talbott is merely a name we created when..." A blank look flickered over her face and she blinked. "I'm sorry, I forgot what I was saying. Where was I?"

I felt Shara's sadness in the bond. She hated that no one could talk about her mother. Even us. I know she'd told me her mother's name… But I couldn't remember it. "We were talking about who was going to move to Eureka Springs with me."

"Oh. Yes." Gina paused, twiddling with her napkin. "I would love to move with you and serve as closely as possible, but if you'd rather have some distance, that's perfectly acceptable. There's nothing I can't handle for you with a phone call, and if I need to fly to you, it'll only take a few hours."

Shara reached over and squeezed Gina's hand. "I'd love you to come, unless you have family here."

"No," she replied softly. "I have no children. I'll be the last Talbott who serves as your consiliarius."

"You're young yet. Maybe you'll fall in love with someone in Eureka Springs."

Gina snorted and started gathering up the blueprints. "I'm flattered, Shara, honestly. But I'm much older than you think."

Shara stood to help. "You can't be that old. You look at most thirty, thirty five."

"Oh honey. That ship sailed nearly twenty years ago."

We Blood stood too. Rik's forehead had a deep slash and I knew what he was thinking. *My queen doesn't clean or tidy up something as insignificant as papers.*

But the women were talking and laughing, certainly not working.

"Marissa has already fallen in love with the town, so she's a definite. Winston, of course. And he'll need to hire a few staff to care for the grounds, prepare the meals, and clean inside. Probably five people. We'll hire from within, offer a few select associates that he's worked with before the chance to move. What do you think of Frank? Has his security team done a good job for you?"

Shara shrugged. "So far. I mean we haven't really gone anywhere lately. But I guess the poor guy has had to dispose of two bodies." She cringed. "Ugh. I can't believe I said that out loud. He's definitely proven his loyalty. If he'd like to provide a security detail in Eureka Springs, I think that will be fine. Rik, any objections?"

He inclined his head. "Not at all, my queen. I agree that he's been loyal and quick thinking when we've needed him. He's not Blood, but he'll do well enough as a human."

"Very good. I'll let everyone know. I'll call Bianca tomorrow morning. Scratch that. Tomorrow's Christmas Eve. I'll call them the day after Christmas. That works better for your schedule anyway."

"Wait, tomorrow's Christmas Eve? Really? We don't have any presents or a tree or lights..."

Rik met my gaze and he didn't need to make the order. "We'll decorate for Christmas first thing tomorrow, my queen."

"And take you shopping again," I added. "You'll want some things for the new house."

"And presents for each of you."

I dropped my gaze to the table cloth, unable to meet the shining glow in her eyes. Not when I'd failed her so miserably.

Rik said what I could not. "You are our present, my queen. We need nothing else but you."

SHARA

Tomorrow was Christmas Eve. I'd totally lost track of time. Gee, I wonder why? I'd only been fucking and feeding and fucking so more the last few days. My cheeks heated at the thought. And yeah, my fangs started to ache and images of naked skin and hot muscle and hard dick started flickering through my mind. Gina left with her crew, and I hoped I wasn't rude to her. I was too distracted. Mutely, I looked at Rik. I wanted to go to bed. I wanted to feed. But I didn't know who or how many or—

"Daire and Xin, you're on the first patrol duty." His voice rumbled the floor beneath my feet as he strode to me. "Guillaume, with me. Xin, trade after six hours. Daire, you're on your own."

He swept me up in his arms and as soon as I smelled his skin, I was lost. Hunger roared through me and I sank my fangs into his throat. He clutched me hard, pausing to lean against the door. His body shook and he groaned, deep and low in his throat. Guillaume caught us, pressing him against the door frame. Like he couldn't even stay on his feet.

Alarmed, I lifted my head, blood dribbling down my lips. "Rik? Are you all right? I'm sorry. I forgot I fed on you already today."

He half laughed, half groaned, leaning heavily against the wall. "Your bite comes with a new gift, my queen."

"What?"

Guillaume pulled me into his arms and started for the stairs. Confused, I looked back at Rik. Why weren't they more concerned for him? He started up after us and wavered like he was drunk. Like I'd taken too much blood again. My *alpha*. His bond felt fine in my head though. Better than fine. He radiated pleasure through me, making my hunger worse. I couldn't hurt him...

"Your bite is orgasmic." Guillaume said in that grave, solemn way of his. But when I looked into his face, his eyes danced with mirth. "At least for our alpha. Though you can try out this new power on me as soon as you'd like."

Orgasmic. Oh geez. I'd bitten Rik and he came? Just like that? Maybe that was why he'd come so quickly earlier with Xin. Not that I was complaining in the slightest.

"Just like that." Guillaume huffed out a laugh. "Keep that in mind, my queen, if you're wanting more than blood. I'm sure Rik will recover quickly but it'd be a shame if you made us all come before we're able to sate your need."

"I'll be ready quick enough." Rik caught up to us.

I took one look at the blood spilling from his throat and reached for him. He pulled me close, tucking his face close to my head as I locked my mouth over the punctures. "Take all you want. I'm nowhere near weakened yet from blood loss."

:*Even after this morning?*:

When I'd killed him...

I shuddered at the memory and burrowed deeper into his arms.

:*Your cobra bite made me stronger. I think you could feed from me a dozen times a day and not endanger me.*:

My mind protested that I surely wouldn't need to feed

on him a dozen times a day. But the more of his blood I drank, the more I wanted. He'd always had that extra punch of alpha, but now... It was addictive. I craved his blood. I burned for it. And once I had his taste on my tongue, I wanted my belly full of his blood. I wanted him spilling down my breasts and dripping down my body.

:*Your wish is my command.*:

I felt hands tugging and removing my shoes but I didn't let go of Rik's throat. I couldn't. My brain insisted if I let go of his blood I'd die. I needed all I could hold and I had a feeling that wouldn't be enough either. The thought made me tremble, my stomach quivering with dread despite the power spreading through me with every swallow of his blood. I didn't want to incapacitate him again. Let alone all of them. But this rising need felt like that night in the tub. When we'd barely had the energy to walk when I was finally done feeding off them.

He laid back in the bed with me on top of him and I rubbed against him. I wanted every inch of his skin against me. But I didn't want to lift my mouth from his skin.

"I can easily cut your clothes away, my queen." Guillaume said. "But I didn't want to upset you."

:*Fuck these clothes. I've already bled on everything anyway.*:

I tore at Rik's T-shirt. The sound of tearing cotton made chills race down my spine, but I liked it. I liked it a lot. I especially liked the tug of Guillaume's knife at my nape. The soft sound of my sweater cutting apart, falling away to bare my back. There was something about the sound of fibers giving way beneath his steel. The gentle kiss of the blade on my skin. I knew he wouldn't hurt me, but it still made my heartbeat quicken. So naturally he stroked me more with that blade.

I remembered the way he'd cut himself for me that first time. And my two other Blood. How quickly and easily he'd made them bleed for me. Before I could even ask, I felt the hot drip of his blood against my skin. It made me writhe against Rik, desperate for more. Every muscle tightened, need hammering with my pulse.

:*Get that big dick in me before I die.*:

Guillaume groaned roughly. The cold tip of his blade pressed against my lower back and then he tugged through my jeans so hard and quick it lifted me up. He jerked the denim out of his way, yanking me up, baring my ass. And then sweet bliss as he started to push inside me. So big. So wide. I groaned against Rik's throat, tightening my grip on him with my mouth. I wanted to bite him again and again, but I didn't know what that would do to him. If he'd just dry come? That didn't sound good.

"Bite me again if you want," he ground out. "Though I'd rather be inside you when you do."

Guillaume slid to the hilt inside of me, his weight heavy on my back. Pressing me against Rik. Two solid walls of muscle. Goddess. It was fantastic. I wanted to sleep like this —if I didn't need to breathe. Then G started to move inside me. The long, slow drag of his full length gliding through me. It made me claw at Rik's chest. He lifted me on my knees to give G better access.

Living several hundred years certainly gave a man plenty

of time to perfect his technique. He'd been on the bottom of us last time and hadn't moved much at all, but this time... He made sure I fully appreciated his size, and gradually, his power. He thrust a bit harder, making my breath oomph out against Rik's throat, but I still had the impression that he was only playing. He was holding back.

:Fuck me. Hard. I can take it.:

His big, scarred hands clenched harder on my hips. Rik had both hands in my hair, one palm clamped to my nape. And suddenly, I realized I was pinned. Locked in place. They paused a moment, waiting to be sure that I really was okay with it.

:Please.:

Guillaume let out a guttural sound and slammed deep. He rocked me so hard against Rik that I would have lost my grip on his throat without his hand locking me in place. G waited a second and I felt his bond slice through me, a quick, hard kiss of steel as if he needed to be sure I was all right. He hadn't hurt me. Then he hauled himself out of me, inch by inch, making me twist and buck between them. He plunged deep again and stars exploded in my head. Thunder rolled in the distance, coming nearer with each heavy thrust. Not thunder, hoof beats. The Dullahan galloped closer in the night, dripping blood down my back.

Rik's blood filled me with power. His volcano rumbled toward eruption, pumping me full of molten rock. My bones were melting, shifting, nerves firing up that had never been exposed before. My scalp prickled, my spine itched, and for a moment, I was terrified I'd shift into the cobra again. I didn't want to hurt anyone. Pressure built inside me. Power. Pleasure. Blood. I strained to hold it all.

G shoved deep and ground against me, stroking deep inside, and I couldn't hold back any longer. I convulsed, power streaming through our bonds. Enough power to light up Kansas City. The whole fucking state. Rik let go of my head and I reared back against Guillaume. I didn't have to ask. He wrapped his forearm around my face and I buried my fangs in his wrist. He let out a thundering roar and came hard inside me, spurt after spurt that sent my pleasure surging higher. Rik held on to my thighs or I probably would have soared right off the bed. It felt like I could fly. Power lifting me up. My hair floating. My body weightless. I'd just float away into the night sky and join the stars.

"No floating away, my queen." Rik pulled me down on top of his chest, and Guillaume crashed down beside him to sprawl on the mattress, though I didn't let his wrist go. Not yet. His blood tasted too good. Clashing steel, thundering hooves, the ancient blood of a warrior.

Rik's arms enfolded me, holding me close. His bond settled down to a fiery red ribbon of lava rather than the rumbling volcano. G's stallion whickered softly in my mind. I felt a soft muzzle touch my cheek. I finally licked his wrist, unable to swallow a single drop more, though he kept his wrist pressed to my cheek.

I shivered a little, my back cold. Which reminded me that my favorite cuddly warcat was absent. Rik drew me down between him and Guillaume and pulled a blanket up over me. G wasn't exactly a purring cuddle buddy, but he spooned tight against me, tangling his legs with mine and Rik without a care. I wasn't sure how he'd feel about touching another man, but he didn't seem to mind.

"Blood are Blood. Male, female, both, neither, it doesn't matter. We're here for you."

"But have you fucked men and women? Do you have a preference?"

"My preference is to fuck my queen whenever and however she wants, in as many ways as she wants. If you find pleasure in Blood fucking Blood, then we'll do that and enjoy the hell out of it too."

"You will? Really? Or only because I ordered it?"

"Really. You forget that your blood flows in all of us now. To touch one of them is second only to touching you directly."

"In most courts, a Blood only rarely gets to sleep with the queen," Rik said.

"I remember you saying that. I guess I'm just trying to wrap my mind around it. For you, it's not uncommon or even unexpected for two Blood to be away. For me... I'm hoping they're not upset. And I miss them."

Just saying it out loud made my throat tighten. Especially Daire, though I didn't say anything. I wouldn't interfere with Rik's command or punishment.

"Daire is upset, but he should be." Rik's voice hardened. "Xin will be here in a few hours. If you have need of him before then, you know how to call him. And if you want Guillaume to stay, then he'll stay."

"Even if Xin has to sleep on top of us, we'll figure it

out," G added with a yawn. "You'll have more room in the nest once we move."

My nest. My manor. Just thinking about it made me smile with wicked glee. All that space in two big beds. We'd all be able to sleep together.

All five of us. Or six. If this king, Leviathan, worked out.

22

SHARA

Something woke me. Not a sound exactly. A presence, a sense of something moving. A quick bond check told me Guillaume was still here, so it hadn't been six hours since we'd gone to bed. I thought maybe Daire was sneaking close, but when I touched his bond, I felt him in the kitchen making a sandwich. No surprise.

Xin was further away, like he was outside.

I turned my attention back to the room. It was brighter in here than it should be. I lifted my head and it took me a few moments to even make sense of what I was seeing. A window. In my room. That had no windows. Between the bed and the door. Soft, golden light spun out in rays from the window, so I wasn't immediately alarmed. Monsters didn't like the light. But then I saw what was crawling out of the window.

"Rik." He stirred, made a low mumble, but didn't wake up. Maybe I was dreaming. Because why would a skeleton climb through a window into my room?

It wore some kind of armor. Light flashed off the silver, making me wince. Suddenly the light was not so soft and pretty, but hard, sharp, and bright enough to hurt.

"G. Rik. Guys. Wake up. Tell me I'm not dreaming."

:*We're coming.*: Xin and Daire both flared brighter in my mind. I felt them racing toward me, Daire closer, coming up the stairs. But it still didn't feel real. Until the skeleton laid its bony fingers on my ankle. That felt pretty fucking real. In fact, it hurt like a bitch.

"Rik!" I shrieked. The damned thing locked a vise around my ankle and wouldn't let go, even when I kicked it in the head. "Rik!"

He moved slightly, as if trying to come awake, but slumped back down heavily. Drugged. Spelled. Something was keeping him from moving. I refused to consider that they might be permanently incapacitated. Or I'd just give up right now.

Magic leaped in my blood, strength and power ready to rock and roll, but I wasn't sure what to try, especially against something that didn't even have a body. I didn't want to burn down the house with us in it so a fireball didn't sound like the brightest idea. I went for Rik's troll strength and slammed my foot into the skeleton again. Bone shattered. And it still dragged me off the bed. I hit my head on the floor so hard that it dazed me a moment. I grabbed at the leg of the bed, hooking my arm around it to hold on.

The skeleton jerked on my leg so hard something popped or tore, I wasn't sure which. Pain burned up my calf and into my knee. Which pissed me off. Fuck it all to hell. If I had to burn the house down, so be it.

I willed fire to engulf the skeleton. So hot that even its armor would melt and bend. I felt the sear on my flesh. I heard an unholy screech. But it still wouldn't let go of my ankle.

Daire's warcat exploded through the door, casting deadly splinters of wood everywhere. He seized the skeleton's arm in his jaws and crunched through the bone, tearing its whole arm off. The skeleton drew a gleaming gold and silver sword with its other hand and stabbed Daire in the chest. He roared, I screamed, and finally, Rik and G scrambled up, dazed, but alive, just as another skeleton crawled through the window.

My tower bedroom had felt plenty big. Until a warcat, a rock troll, and a hell horse started tearing a bunch of skeletons apart. Xin's silver wolf crouched over the top of me, shielding me with his body. I wrapped my arms around his neck and tried to stand, so I could get out of the way, but my leg wouldn't hold my weight. He dragged me over to the wall and pressed against me. :*Can you shut the portal?*:

I focused on the gleaming window. Five skeletons had crawled through. All armored and fighting with swords. They were actually very good, too. I could smell my guys' blood. All of them but Xin. Another skeleton started through. A couple of more, and we'd be seriously outnumbered.

I tried envisioning the portal smaller, but I strained until sweat beaded on my forehead and nothing happened. It was like the harder I pushed, the firmer the window stood. From the side, it looked silvery, kind of like a flat bubble hovering in space. I crawled a few steps to the side so I could see the back better, and it definitely looked like a bubble, gleaming and slightly rounded.

Bracing myself, I tapped on my period blood. Power surged through me like a million-volt generator came on line. I pushed that energy like a lightning bolt to prick that bubble. Something exploded all right. Light blazed like we'd blown up the sun. My eyeballs burned, seared and tender. I blinked, and I was looking up at the ceiling. Xin rolled over beside me, blood leaking from his ears and eyes. He touched his muzzle to my cheek, and I could feel his pain. All of their pain. They were all down. All hurt, bleeding, damaged. I forced myself upright, slowly, holding my head. Pain splintered through my skull, whether from the explosion or when I'd hit the floor, I wasn't sure.

Bones littered the room. It looked like a graveyard had been torn apart by an earthquake and coffins had just emptied out all over my bedroom. Rik's rock troll pushed up to his knees, one hand braced on the floor, his head hanging low. Daire was sprawled and twisted half under the bed. He was the one I was most worried about after taking a sword in the chest. I couldn't see G, but he was on the other side of Rik and the bed. Banged up, but okay, at least his bond felt the most solid and least pain. It'd take a hell of lot to kill the headless knight.

I crawled over to Daire and laid a hand over the gaping wound in his chest. He was still alive, but weak. The sword had punctured a lung. His breathing sounded too wet and heavy. Though he still managed to lick my cheek.

:*Don't cry, my queen. We're all alive.*:

I didn't realize I was crying. "Can you feed? Will that help you?"

Rik pushed up, lurched a step, and finally made it to us. "Your blood will always help."

:*I can't shift, and if I bite her like this, it will hurt her.*:

G came to me, a small knife in his hand. Silently, I offered my wrist and he made a quick cut. I let my blood drip directly onto the horrible wound in Daire's chest, and then offered him my wrist. Rather than lick, he took my whole arm in his mouth, cradling my wrist so gently that he didn't even break my skin, and let my blood flow down his throat.

I held my other wrist out to Rik. He hesitated a moment, bowing his head.

"We failed you, my queen. *I* failed you. You should feed Daire and Xin first since they were quickest to your aid."

"You're alpha. We need you up quicker than them. And you didn't fail me. You kept trying to wake up, but you couldn't. Something was keeping you from helping me."

"You know who it was." G's mouth turned down in a

grim slant. "So how is she supposed to hold you accountable for not responding quicker?"

Rik grunted an acknowledgment and cradled my left wrist. He bent over my arm, but looked up at me, meeting my gaze. "I still feel like I failed you, though Guillaume's right. We're all lucky to be alive."

"Who was it?" He bit into my wrist and my eyelids fluttered. Time seemed to still. Eons passed in between my heart beats. All that mattered was my blood. In them. In them all. I looked at Guillaume, a silent request. No, order. I willed him to come to me, now, and feed.

He walked around behind me and took me in his arms. I relaxed into him, letting him hold me up, as he sank his fangs into my throat.

Xin's wolf crept closer, head down, though not because he was injured.

"Can you shift?"

:Not yet, my queen.:

"G, I need you to bite me again so Xin can feed too."

I sensed a heaviness in his bond. Concern for my welfare, with four of them feeding at the same time. Especially after I'd just shattered whatever that portal thing was. But I tugged on his bond. Willing him to do as I asked.

He shifted me up so he could bite through the upper swell of my breast. I shuddered, so close to coming, just from the bites. From taking care of them. Healing them. G returned to his bite on my throat and Xin's wolf licked my blood from the second bite.

Connected. All five. My blood pulsed in them, setting off a cascading power surge. I didn't have to do anything but lie there in G's arms and bleed. My blood knew exactly what to do. One by one, I healed them. I closed the wound in Daire's chest. The skeleton swords had managed to gouge several deep cuts into Rik's troll hide, and the explosion of the portal had hurt something inside him. Bruised his organs. My blood flowed over those injuries and took away his pain.

I sank into Xin, easing his wolf's sensitive senses that had been scorched by the brilliant light. Then Guillaume. Skilled with sword and blade as a knight, he hadn't taken any direct wounds—until I'd tossed him on his back and broken several of his ribs.

Footsteps pounded up the stairs and all four men went rigid with tension. G held knives in both hands and even Daire scrambled to a crouch, tail lashing.

A very human and suddenly very scared man stumbled to a halt at the door. "Oh shit. We heard... We saw... No alarm but..."

He looked at each of us and I finally realized who it must be. "Frank, right?"

He nodded and tried to keep his gaze locked on my face, but yeah, I'm pretty sure he thought he'd just stumbled into a crazy orgy. I was naked and bloody and stretched out between two men and two animals. "There was an explosion," he whispered. "Thought maybe a gas line. You didn't answer your phone."

Dismissing the man as a threat, Rik picked me up and

carried me to my bed. "And now you need to heal yourself, my queen."

I didn't remember what he meant, until he touched my right knee. I sucked in a hard breath and bit back a scream.

"I think it's dislocated," G said. "While she can heal it, it might be best to have a doctor set it for her first."

"You did the right thing," I said to Frank, pleased my voice didn't quiver, though I sounded a bit breathier than normal. "Can you call Gina and ask her to come with Dr. Borcht, please? Tell them I hurt my knee and it might be dislocated."

"Of course, ma'am." He took a step back, eyes still frantically locked on my face. "Right away, ma'am."

He disappeared and ran back down the stairs quicker than he'd come. I sighed. "Money says we'll need to hire a new security firm tomorrow."

"You never know." Xin sat on the edge of the bed, fully human. "He seems to be more invested in you than the average human. He may very well ask you to bond him."

"A human?"

"Not as Blood, but as… what's the word?" He looked to G and Rik for help.

"Thrall?" I asked, but he shook his head.

"Servant, but they don't really have servants in this day and age," G replied. "Back in the old days, all humans working for the nest were sworn to the queen, even if they weren't Aima. That way she knew who she could trust, and who might be a plant of another queen."

Daire sat on the floor beside the bed. He didn't ask, but I

wanted him up with us. I didn't ask Rik, but he felt my desire in the bond and gave a nod to Daire. He hopped up and cuddled into my side, careful not to bump my knee, which was swollen and hurting more by the moment.

"So which one of you is going to tell me who attacked us with skeletons while we wait on Dr. Borcht?"

23

RIK

I hurt all over and not because of any physical injuries.

I'd failed her. I'd failed to protect my queen when she'd needed me.

Sure, some magical shit had to be going down to keep me from responding to her, but I wouldn't soon forget the horrible feeling of hearing her scream my name and being unable to move. Without Daire, she would have been dragged through that portal.

We never would have seen her again. I had no illusions what would have happened to her on the other side. Our bonds would have been severed. The thought made me want to smash this whole house down and kill everyone who tried to stop me.

Guillaume and Xin looked at each other like they were silently daring each other to be the one to tell her. As the oldest Blood, they'd seen the most shit. And while I'd been fully prepared to deal with court politics and queen wars, I'd never in a million years expected we'd be facing off against a god.

"He has many names," Guillaume finally said. "Out of all the old gods, he's found a way to still be meaningful in the world today. He's not worshiped, exactly, but he's conflated with other religions, feeding off them, confusing people, turning good intentions wrong. All the ancient mythologies featured a father god, usually a god of the sun, or god of light. That's who we're dealing with."

"The Egyptians knew him as Ra, or Amun-Ra, or even Aten," Xin said. "The Greeks usually called him Apollo. He influenced both, though not as directly as the Egyptian mythologies. Perhaps that's why he was so quick to strike at you, my queen. He's closer to Isis than the other queens' goddesses."

Shara frowned. "Nobody worships Ra today, do they? Light is supposed to be good. That's why I wasn't afraid at first. The monsters don't like light, and the golden light shining through the window was so beautiful. How could something that beautiful send skeletons that tried to kill us all? What the hell were those things, anyway?"

"Soldiers of Light, the best warriors from all the ages who died in service to him. Samurai, Pharaoh's personal guards, even a few Templar knights I'm sure." Xin paused when Guillaume grunted with disgust, but he nodded. "The sun is good, yes? We must have the sun to survive. But the sun can also cause cancer. It can burn your skin, cause sun poisoning, heat exhaustion, and extreme dehydration. You can die from sun exposure, even though we need the sun to survive. Light is wonderful, until it's focused into a laser that sears your eyes or cuts through a foot of metal like butter."

Guillaume laid his hand on her left thigh, his touch gentle. "In the world today, any time you see something good twisted to hurt another, it's his influence. Supposedly good men who excuse killing people who are different from him. Gunmen killing people in church or at a concert at random. Men spewing obscenities to women on the street. Tyrannical purity, racial injustices, fanatical extremists. He revels in patriarchy, misogyny, racism, and hatred."

She shivered and we all drew closer, pressing against her, shielding her. "Why would he come after me?"

I pressed my lips to her forehead. "Can you think of anything a patriarchal god would despise more than a woman reveling in blood and sex and her own growing magic?"

"Then why not all the Aima queens?"

"I'm sure he's spun out his fanatical plots against them as well, but I have a feeling you will be his focus."

She pressed tighter to my side and I wanted to die at the thought of losing her. Of failing her again. We had to find a way to counteract whatever spell he'd sent ahead of that portal. "My mother said I was controlled chaos. If Ra is order to an extreme... then I suppose it makes sense that he'd hate the chaos I bring."

"And that's probably why you must find Leviathan," Guillaume said. "Remember those old myths? They feature the father god defeating the mighty serpent and either killing him or chaining him in the depths of hell or the ocean, far from mankind. Or in this case, far from you. That's probably another reason he targeted you now, before you could find the king and free him."

I felt her fear trembling in the bond. Her core was shaken. All the political plots and queen games suddenly paled in comparison to an epic battle of light versus dark proportions. "If you'd all been in here sleeping with me..."

Rage crawled through me, lowering my voice to furious bass. "You'd be dead. Gone. Lost forever."

SHARA

Great, just great. While I thought I had a bit of a handle on the whole Aima court politics mess, now I found out a patriarchal god of light was gunning for me.

I felt pretty confident in fighting back against other queens. I was starting to understand my magic. I trusted my Blood to guide me, protect me, and know when to stand back and let me do my thing. But how do you fight a god who'd once been worshiped by ancient Egyptians as Ra?

"Shara, we're coming up!" Gina called from downstairs.

I looked around the room, dismayed. Again. Busted bones, pieces of armor, and weapons littered the floor. Blood everywhere. Of course. The guys were all buck naked. I loved Gina and was definitely getting fond of Dr. Borcht too, but I sure as hell didn't want two other women getting an eyeful of my men.

Rik flashed a cocky smile. "Let's at least put some pants on."

I dragged the sheet up to cover my midsection and breasts, though I didn't know that was any better with all the blood splattered all over it.

Gina hesitated at the destroyed door and surveyed the room. "Oh my. I guess you've had some difficulties."

"You could say that."

Poor Frank followed the women carrying two black cases. Dr. Borcht stepped around and over the broken skeleton soldiers and made her way to my side of the bed. Her gaze immediately locked on my right knee and she gently began to manipulate my leg to see how badly it was damaged. "If you could set the cases over here close, that'd be great."

He brought the two cases over to her and set them down, but I was surprised when he didn't immediately bolt for the door. He looked at each man and then focused on Rik, correctly reading him as the man in charge. "I get that my team's strictly outside security, but if we can help with whatever this situation was, we're willing. Or if there's any debriefing you can give me, so we can improve our response…"

Rik nodded. "Yeah, we should fill you in on what happened. All of you. It's going to affect Her Majesty's security going forward." He looked at me, though, a slight frown wrinkling his brow. *:Do you mind a human included in this discussion?:*

:He's willing to stay. I guess we give him a shot.:

"Here's what happened tonight. Guillaume and I were up here with Her Majesty. Daire and Xin were on watch downstairs." He paused with a glance at Daire.

"I was in the kitchen. Xin went outside to make a quick circuit around the house."

Frank nodded. "We saw him, said hello. That was at 2:04 AM."

Rik looked at me. "Were you asleep, my queen? When it started?"

"I had been, but something woke me up. The room was brighter than it should have been and when I started to sit up, I saw what looked like a window in the center of the room and a armed skeleton climbing through it."

Frank paled but impressed me again. If he doubted my story, at least he didn't express any doubts. Though he made a quick look about the room, saw the bones, and I'm not sure how he could think I'd made the whole thing up. Gina sat on the edge of the bed and took my hand.

"I couldn't wake Rik and Guillaume. Rik moved and groaned, but he couldn't wake up. I heard Daire and Xin coming, but the thing grabbed me."

Dr. Borcht touched my ankle, which bore an ugly ring of bruises. "The skeleton had quite a grip on you."

I shuddered and nodded. "I kicked it two or three times and broke something in it, but it still wouldn't let go of me. It pulled me off the bed. I grabbed the leg of the bed and held on for dear life, and that's when it hurt my knee tugging on me. I tried blasting it with fire, and it definitely howled, but still wouldn't let go of me. By then, Daire came through the door and attacked it. Xin dragged me to safety, and Rik and Guillaume were finally able to wake up and join the fight."

Dr. Borcht lifted the largest case up on the bed and opened it up. Inside was some kind of medical equipment. She lifted up an inside shelf and the whole thing lit up. "This isn't quite as good as the full-body MRI, but it'll at least let me see what exactly is torn inside. I think your ACL is okay, but you've torn at least the meniscus." She looked over at Rik on the other side of the bed. "If you can help me lift and support her injured knee, I need to get it underneath the scanner."

Daire moved out of the way and Rik crawled across the mattress to kneel beside me. One big hand cradled my calf, while the other slid beneath my thigh. He lifted my knee up smoothly and Dr. Borcht moved the scanner into place. I winced a bit, but it didn't hurt too badly. "I should be able to heal that, right?"

"Oh yes. You could heal an ACL too or a broken bone. I just believe it'll be easier for you to heal it if you know exactly what the injury is. There's no sense in you trying to mend back a bone if all you have is ligament damage. It'll take a few minutes to get a good image. Try to hold still and let Rik support your leg."

"The first skeleton was probably a high priest," Gina said, drawing my attention back to her. "He knocked out the Blood, making it safe for them to come through. How did you finally close the portal?"

I forgot that Gina had been around Aima courts her entire life. She probably knew almost as much as the guys, even though she wasn't full Aima. "I couldn't close it. The harder I pushed on it, the stronger it got."

She nodded, her gaze locked on me. Her intensity started to freak me out a bit. Nothing had managed to rattle my consiliarius yet. So if she was worried, or goddess forbid, scared, we were fucked worse than I'd already imagined. And I had a damned good imagination.

"Xin had pulled me over to the side," I continued slowly, watching her reaction. "It looked like a bubble. Kind of shiny and floating, moving like the surface of a bubble. So… I popped it."

"From the back?"

I nodded and she sat back, stunned. She opened her mouth, closed it, and opened it again, but couldn't seem to find the words.

"You do realize who was behind the attack, yes?" Dr. Borcht asked.

"The guys explained it to me," I said vaguely, not sure how much supernatural shit I wanted to discuss in front of my human security guard. Though he hadn't bolted for the door yet, even as he heard my story.

"You did the impossible," Gina finally whispered

hoarsely, shaking her head. "A portal can only be closed by the one who opened it. When Daire attacked the high priest, he freed Rik and Guillaume from the spell, but the portal stayed open. So the first skeleton hadn't opened it. Someone on the other side did. *He* did. The god himself. And you shut it right in his face."

"Goddess," Dr. Borcht whispered, her eyes widened.

"Holy fuck," Gina said, startling a laugh out of me. I'd never heard her curse before.

Suddenly we were all laughing like we'd heard the funniest joke ever told.

Gasping for breath, I lay back against the pillows. Tears filled my eyes but I didn't cry. It was just too much, too sudden, too overwhelming. They sensed my changing mood and quieted too. Rik kept my knee steady. Gina held my hand. Daire started purring, even though he wasn't touching me. Always the knight, Guillaume started piling up the weapons and shields, testing out each sword to see if he wanted to keep any of them. Silent Xin only watched me, his eyes shimmering, crackling ice. If I hadn't taken him…

I didn't think I'd be alive.

But I had to wonder… If Rik and Daire hadn't found me, how much longer would I have lasted on my own? Had the king started to wake up before I came into my power? Was I even on the patriarchal god's radar when I was living on the run and powerless? Certainly Marne and Keisha hadn't known who I was. I'd never have found Gina. I'd never have needed Dr. Borcht's care, either. I'd have never seen skeletons climbing out of a golden window to another plane or world. Or dreamed of a massive snake-dragon creature who'd been chained for thousands of years.

Or stroked a warcat, or a ghostly silver wolf.

Or been held by a massive rock troll.

Or loved the last Templar knight.

The machine dinged and Dr. Borcht said, "Okay, let me slide the scanner out of place, and you can set her knee back down. A pillow underneath to support would be best. Yes, that's it."

I heard the clacking of a keyboard and she hummed beneath her breath. "All right. Yes. Meniscus tear and some MCL damage it looks like. The joint itself is undamaged and the ACL is intact."

I opened my eyes and sat up a little. Gina stuffed another pillow under me so I could still rest but remain upright. "So what does that mean?"

Dr. Borcht pulled up the gray and white scan of my knee. She pointed to some white blobs and rattled off some more medical words but all I really caught was fluid, swelling, and tear. I waited until she paused and said, "I guess I should have asked how do I fix it?"

She touched my knee with her index finger in the center, the outside, and the inside of my knee. "You have some damage in these places. If you flood that area with power, and concentrate on removing the swelling and knitting things back together, you should be up and walking tomorrow."

Frank made a low sound under his breath, making us all look at him. He blushed and stammered, "Sorry, my friend's daughter tore her meniscus a couple of years ago playing basketball and they recommended surgery. She had pain and swelling for weeks."

"In case you hadn't realized, I'm not exactly human."

He met my gaze steadily. "I got that. Um, Your Majesty."

Daire snickered. "What was the clue: the giant warcat or the skeletons or the dead bodies?"

"All the above." He came closer and though Rik didn't move, I felt his readiness in the bond. If this human so much of flinched in a way he didn't like, Rik would tear him apart with his bare hands. Frank went down on one knee. "I'm willing to do whatever you want to stay and make sure you're safe."

I tried to keep the surprise and doubt off my face. It was a really sweet offer. But I wasn't sure what a human could do for me that my Blood could not.

Gina said softly, "Humans are generally beneath other queens' radar. And they have access to places where you may not want your Blood seen."

:What do I do?: I asked Rik. :Is this like that human servant thing? Or do I just say fine, okay, and let it go?:

"I've seen things before," Frank said, drawing my attention back to him. "Things I couldn't explain. Things that..." He sighed, trying to find the words. "It's like they tugged on me. Just a string, a thread, but I felt it. I always knew there was more out there. Like if I just turned my head fast enough, I'd see it. I want to see it, Your Majesty."

:He must have some Aima blood in him,: Rik said through the bond. :It would respond to your magic.:

:How?:

:If you want to magnify his gift, you would need to give him some of your blood. If he's willing. That will make him wholly yours.:

I let the idea rattle around in my head a minute. :You wouldn't care?:

:It's your blood, my queen. We Blood will always be your first and closest servants.:

"There is a way." Gina met my gaze, her eyes gleaming with intensity. "And if you give it to him, I'd ask for it too."

:There are ramifications,: Guillaume said. :They will live longer. Their appearance won't age the same. They will not willingly leave your service if you change your mind later. Gina has proven herself, but I'm not sure that the man won't regret it later.:

Frank stared up at me. He was forty, maybe forty-five, I thought. A good looking tough guy, probably ex-military by the way he held himself. Maybe an ex-cop.

"Do you have any family?"

He shook his head. "Only my business and the people who work for me. My partner and I served together two decades ago. He was the brother I never had."

"Was?"

"He died last year. Cancer. I've got nothing but my business. My people. They're good, loyal, smart people not afraid of anything. Even skeletons that crawl out of windows that don't exist."

"I wouldn't do this for anyone that I didn't know. And I don't even know if this is something you'd want to do."

He looked at Gina a moment, weighing her reaction.

She was entirely focused on me, no doubt in her manner. "You know I'm more than willing."

"What's required?" He finally asked.

I looked at Guillaume and he immediately came to me with a blade in his hand. I held out my wrist and he made a small cut, so quickly that I didn't even feel it.

Blood welled. I felt a surge inside me, as if a gigantic wave swelled higher, lifting me toward the sky. Guillaume's nostrils flared and all my Blood's intensity sharpened. I held my wrist out to Gina.

Her icy fingers trembled on my skin but her eyes gleamed with excitement. Joy. "I swear my life to Shara Isador, last daughter of Isis. I'll serve you faithfully, as my grandmother served before me."

I wasn't sure what to expect as her lips touched my skin. When one of my men tasted my blood, even from someplace as innocent as my wrist, it felt like he was licking my pussy or nipples or hell, both. It was purely sexual, stirring my lust as easily as a kiss.

I didn't feel anything really as Gina swallowed my blood, just the rising power. She swallowed several times, but I didn't count. I didn't know how much was appropriate, but trusted that she knew.

She lifted her head and her eyes swum with tears. "Thank you, Your Majesty. I never thought..." She cleared her throat and gave me a brilliant smile. "Thank you."

Looking at her, I could see my blood in her. I could feel it spreading through her like a soft, warm glow. She carried a piece of me now. I suspected that if I closed my eyes and felt for her in the tapestry I carried in my mind, that I would see her. Wherever she went in the world.

I looked at Dr. Borcht and she smiled apologetically. "I'm a doctor, Shara. I've studied blood-born diseases all my life. I'm afraid that the thought of sharing blood is too risky for me. I'll still serve you as faithfully as I can."

I nodded and smiled back. "Yeah, it never occurred to me either. Not until Rik and Daire showed up. I understand." I turned to Frank. "No pressure. If you change your mind, I'll understand."

"Are you really Isis's daughter? The goddess?"

"Yes."

"I'll swear." I held out my wrist and he came closer, taking my hand in his. "Your Majesty." He pressed his lips to my skin, shuddered a little, but swallowed. Again. And it was the same as with Gina. I didn't feel anything but my blood glowing inside him. Nothing sexual.

Relieved, I smiled at Rik. I didn't want to be some kind of sex fanatic anytime someone touched me.

His bond rumbled with low laughter. :*You can be our sex fanatic whenever you wish, my queen.*:

Frank lifted his head, his eyes wide, his pulse thumping rapidly in his throat. I felt all that, now. I felt the tremor of nerves in his stomach. He was afraid he'd throw up and embarrass himself. Or worse, crave my blood like some kind of beast. But as each moment passed, his nerves settled. He didn't feel any different, other than a spreading warmth, like he'd drank a shot of whiskey.

"I, Frank McCoy, swear my life to Shara Isador, daughter of Isis. Is that right?"

Smiling, I nodded. "As far as I know. This is a first for me too."

Rik took my wrist and licked the small cut. One swipe of his tongue and my eyes fluttered closed and my nipples hardened. I was very aware of being naked, in bed, and surrounded by a bunch of people. Three of which I didn't really want to have see me in the throes of passion.

"Are you ready to heal your knee?"

I was so tired. All I really wanted to do was sleep.

He scooted closer and eased me back on the pillows, still holding my hand. "It doesn't have to be hard or take long, my queen. There's plenty of blood in this room already. Draw it to you and let it heal you."

I closed my eyes and brought up the billowing fabric. Everything glowed, blood like fiery rubies, but the bones and weapons gleamed with liquid sunlight. It was so beautiful—I still couldn't quite wrap my mind around the fact that it'd been used to try and kill me.

:*Do you see this?*: I asked Rik.

:*Fuck. It's like a beacon, telling his servants exactly where to come. We have to get rid of it.*:

:*How?*:

Aloud, he asked, "Everything they left behind is glowing with his magic. I'm surprised every light fanatic in the state isn't camped outside. Is it safe for her to pull that magic to her, like her blood?"

Xin frowned. "I don't know that she can. If it will respond to her call, since it's not hers."

"But will it hurt her? Otherwise how do we dispel the magic?"

"The fuck if I know," Guillaume grumped. "Xin and I are old, but we've never messed with the sun god before."

I knew someone who might know. If I dared ask Her.

24

SHARA

For the first time, I tried to deliberately enter the dreamscape. The place where I'd met a goddess and seen Her pyramid and tasted Her blood.

Closing my eyes, I brought up the pyramid in my mind. Gentle breezes across the sand dunes. Incense and night-blooming jasmine on the air. The gleaming golden pyramid rising in a night sky, a crescent moon hanging above, almost hooked over the tip of the pyramid.

I was there. Barefoot. Hair blowing in the breeze. I called out. "Isis? This is Shara Isador, your last daughter. Your queen. I need your help."

A gust of wind whipped my hair around the opposite direction, right into my face. I started to brush the hair away, and not all of it was mine. It was dark like mine, but heavy with oil and sweet perfume. Her hair tangled with mine, Her arms drawing me back into Her embrace. She wasn't warm or cold against me. Only hard. Like a statue come to life.

"My child. What may I help you with?"

Closing my eyes, I pictured my bedroom at home with the golden glow blazing from bits of skeleton and armor.

Her arms tightened against me, crushing me to her. "Ra has marked you. He tried to take you. How did you escape his net?"

I let the memory of how I'd broken the portal flicker through my mind.

She laughed and white roses suddenly burst up from the ground and wrapped around us, their perfume divine. She loosened her fierce grip on me. "I would have dearly loved to see his face when you broke his magic."

"My Blood are afraid the lingering magic will draw his fanatics to us. That it's like a beacon. So how can I get rid of it?"

"It will, left unchecked." She sighed against my ear. "One thing to remember about light. Everything living needs it to an extent. Everything living can use its warmth and glow for themselves. Just control how much sunlight you take. You'll feel when you've had too much sun."

She kissed my neck, her lips hard and strange. Again, all I could compare it to was a statue, coming to life. I wondered what it would take to make her warm and soft again.

"More blood than you have in your body, dear one. And I

need you alive and well too much to indulge in even one small taste of your blood, even though you tempt me. You tempt me greatly. So alive. So sparkling and rich and pure."

"My mother said I'm controlled chaos. Is that why you need me?"

"Yes. One reason. And someday I hope you'll continue my line with many daughters."

The thought of children almost made me run in the opposite direction. I'd never been around children. Never wanted one of my own.

"Someday you may."

I liked that She didn't make demands of me. It was my choice. Even if Her line died with me.

She loosened her arms, slowly moving away, and I didn't want her to leave. Not yet. There were so many things I wanted to know. I wanted to ask her about my mother, my father, the king—

"Take your king." Her voice sounded further away, though I still smelled the perfume of her hair. "And build a place of safety that Ra cannot penetrate."

I opened my eyes, startled when I realized everyone was staring at me.

Rik's face softened, the lines between his eyes smoothing. "My queen."

"She told me what to do." I paused a moment, looking at my two human… servants. I was going to have to get rid of the negative connotation that word carried in my head. Gina was my friend, not someone I wanted to order around. Even though I was her employer, her queen, it felt demeaning to think of her as a servant. "Brace yourself. When I do this... I don't know what it'll feel like for you. If you'll feel anything at all."

Gina nodded, settling more firmly on the bed. Frank braced a hand against the bed, still on his knees beside us.

I looked up at Rik. I hadn't felt so tired in a long time. My eyes were already heavy, and I had to concentrate on putting words together. "This is probably going to knock me out awhile."

He lifted my hand to his mouth and kissed my knuckles. "Sleep well, my queen."

I closed my eyes and took a deep, steadying breath. Some of the blood here was period blood. I knew what that would do. I wasn't sure how hard the sunlight would hit. So I decided to deal with it first.

In my mind, I carefully touched one of those glowing bones. Golden light clung to me, but it didn't burn or hurt. I rubbed my finger and thumb together, spreading a pleasant glowing warmth into my skin.

I spread my arms out, palms up, and pulled the light toward me, concentrating on my hands. Droplets of liquid sunlight floated to me, dancing through the air like fireflies. My hands glowed brighter, almost like twin suns. There was a lot of golden energy in the room. I could feel the power coursing through my hands. Enough solar energy to power the house. Maybe the whole city. I pulled all the light to me, until the landscape in my mind was dark, lit only by the deep red glow of blood and the light of my bonds.

Rik's molten lava swirled around me. I carefully poured some of that golden light directly on his bond. I heard him inhale at the touch of warmth spilling through him. Then Daire's purring warcat and Xin's silver wolf. His eyes flashed like golden lamps in the darkest night. Guillaume's snorting stallion pawed the ground as I neared. I stroked liquid sun into his black fur and it rippled, gleaming like a burnished coin before sinking down into his hide.

I still had a whole handful of light to dole out, so I moved to Gina and Frank's bonds. They were thin, like threads, but I could feel them. I trickled light onto their bonds, but it didn't seem to hold much. Hopefully it was enough to help them.

Some of the golden warmth sank through my skin as I worked. My blood heated, like it danced and sang in my veins. It was nice, yes… but deep down, I couldn't forget that skeleton's bony grip on my ankle. I wasn't entirely comfortable with that magic touching me, so I didn't take much of it.

I thought a moment, trying to decide what to do with the rest. It was a lot. I had to get rid of it, but that much might hurt even my Blood.

Thousands of miles to the south, I felt a tug. Chains rattled in a deep, dark space that time had forgotten.

Of course. It would be fitting revenge against the god of light if I gave his power to his greatest enemy, Leviathan. I had no bond with him, but I could point in his direction. I knew exactly where we needed to go in order to find him. Focusing on the liquid sunlight swirling in my right hand, I willed myself south with every drop of golden magic. I pictured the great beast in the dark, chains rattling, claws scratching aimlessly against the stone. Sunlight never reached so deep or so far beneath the earth, so this would probably hurt his eyes. If he was even awake. Hopefully I could drop the golden ball of light onto him and be gone before he even realized it'd happened.

I didn't move physically, but my awareness flew through time and space. I saw the steep cliffs of the mountain. Water cascaded over me as I passed through a crisp, cold waterfall. Deeper, and faster, now, I flew through the dark, homing straight to him.

"It's you again."

I froze at the deep, rumbling tones of his voice. I'd never heard him speak before.

"What do you want with me this time? Did you come to torment me with what I cannot have, while I lie chained another thousand years?"

"I have a gift for you," I whispered, holding the ball of light out in front of me to light my way. Wet, black stone glistened in the soft light. Something crawled in the darkness, the sound of scales rustling over stone.

"You stink of Ra. Get the fuck away from me before I eat you."

"Ra tried to kill me."

He chuckled, a luscious, low laugh that did crazy things to my very healthy libido. It felt like he'd reached deep into my belly and strummed a chord. "Yet you're still here. Either you're very good," and his tone said he meant very, very bad, "or the stick-up-his-butt sun god is getting lazy in his old age."

"I prefer the first."

He blew out a deep breath, a beast-like pant so at odds with his smooth, chocolaty voice. "Maybe. Maybe not."

"Maybe you'll find out for yourself."

He let out a long hiss. "Maybe so. Or, like I said, maybe I'll eat you. It's been a fucking long time since I had anything but rats and worms to sustain me."

"Which is why I'm bringing you this." I sent the ball floating forward though I couldn't see exactly where he was. "Is this enough to free you?"

The golden ball winked out of sight a second before the clash of teeth warned me that he'd engulfed it. A low rumble shook the ground beneath my feet. Rocks and pebbles rained down and I fell against the side of the cave. My first panicked thought was that he'd broken free and was going to bring the whole fucking mountain down on us.

But then I realized he was laughing.

"You think this is enough to free me? That was a taste. Just another torment you've brought me."

"What will free you?"

Chains clattered on the stone and I had a sense of something dark and large scuttling toward me. I trembled, my heart pounding, but I didn't move. I wouldn't run. Not from him. Not from anything. Never again.

He crashed at the end of the chains, inches away. I

could feel the strength radiating from his body, an impression of exactly how massive he was. He made Rik's rock troll look like an action figure a kid would play with on the floor.

"You. You will free me."

"How?"

"The fuck if I know."

He sucked in great bellows of air, blowing my hair around. His head lowered as he breathed in my scent. My blood.

Something brushed my belly. His tongue maybe. I trembled, scared, but also turned on. I didn't want to be eaten or bitten by whatever monstrous dragon-serpent thing he was... But for all his threats, I had a feeling he'd much rather eat me *out*, than actually eat me.

"Give me some of this power and that might be enough to allow me to shake the foundations of the world."

I closed my eyes and pictured my room, both around me, but also thousands of miles away. Blood shimmered all around me. On me. I opened myself to that blood and called it home. All of it. Every drop.

Magic rushed through me, lifting me up, tossing me about like a tornado swirled through me. So much power. Gritting my teeth, I let it build. I held it until my bones throbbed, my teeth ached, my skin felt like it was going to tear open under the force. My blood boiled in my veins, eager to work its magic.

I shoved all that power toward Leviathan, hoping he knew what to do with it. I couldn't drop it to him through a bond and that much… I was afraid I'd kill him and not even mean it.

He gulped it down like a crocodile eating an antelope whole. Roaring, he rolled and thrashed in the depths of the earth, and yes, the entire mountain rattled above him. I was terrified he'd bury himself in a landslide and I'd never be able to dig him out.

I had just enough magic left to drop some on my knee. I tried to imagine the torn flesh knitting itself back together, the swelling easing, but I was no doctor. I really didn't know what meniscus or MCL meant exactly.

Exhaustion sucked me deeper. I strained to hold on, to open my eyes and let Rik know that I was okay, but I don't think my eyelids even cracked a slit.

A brush of scales, the tick of claws on stone. Leviathan brushed against my mind, reaching for me this time. "What is your name?"

"Shara."

He paced in my mind, his claws digging into me. I flinched, both mentally and physically, but I didn't try to push him out. His loneliness ached like a foot-long thorn in his massive paw. "Come and find me. Now, Shara. I won't last much longer, even with that sweet dollop of power melting on my tongue. You must come soon or all is lost."

"How long do we have?"

"Hours. Days. No more."

"Why? Why are you dying now?"

"I felt the moment you took the first breath on this earth and the countdown started."

Oh fuck. Knife straight to the heart. Me. I was killing him, just by being alive. Worse, because I'd been on the run for five years, lost to my consiliarius and the legacy, I hadn't had the power to know that the king needed me. *My* king.

I must have made some sound of pain, because I felt Rik pressing tighter to me, all my Blood in fact. Daire's warcat was draped on my legs. Xin and Guillaume on my right. Rik on my left. Distantly, I felt Gina and Frank leaving the room, probably with Dr. Borcht, though I didn't feel her directly.

I wanted my Blood crowded close. Definitely. But the horror of the skeleton grabbing me was fresh in my mind. If they were all here, unable to wake…

:*We're all taking turns on guard duty even in your bed. He won't catch us unaware this time, my queen.*:

It felt like Leviathan's chains were tangled around my legs, dragging me deeper. I fought to stay awake. I needed to make plans. :*He's dying. He doesn't have much longer. I don't think we can wait.*:

:*We'll tell Gina. We'll go tomorrow if you must. Sleep. Rest. All is well, my queen.*:

No. All was not well. My very existence was killing him.

:*I feel him in your mind,*: Rik's bond glowed brighter, and for a moment, I was afraid he'd try to drive the massive beast out. Leviathan watched him from the darkness, one great slitted eye that gleamed in my mind. :*Did he taste your blood?*:

:*I gave him power, but he hasn't had my blood directly.*:

Distantly, I felt Rik giving Xin a silent order to race after Gina and tell her we needed to move our travel plans up.

I guess we wouldn't be decorating or shopping for Christmas.

I'd be unchaining a monster the god of light had chained up thousands of years ago.

Let's hope he didn't destroy the world when I freed him.

25

SHARA

I never thought I'd spend this Christmas Eve on a gorgeous jet—that I actually owned—on my way to Venezuela.

My team was assembled: my Blood, consiliarius, human head of security and three guards, and my personal doctor. I was glad Dr. Borcht came, even though she hadn't wanted to become a blood servant. I was fine with that. More than fine, actually, as long as she was willing to help.

I didn't know how bad off Leviathan would be when I freed him. Or if he'd try to kill me or injure someone. Having a doctor close made me feel like we might have a chance of pulling this off.

My knee was much better today, though it felt weak. I

wouldn't want to run or do jumping jacks on it, but I could walk without a limp or pain.

Gina hung up a call and gave me a nod. "Angela is taking care of locking up the Kansas City house, and I returned the legacy to the safe first thing this morning. Though the main house in Eureka Springs won't be ready for a couple of more weeks, Winston recommended a smaller guest house as a temporary residence on the property. That way you can establish the nest and begin powering your defenses as soon as possible."

"Good," Rik replied. "Once she establishes the nest, it'll be impenetrable. Ra won't be able to open a portal inside again."

"That sounds great," I said, drawing his gaze to me. "But how do I establish the nest again?"

He took my hand and kissed my knuckles. "Easy. All you have to do is bleed."

"Then why didn't the house in Kansas City work as a nest? I think I bled all over that place."

Chuckling softly, Gina covered her mouth.

Yeah, she'd seen enough to have an idea of how bloody some of our lovemaking had been, but really, she didn't have a clue. Like that night in the tub. I don't remember how many times we changed the water because it was too bloody. We all wanted to taste each other, sure. But that didn't mean we wanted to sit in cold, bloody water.

"Intention," Guillaume said. "Your intention sets the magic and invests part of yourself into the nest. There was no need to do that in Kansas City, since you intended to leave. You wouldn't want to leave part of your soul, your magic, unattended, left behind and unguarded. While you could have dismantled a nest and reestablished it again, it takes much more effort."

Just the thought of leaving behind some part of me made me queasy. I could only imagine how hard the monsters would work to break through the defenses in order to devour what I'd left behind. They'd destroyed that dressing room for a few drops of blood on a pair of underwear. "I really wish we had time to set the nest now before we go on this crazy mission."

"It's *your* crazy mission," Daire said, flipping tawny hair over his shoulder. Yes, it was that long now. I think it'd grown six inches since yesterday.

"It's still crazy. I don't know what I'm going to do once we get there. Let alone *how* we're getting there."

Gina patted my knee. "I've got that part covered. A local guide is making a hefty bonus to take us to the mountain on Christmas Eve. Because of the holiday, we should have the area to ourselves. He said we may have to hike the last mile or so, though he'd try to hire enough horses for our party. Will your knee hold up okay?"

"I think so. As long as we don't actually have to climb much. We don't have to go up. I have to find a way *down*. He's inside and under, through a waterfall. That's all I know. I'm hoping I'll feel him once we get there."

I listened inside my head, waiting for the click of his claws, the pant of his breath, but I found only silence. I hoped that meant he'd retreated to his prison, and not that he was dead.

Gina proved herself once again to be an excellent consiliarius. Cars were waiting for us at the small private airport, and a guide met us on the dirt road to Roraima. He'd managed to find enough horses for everyone, saving my knee any stress.

The guide looked at me, Gina, and Dr. Borcht, and then the sun hanging low in the sky. "Are you sure you want to go this late in the day? It'll be dark before I can get you back to your cars."

"Yes," I said at the same time as Gina, confusing him even more to who was in charge.

I'd never ridden a horse before, and riding up the foothills at dusk might not be the best time to learn. In the end, Guillaume lifted me up on Rik's horse. I could have figured out the basics and the horse seemed tame enough, but I didn't want to waste any time. Every minute they spent trying to tell me which rein did what was another minute Leviathan might have died. How stupid would it be to know that I could have freed him if I'd swallowed my pride and ridden with one of my Blood? Though I would like to learn to ride someday.

Rik pressed his mouth against my ear. "It will be our pleasure."

Daire snickered as he trotted past. "Maybe Guillaume should just shift and let you ride him."

Guillaume rode easily beside us. "Our queen can ride me anytime she wants, shifted or not."

My cheeks burned and our poor guide looked at each of us like we were crazy. Hopefully he didn't understand all that, but his English had been excellent.

The mountain loomed on the horizon, its top wrapped in clouds. Sheer cliffs towered above us as we neared the foothills. I couldn't imagine climbing something that steep, though evidently, people did all the time. The view from the top must be incredible, if the clouds and fog weren't too thick.

The guide stopped, turning his mount to face us. He glanced at each of us and finally settled his gaze on Gina, who'd arranged everything. "There are two approaches, depending on which side of the mountain you would like to see."

Rik nudged his horse forward and the others moved out of the way so we could get closer to the split trail. "Which way, my queen?"

I closed my eyes, listening with my whole body. Trying to sense a pull. Some hint of where Leviathan was. I didn't feel anything myself, but the horse whickered softly and turned its head toward the left path.

"Is there a waterfall that way?"

"Yes," the guide replied. "The closest one is not far. The other path has a waterfall too but it's at least a two hour ride to get there."

"Then let's go this way. I know I need to see a waterfall."

With a nod, he guided his mount past us to the left and we followed closely. The rest of our party trailed along behind. The further we rode, my urgency increased. I wanted to yell and race up the trail, even though I had no idea where we were going. Or how hard it'd be to ride at such a break-neck speed.

My scalp prickled, nerves screeching. Even my heart seemed to pound heavier, harder. Telling me to hurry. I still couldn't feel Leviathan. At all. Were we already too late?

"Can we go a little faster?" I finally said.

"Yes, some." The guide looked at me doubtfully. "But it won't be a comfortable ride. Very bumpy."

"Please. I can deal with bumpy."

He signaled his horse and we started trotting and bouncing up the gradual incline. "We won't be able to go all the way like this, but some."

"Okay." Jounced back against Rik, I didn't try to say more than that. I didn't know if all horses had such a hard gait or if we were just unlucky.

The trail steepened, sometimes running us so close to the cliff that I could reach out and touch the stone. Although it was December, it was seventy degrees and sunny, though it was almost dusk. A huge change from the chilly Kansas City temps. Moss and plants grew out of the stone, clinging to rocks. Water trickled down the rocks, creating a moist, green living carpet.

Our guide slowed his mount to a walk and I ground my teeth. Fuck. I was going to lose my mind. If I'd been on my own horse, I probably would have kicked it in the flank and galloped ahead.

Which I knew was stupid. Though the trail was easy to follow and clearly marked, I had no idea what pitfalls might lie ahead. It'd help nobody if I accidentally broke a horse's leg in my rush to find the waterfall I'd seen in my dream.

As the horse worked harder, scrambling up a steeper section of trail, I understood why he'd slowed our pace. We had one scary moment where the horse's hooves slipped on rock and we started to fall backward. Rik stayed calm and gave the horse his head. With a hard lunge that threw me back against Rik's chest, we finally made it up to a relatively flat section of dirt trail.

"Here's the waterfall, ma'am. Is this where you needed to go?"

Rik guided our horse around on the left to give me a good look. I wasn't sure, honestly. It'd been just a glimpse last night and it'd been dark.

:I'm not sure,: I said to Rik. :I can't feel him anywhere.:

He swung down and reached up to help me dismount. :Walk around a bit. See what you feel.:

The rest of my Blood fanned out, taking up protective positions down the trail and up ahead, in case anyone came down from the top. Gina stood talking softly with Dr. Borcht and Frank's team. I turned back to the water splashing on the rocks. I tipped my head back and marveled at how tall the waterfall was. I couldn't even see the top.

Closing my eyes, I laid my palm on the wet rock. I pulled up the surrounding tapestry in my mind and searched for anything that might confirm this was where I needed to start. My bonds all glowed, bright and healthy and strong, even my two humans. After giving them some of the golden energy last night, their faces glowed and everyone's moods today had been positive and warm. No signs of anything negative at all.

Trying to block out those shining bonds was difficult. I finally managed to dampen my awareness of them somewhat. I didn't feel anything shadowed approaching, even though dusk was falling fast. Chills rippled up my spine. I hadn't been outside, at night, in days. My period was still flowing but had slowed considerably. I'd used a tampon for the trip, so hopefully my scent was well contained at the moment. I didn't know how many thralls might be in Venezuela but I didn't want to find out if I could help it.

I looked deeper, searching under our bonds. I felt the prior bonds Daire and Rik both had with the Skye court. Though I'd killed Kendall, they had other connections that Keisha would be able to use against us. Though hopefully she'd learned her lesson.

But nothing felt like Leviathan. No scales, no claws, no snake scent, no rumbling beast hidden deep in the ground.

I shivered, hugging myself. Maybe I was too late. Maybe the king was dead. I didn't know what that would mean going forward. If Isis had sent me here for a reason, then Leviathan was important. Why? Why did I have to find him?

"There's a legend," the guide whispered, his tone reverent. "Some believe there's a portal here that takes you to another world."

"Here, at the waterfall?"

He shrugged. "No one knows for certain. Most say it's at the top of the tepuy, but people have disappeared from this area for centuries."

Had they disappeared… or had Leviathan eaten them? If there was some kind of portal or gate here, it might need magic to open.

Which for me, meant blood.

I didn't want to flash fangs and scare the guide away. Before I could even think, Guillaume stood beside me, a small blade in his hand. Unobtrusively, I swiped my left palm across the razor sharp edge. Blood dripped down my fingers.

I heard him inhale. All my Blood did. Their bonds sharpened. Rik's molten lava flowed brighter. Daire's warcat prowled in his bond. Guillaume's hoof beats rumbled like thunder on the horizon. Xin's wolf paused and looked at me, a silver flash against the darkness.

No snake or dragon or monster.

My blood plopped onto the ground, and suddenly my ears roared like I'd stepped into a wind tunnel. A gust blew my hair back and water sprayed me.

Wind… from the waterfall.

"It's true," the guide whispered, his voice shaking. "You opened the portal."

I couldn't respond. Too many emotions and sensations pounded through me. They weren't mine, though I felt them intensely.

Rage, despair, hatred, desperation, agony. But most of all, glee. I had come. Exactly as he wanted.

Leviathan was pissed, hungry, and so fucking *strong*. Not weak or failing. Certainly not near death. At least it didn't feel like it.

In fact, I was pretty sure there was no way in hell I'd be able to get anywhere close to him without dying.

"Then you won't get close to him," Rik retorted.

"I must," I replied softly.

"I thought you said he was dying."

I could only shrug. I'd felt urgency, yes, but maybe I'd misinterpreted it. Maybe it was my human upraising that had leaped to the conclusion that only I could save him. That he'd die without me.

Oh, the arrogance. The stupidity. He wanted me here for one reason only.

So he could wreck vengeance on the world and destroy what Ra had wrought. And nothing was going to get in his way.

Especially me.

26

SHARA

Rik grabbed my arm and pulled me against him. "Don't do this."

I was scared. Sure. I was probably going to fail. But the hell if I'd stand here and let him tell me what I could and could not do.

No matter how much I loved him.

He pressed his forehead to mine and held me tightly. "I know," he whispered. "My queen."

Daire pressed against me too, wrapping his arms around us both. "At least allow us to go with you."

"There's no way I'm letting you die too. Besides, I need someone to protect our friends if something happens to me."

"If you die, we die," Rik replied, his tone as even and

emotionless as if he'd said the sky was blue. "We won't survive your death."

I forced my voice lighter, brighter, as if I wasn't scared to death. "Then I had best not die."

He pressed his lips to mine in a soft, gentle kiss. He could have thrown me over his shoulder and hauled my ass back down to the cars. Or he could have tried to use my passion against me. He could have taken my mouth deep and hard, stirring my desire, or even nicking himself to tempt me with his blood.

But he did none of those things. For being so big, my alpha could be especially tender.

I kissed Daire and his rumbling purr made my eyes burn. I turned to Guillaume, my grim, silent knight. He shocked me by sweeping me up into a fiery kiss, his tongue twined with mine. He pulled me up against him and then twisted to the side over his arm, like an old fashioned dip.

"Shit, G," Daire finally said. "You've been holding out on us."

Guillaume smiled against my lips and pulled me back upright. Breathless, I stared up at him, shocked as much by the twinkling light in his eyes as the dramatic show of affection from the normally stoic man.

"I expect more kisses like that in the future."

He inclined his head. "It will be my pleasure, my queen."

I turned to Xin. He took both my hands in his and kissed both my cheeks. "We all hunger for your blood, and he will be no different. But remember that your blood is also a weapon, my queen. You have magic that he will not be able to withstand."

His words reminded me that my hand was bleeding. Might as well make use of it. So I lifted my palm to his mouth. His eyes darkened, his nostrils flaring, but he only took a quick swipe with his tongue. "Thank you, my queen, but save it. I have a feeling you'll need every drop to bend the king to your will."

If that was even possible. *It has to be possible.*

I hesitated, trying to think of anything I could do to better my chances. Salt and iron weren't going to help bring Leviathan to heel, not that I'd brought any. Absently, I patted my pocket, felt the small knife there.

Guillaume snorted. "I need to give you a lesson in knives when you establish the nest."

"I'd like that. And a forge for Rik so he can make some ketars for me."

"Done," Rik said. "I'll hold you to that promise."

The ground rumbled beneath my feet. I thought it was his rock troll, but he shook his head slightly.

"If that was an earthquake, we need to get down off the mountain," the guard said. "Now."

Turning toward the waterfall, I took a couple of deep, centering breaths. "I'll be as fast as possible."

He rushed toward me, his hand out like he was going to touch me. Rik growled and stepped closer, protecting my back as always. I don't think the man meant me any harm. He just wanted to escape landslides or whatever destruction might happen if we were up here when an earthquake hit.

Rather than let him grab my arm, I stepped into the waterfall.

Cold water splashed down on me, stealing my breath, but with another step, I was through. Absolute darkness closed in. With the roar of the waterfall behind me, I couldn't hear what they were saying outside. If I was still even in our world. In my head, my bonds still gleamed, but they felt... stretched. Less substantial somehow. Almost like I was looking at a reflection of them through water.

Hands outstretched, I felt around until I found the side of the tunnel. Just as in my dream, it led downward, though it felt wider and definitely steeper. Water trickled down the walls and the floor, making the rock slippery, and this time, I didn't have a golden ball of sunlight to light my way. I thought about calling a fireball, but I didn't want to flash a lot of power. Ideally, I'd keep him guessing about how strong I was. I really had no idea how my power would hold up against something thousands of years old, but I had a feeling I'd be able to hold my own. I was well fed, and he surely wasn't.

Though now I was kicking myself for giving him power last night.

I slipped and fell on my ass, bruising my hip.

:*My queen.*: Rik's bond vibrated with concern. He hated being left behind. He hated my back unprotected as I approached danger. A little bit of my pain had him standing at the edge of the waterfall, ready to shift and come after me.

:*I'm fine. Just slipped.*:

The further I went, the harder it was to stay on my feet. My thighs and heels ached from keeping my weight shifted back as much as possible, and my palms were raw from the rock side. I had no idea how I was going to climb out of here.

:*I'll come get you.*:

A sense of space opened up in front of me, though I couldn't see anything with my eyes. I eased my foot out and felt the edge of a drop.

Crap. I had no idea how far down it was. I listened a moment, trying to hear the chains or deep, rumbling sounds of the beast's breathing, but all I heard was the heavy pounding of my own heart and the steady drip of water.

He was close, though. He had to be.

I lifted my injured hand and willed a small ball of fire to fill my palm. Golden flame instantly glowed in my hand. *Golden*, like Ra. It made me shiver. How much had his power changed my own? Was it enhanced... or twisted? Tainted? I had to admit that the brighter flame made it easier to see. I sent the small ball out into the void and slowly brightened it.

A cave loomed straight ahead, with both the ceiling and floor widening into a dome. The drop was only ten feet, but the bottom was littered with bones as if all the graveyards of the world had been dumped here. It was too far for me to make out the details. Some of the bodies looked like animals, but there were definitely human skulls jumbled among the bones. How long did he have to wait for an unwary tourist to wander into his domain?

"The last was two years ago."

I jerked my gaze up to the opposite side of the cave. Eerie green eyes glittered at me from a shelf about two stories higher.

Now that he had my attention, Leviathan made a great show of coming out of his den. Wings outstretched, he glided toward the bone yard below in a slow spiral.

No chains. That was the first thing I realized. He wasn't chained at all.

And fuck, he was big. Long, sleek green-black body, four legs with powerful rear haunches, sinuous neck, and spiked tail. My tiny fireball floated down his side and he gleamed like an iridescent oil slick in the faint light.

Circling around toward the floor, he didn't even look in my direction. Wary of his teeth and claws, I should have been watching his tail. It crashed into my ankles, wrapped around both legs, and dragged me off the edge. I didn't even have time to grab for the side or duck.

He landed and swung me around in front of him, dropping me with an oomph in front of two giant clawed feet.

"Shara." He drew out the first syllable of my name in a hiss. "So kind of you to visit me in person this time."

Bones poked me in the back. I scrambled up, trying to get to my feet, but he casually planted one big foot on my stomach and pinned me to the ground.

Six-inch long claws dug into my belly, pricking my skin. His threat was clear. With a twitch of his foot, he'd eviscerate me before I could scream.

Time seemed to slow. Or maybe my mind was firing

super fast. I thought through my options. Whether I should blast him with a giant fireball now—though fire would be pretty useless against a fire-breathing dragon. Or use Rik's troll strength to push him off me. Or Xin's ghostly invisibility. I was pretty sure I could make myself disappear, but I'd feel pretty stupid if it didn't work.

On the other hand, Leviathan wasn't hurting me. He hadn't even let me bang too hard on the ground. The skeleton had hurt my knee and ankle way more than his tail had. He'd scared me a little. That was it.

So I'd play along. Let him think I was as scared as he wanted me to be. Other than what he'd gleaned from my dreams, he had no idea what kind of power I had, or what my personality was. Whether I'd fight, or surrender. Plot his demise, or capitulate at the first sign of force.

I forced some smart-alec bravado into my voice. "Seems as though I forgot the key for your chains. Oh wait..."

He lowered his giant head and let out what I thought was a chuckle, though it sounded like a bear waking up after a long winter of hibernation. "That was a nice touch in your dreams, wasn't it? I thought you might feel safer approaching me if you thought I was bound."

The strong musk of his snake scent filled my nose. My spine itched and my fangs ached, like the cobra wanted to slither out of me and roll in his scent. I shuddered, fighting down that thought. No cobra. Though the massive fangs that had left fist-sized wounds in Rik's stomach might be a nice weapon to use against Leviathan.

He lowered his massive head closer. "Do you have any idea how long I've waited for you?"

"It couldn't be that long. I'm only twenty-two."

He snarled and snapped his teeth close to my ear, making me flinch away. "Not *you* in particular, but any Aima queen stupid enough to try and free me."

"So you don't want to be free?"

"Not if my freedom comes with the kind of hooks that queens try and put into me. I'd rather be here than chained to obey like those morons you call Blood. I don't live to serve. I don't live to protect. I don't give a fuck about you."

Yet he'd been so careful so far. He hadn't even scratched me. "Fair enough. I don't give a fuck about you either. I already have Blood to feed and protect me."

"And fuck you."

"Of course. So if you don't want your freedom, I'll be on my way."

"I want my freedom more than anything, but I won't trade one prison for another."

"I wouldn't—"

He threw his head back and roared out blistering-hot flames that crackled to the cave's ceiling. "Don't lie to me. You would. All queens would."

Such rage. He didn't only want revenge against Ra. A queen—maybe several—had hurt him just as badly as the god who'd locked him away from the world for thousands of years. "You don't know me," I said softly. "You don't know what I want."

"Queens want the same thing."

"What do you want? Why did you want me to come here, if not to free you?"

"Oh, I never said you weren't going to free me." He tightened his claws on my stomach, deliberately breaking my skin. "But it will be on my terms."

I had a feeling I knew what his terms were. "Let me guess."

"I need queen's blood to leave this plane, but I refuse to be bound to a queen. So what does that mean, Your Majesty?"

He wanted my blood. And he didn't mean to let me walk away, because I would own his ass then. So the only way he could take my blood and not have a bond... was if I was dead.

I toned down my sense of my Blood bonds as well as I could. Like Xin, I let fog fill me. Not to disappear, but to shield my Blood from the undeniable pain that was coming. If they felt what Leviathan did to me, they'd come after me. He'd kill them, or they'd kill him, and in the end, someone that the goddess had sent to me would be gone. A hole would live in my heart.

I didn't know Leviathan. Not really. But Isis had said he was my destiny. To me, that meant he was mine to love.

Even if he hurt me.

27

SHARA

His jaws crunched down on my bleeding hand and the rest of my left arm below my elbow. Bones snapped and I screamed, but I didn't pull away or fight. Blood frenzy burned in him. He growled and rumbled and hissed, lapping my blood from my skin, but he could have thrown his head back, ripped my arm off, and gulped me in one big swallow. There was something in him that wasn't twisted and dark.

Something that I could touch. Call. Love.

If he would only listen.

:*Shara!*: Rik's rock troll roared in my head.

:*No,*: Panting, I breathed through the pain. :*Stay.*:

Already, I could feel my blood inside Leviathan. My power slid down his long throat, heating his body. With every swallow, he took me deeper into his consciousness. Giving me a foothold in his mind. I needed a good hold in him. Enough to bind him to my will. I had to let him take enough to almost kill me.

Almost. That was the trick.

My head swam, my heart thudding heavily. It wouldn't take him long to drain me, and if I was too weak, all of this would be for naught. I needed blood. His blood. If I could feed...

I lurched up, trying to get my fangs in his leg. His neck. Anything.

He didn't lift his head, but shifted his paw on me, keeping me pinned to the ground. One slitted eye glared at me. He knew very well what I wanted, even if my fangs hadn't descended.

I needed him to bleed. My brain raced.

Fire wouldn't help. His hide was too thick and protected him against his own flames.

Rock troll strength wouldn't make him bleed quickly enough to save me.

Daire's claws? Maybe. But I'd never tried to use one of my Blood's shifters and I had no idea if it would work or not. I didn't have time for experiments and no plan B if it failed.

I ran my other hand along the ground, trying to find a sharp bone. Something I could use to stab him with.

Wait. Of course. I dug into my pocket and found my puny knife. Hiding it alongside my leg, I worked the blade open and eyed his underbelly, looking for the best place to stab him. His scales were lighter and softer on his belly, a deep, emerald green mixed with pearly white. The scales interlocked together, making an impenetrable armor.

Except where his front leg met his body. That delicate hollow didn't have any scales.

Focusing on my target, I took a deep breath and gathered my will. My power. I had to strike fast and hard. His hide would still be tough. My aim had to be true. I wouldn't get another shot. It had to be deep enough that he'd bleed, and bleed enough to drip down on me. My hand couldn't shake. My vision couldn't waver.

With all my power, all my will, I slammed the pocketknife into that joint.

He growled against my skin but didn't lift his mouth. In fact, he winked at me, as if to say, *"Good try, honey. I felt your little bee sting."*

And yeah, it wouldn't make him get off me. Let alone kill him.

But his blood poured over my hand. I cupped my fingers, catching as much as possible, and poured his blood over my mouth.

He tasted like the blackest night, the deepest part of the ocean where sun never shines. Cold, empty, forgotten, lost on the mists of time. He'd endured silence and loneliness for centuries, plotting his enemies' demise. Planning exactly how he'd lure his queen to his side.

Only to kill her.

Yet my blood slid into that cold, empty space. Blood,

spreading in the water. Stirring his hunger. Reminding him of all the things he'd been denied.

Sunshine. Air. Green grass. Blue sky.

A queen's blood.

A woman's skin against his human body.

The dragon shape was his prison. He couldn't ever be a man again...

Without me. His queen.

And that's what he wanted most of all. He wanted to be able to walk on two legs. He wanted to touch another living person. Hug, fuck, kiss, everything. He was starved for affection, the same as Guillaume and Xin, and even Daire and Rik. They'd at least had sibs to touch, but it hadn't been enough.

Leviathan tried to scramble back to save himself. But it was too late.

The ancient blood of an Aima only a step or two away from the god and goddess who'd sired him now flowed in my veins. I lurched up and wrapped my good arm around his neck with all Rik's troll strength hammering through my muscles.

The cobra queen's brutal fangs descended and I sank them deep into his neck. His scales couldn't keep this queen out.

He surged into the air and shot up the tunnel. Wind tore at me, but I clung to him, my fangs an anchor in his hide.

Flee. Dread. I read his emotions, his mind open to me like a book. He feared me more than anything. More than Ra, the great blazing god of light. More than his queen mother who'd banished him for fear he'd kill her and the rest of her brood.

He'd raged. He'd bled. He'd fought.

Queens had tried to calm his beast and return him to his human form, but they'd failed.

Each failure like a sword in his heart.

I tightened my grip on him, wrapped my legs around his muscled neck, and used our new bond for the first time.

:*I will not fail you.*:

28

RIK

Agony. To stand here and know my queen was in danger. That she was hurt. That she feared for her life. And do nothing.

But that's exactly what she wanted.

And so I would do it. No matter how difficult it was.

The mountain rumbled like it was a volcano ready to spew any moment. The guide finally gave up on us and hightailed it back down the trail. Our horses screamed and reared, milling about frantically. Guillaume let his and my mount go and they tore off down the steep path. Hopefully they didn't break a leg on their way down.

:*We're coming,*: Shara said in our bond.

We. She'd done it. She had the king.

He came boiling up out of the waterfall, a massive dark

shape that shot into the sky. Wings beat the air frantically and he soared up into the darkening sky, gone so quickly that I'd barely caught a glimpse of my queen.

Shara clung to the great beast's neck, her small form like a child against his bulk. Her bond blazed with strength and I realized she was feeding on him. In fact, she was draining him, like he'd tried to do to her.

Like her cobra had done to me.

I let the rock troll bulge free of my human shape, and the other Blood shifted without my command. "She's going to try and drain him back to his human shape."

:Then how will they fly?: Daire asked.

Guillaume's warhorse reared and screamed a challenge up at the sky. :Exactly.:

Nose in the air, Xin's wolf sprinted off into the night, following her scent and her bond.

"Get down the mountain," I told Gina. "Follow the guide. We'll catch up as quickly as we can."

Using Shara's bond, I lumbered after Xin as fast as I could. Daire ran at my side, but Guillaume easily galloped ahead. Xin paused every once in a while, a silver flash in the growing murk to guide us. Her bond was still strong, but she felt too far away. Too high. Fuck. If they started to fall from the sky at that height, it'd kill them both. I didn't want to count on her resurrection power to bring her back from smashed and broken. The thought made me scream with rage and shake a giant fist at the sky.

Not that either of them could see it.

Holding on to her bond, I felt the dragon's wings slow. The air was thin and cold. So high.

He tucked his wings around her, folding her close against him. :*It is finished. So we end, my queen.*:

They hovered a moment, sliding to a halt. And then they started the long fall back down to earth.

Faster. Picking up speed. They plummeted toward the ground at a speed that made me want to vomit.

Shara sucked on his throat, straining to take more of his blood. Fuck, she was so strong. Stronger than ever. Her power blazed like a beacon in the night, rising higher and higher. The ground split and cracked open. Trees quivered and crashed. Boulders rumbled down the steep sides of the mountain. The stars dimmed in the sky, unable to shine against the bright supernova that blazed from her.

Ears pinned flat, Guillaume galloped in a dead run toward her, but I didn't think he'd make it. Even if he managed to catch her, I didn't think it would help. He'd only be dead too.

:*Let go of him,*: I roared through our bond. :*Use your power to slow your descent.*:

:*I can't let go of him or he'll die.*:

:*Then let him die! We can't lose you!*:

Grim determination shone in her bond like a naked sword hot from the forge. :*No one's dying. Not today.*:

I felt Leviathan ripple against her. Spiraling ever faster toward the earth, he started to shift. Wings dissolved. Scales melted. The dragon swallowed up by our queen as she drained him dry. She literally took the dragon into her. I could feel its massive form slithering inside her. It hissed and roared and blazed with all its wrath inside her. Tearing at her bonds, her heart. I felt her bleeding inside. Battered. But she wouldn't let go, not of the man in her arms, nor of his dragon that was trying to tear its way out of her body.

Seconds slowed. I had time to gauge how hard she would hit the ground. Guillaume was close… but he wouldn't make it. Xin's wolf leaped into the air, soaring higher than I'd ever seen a wolf jump, but he fell short and landed hard, rolling and tumbling into a steep ravine with a yelp.

Ten feet. Nine.

Horrifying visions filled my head. Her bones broken. Her blood splattered everywhere. Her screams of pain, but worse, would be her silence. Helplessness ate through my gut like acid. I couldn't save my queen. I couldn't catch her. None of us could. We were doomed to love her, to hear her call, and enjoy her sweet blood and spirit this short time, only to watch her die a horrible death before our very eyes.

Eight.

Her power surged even higher. Light blinded me, but it wasn't Ra's golden glow. Shara was white-hot. Lightning and ice, moonlight and cold, water and pure. She glowed brighter, so fierce, I had to shield my eyes. Something grew in that brutal light but I couldn't make out its shape.

The dragon finally clawed its way out of her, but it was changed. It didn't have hind legs at all, only a long, black body and massive hood like her cobra queen. A ruby-red diamond gleamed on that hood, the same as when she'd envenomed me.

Cobras couldn't fly. Even my cobra queen.

Seven. Six.

Guillaume leaped toward her, neck outstretched, jaws wide, as if he could catch her in his mouth. The tip of his nose brushed the end of her tail, but he too fell short. He landed hard, whirled, ready to try again.

Wings unfurled, knocking him aside. With a mighty snap, her wings caught air and she swept away from us and back up toward the sky.

:Wyvern: Guillaume panted in our bond. *:Never saw that coming.:*

My lungs burned, my massive thighs aching like I'd run a marathon. I was built for strength, not speed, and rock weighed a ton. Literally. I stumbled to a halt and braced my hands on my knees, head down, and just breathed deep and hard a few moments. Daire wormed his head under my arm, panting just as hard as me. *:I'm going to go check on Xin.:*

I gave him a single nod, too tired to even respond in the bond. He loped over the edge of the ravine to find the wolf.

Guillaume trotted over, his sleek sides wet and splattered with foam. Blowing hard, he scanned the sky. *:Do you see her?:*

I straightened and looked too, but she was impossible to see against the night sky. "She's close. I think she's coming back."

Straining to hear the beat or rustle of her wings, I listened to her bond, trying to pinpoint how far away she was. Goddess, it felt like she was right on top of us but I couldn't see a fucking thing.

A black shape dropped in front of me, so close I flinched back involuntarily. Tucking her wings tight to her body, she dropped into a neat coil with a dark-skinned man in her smaller forearms. He didn't move. I wasn't sure that he was alive. His throat was a mess, torn open by two huge punctures. Blood coated him and her muzzle, dripping down her chest.

She arched up, her hood flared wide. The ruby stone caught fire and she swayed, eyes closed. A sound filled the night, almost like singing without words, music without notes, rhythm without actual beats. Like if I could just hear it a bit more loudly, I'd recognize it. I'd know the song and remember its melody. It stirred something deep inside me. Something ancient that had slept as long as the mountains and had only just realized it had opened its eyes.

That music pulled our beasts back inside before we'd even realized we'd shifted. Including our queen.

Bleeding but whole, she shifted the man's head up with her good arm, lifting him to her throat. "Rik, can you—"

I was moving before she could finish the thought, eager to hold her, touch her, taste her. Relieved that she was alive and well and victorious. I wrapped my arms around her and pressed against her back, taking my spot. And then I leaned over to bite her throat, so she could revive the man she'd saved.

She always tasted magical, addictive, and vibrant with power. Now there was an edge in her blood. A blade that would cut, that would face the hardest test and come away marked, scuffed, perhaps, but her edge true and sharp. Her blood dripped onto the man lying lifeless in her arms and he stirred. He sucked in a rasping breath and opened his eyes.

For a moment, I thought he'd lunge up to try and rip her head off. His eyes blazed with fury and hatred. He'd wanted to be free, even if that meant our queen was dead. He'd rather be dead than here, looking up at her, tasting her blood. Chained. To a queen.

A fate worse than death, for him at least.

She said nothing. Didn't move a muscle. Didn't use her bond to command him. She didn't give him arguments or promises or excuses. She just waited. Looking into his eyes. Letting him decide.

If he didn't feed, she'd let him die. She'd lay him on his back on the ground and walk away. It was his choice.

He tore his gaze away from the blood dripping down her throat and met my gaze. I stared back at him as evenly as she did, refusing to drop my eyes. I was alpha. If he stayed, he'd accept me too. Or I'd be more than willing to pound him back into the ground, flat on his back, and leave him bleeding. I didn't care how old he was. How powerful. I had him beat, and I knew it.

Because I loved my queen with every muscle and bone in my body, and I'd willingly die to keep her safe.

This slimy fucker had been willing to kill her to save his own scaly hide. I wouldn't soon forget it. Let alone allow *him* to forget.

Certainty hardened in me. Shara needed him for some reason. Her goddess had said so. So she would have him.

Even if that meant I had to bash his head in for him until he saw the error of his ways.

His breath sighed out and he dropped his gaze from mine to hers.

"Say it." She kept her tone soft, but her bond gleamed sharp and strong, ready to cut him down.

He swallowed hard and closed his eyes, averting his face.

"Look me in the eye, and say it."

He lunged up toward her throat, but she didn't have to move a muscle to defend herself. I wrapped my fist around his neck and squeezed. "She gave you an order."

He shuddered in my grip, all the fight bleeding out of him. He'd used the last of his reserves. Through her bond, I felt his heart skip and flutter in his chest, desperate for blood. For life.

Emerald green eyes glittered up at us. His throat worked beneath my hand, as he struggled against his own pride.

"My," he snarled out, his voice raw. "Queen."

I released him and she lifted him up to her throat. "Take what you need from me, my king."

29

SHARA

Wounded and weary, we slowly made our way down the mountain. Rik had to carry me because my knees wobbled every time I took a step. Pulling an Amia as old as Leviathan back from the grave had taken the last of my reserves and I hadn't been able to heal him all the way yet. Poor Xin limped beside us, refusing even a drop of my blood for healing. Leviathan stumbled along, slung between Daire and Guillaume. From the dark looks they both kept giving him, the man was going to be lucky to make it down to the waiting cars in one piece.

My broken arm throbbed with every step Rik took. Although I had my face pressed to his throat, I could sense him glaring at me. "If you would feed, you could heal it now and no longer be in pain."

I was tempted. He smelled so good. So strong. But I knew that I'd want more than his blood, and if I bit him, he'd come. And when he came, I wanted him to be inside me. And while I loved him more than ever, I wasn't too excited about making love on the side of a mountain. Especially when I was so tired. I couldn't remember ever feeling like this.

Just… drained. Not in blood, but spirit.

I was fucking exhausted and all I wanted was a huge bed and a lot of sleep. With my guys all crowded around. And then when I woke up, I'd be more than happy to get to the blood and sex part.

The new man lifted his head. "Unless things have changed a great deal from my time, feeding doesn't have to involve sex."

Daire gave a jerk on the man's arm hard enough he groaned. Guillaume somehow managed to step on his foot.

It almost made me laugh… but I was too tired for amusement. "I know. But that's how we prefer it."

"You mean that's how *you* prefer it."

Rik snorted under his breath. "Are you honestly going to claim that you'd rather not have sex when you feed?" The man scowled at him, making him laugh again. "That's what I thought."

"Do you have a name other than Leviathan?" I asked.

"Leviathan is my beast. My name…" He hesitated, and I felt his bond shutter, like he was slamming windows and doors, locking up for the night. And then he realized that it was too late. The monster was already inside the house with him.

"You don't have to tell me. I was just tired of calling you the new guy in my head. I'll go with Levi."

He scowled again, which improved both Daire's and Guillaume's mood considerably.

:*You have a bond with Gina now,*: Rik reminded me, his bond a low whisper. He'd targeted that thought to me only, none of the other Blood. It made me sad, because there was doubt now. Distrust. He didn't want the new Blood to hear him. :*You can tell her we're coming and she can bring clothes and the doctor up to meet us.*:

Sorting through the bonds in my head was almost too much for me to manage. Worse, Levi's bond was heavy and dark against Rik's molten lava, a hissing, angry dragon I'd chained with my blood. His power was mine now. Literally. I would be able to refuse him access to his own beast, something no queen had ever been able to do for him. Or *to* him, depending on how he felt at the moment.

Finally, I found the threads that belonged to Gina and Frank. :*We're coming down the trail now. Can you bring clothes and Dr. Borcht?*:

I felt Gina's flash of shock at hearing my voice so clearly in her head, but she was already giving orders and gathering up supplies. Bless her. It was so nice to have someone take care of the details of getting from point A to point B.

I dozed despite the pain in my arm. It felt like I hadn't rested in days. I guess I hadn't. Not with the sun god sending skeletons out of nowhere, and getting up early to make plans to come here and find Leviathan. My stomach rumbled and my fangs throbbed and honestly, it all made me want to cry a little. I was too fucking tired for this shit. Even eating.

Rik went down to his knees and I opened my eyes.

Dr. Borcht smiled at me. "You must stop hurting yourself, young lady."

"I'll try," I mumbled, fighting to get my eyes open. "If you can clean it up a bit and wrap it, I'll take care of it in the morning."

Frank set a small lantern down to provide light for the doctor's examination. She frowned, clearly not happy with leaving the actual healing to tomorrow. Or maybe it was my condition over all, because she felt my head and peeled back my eyelid to flash something in my eyes. "I didn't think Aima could suffer from shock, but you're definitely more exhausted than you should be. Even after these injuries, you should be able to stay awake."

"She's too tired to eat or feed," Rik replied. "Is it her period? Making her anemic?"

"Could be. Or it's just a matter of too many things stressing her body right now. New powers, battles, trials, injuries. They all take a toll. I'll feel much better once we get you into your nest and let you rest for several days."

"Yeah," I drew the word out. "That sounds great."

My nest. My first place of safety. My gorgeous manor house. I couldn't wait to get there.

Dr. Borcht poured something on my arm that made me

gasp despite my exhaustion. "Sorry, just applying some disinfectant. Was this a bite? It looks like it's already infected. You really need to heal this, Shara. Now would be best."

"Yeah, that was one nasty motherfucking bite," Daire drawled, sidling closer. "You haven't fed on me yet today, my queen. I'm more than happy to help you heal."

I started to lift my arm toward him, but forgot it was my injured one. I gasped, my eyes flying open at the pain. My stomach pitched and I fought the urge to throw up. Rik rumbled, deep in his chest, chastising Daire for me hurting myself, which was ridiculous.

I started to fumble through my bonds, trying to find G's, but he approached without me having to ask, knife in hand. He sliced his palm open and pressed the cut to my mouth, earning a snarl from Daire.

"Bring your own knife, dickhead. Or wait until she's done and I'll be happy to cut you."

His sweet blood flowed into me, decadent and rich. Almost like eating dessert before supper. Then Daire gave me a taste, purring against my side, his fur swishing through my mind. Xin, soft and silent, a whisper in the night, the hush of a snowflakes falling on pine trees in the dead of winter. Before he left, I felt through his bond, searching for his injuries. He'd sprained his ankle and gashed his shoulder in the fall. I wiped those injuries away with a thought.

Rik, strong, steady, my rock. Literally. The one I would build my court upon.

With his blood on my tongue, I sent power flowing through my arm, pushing out the toxic bacteria I'd picked up from Leviathan's bite. If I'd been human, I think the infection alone would have killed me already. I'd have to remember that his beast's bite was a hefty weapon, even if he didn't kill his victim right away.

His bond shimmered with rage, his dragon hissing. Surprised, I forced my eyes open and met his gaze, glittering like chips of dark emerald. Hunched with pain yet still defiant, he stood by himself off to the side glaring at us all.

"I won't *make* you feed me. Ever."

His eyes flickered, doubt chasing across his face like shadows. "You're queen."

Ignoring him, I turned my head and found Dr. Borcht, hovering behind Daire. "Can you check it now and see how it looks?"

Daire scooted out of the way so the doctor could take a look at my arm. "Much better. The wound is closed, though the skin is still pink and fragile. You may actually have a few small scars."

"A small price to pay. Thank you."

While she wrapped my arm in a clean bandage to be safe, Gina filled me in on her developments.

"I know you're tired, but this could be really important. I spoke to Bianca Zaniyah, the consiliarius for Mexico City's queen. Her queen is very eager to meet you and offers her nest to you. Shara, that's… unheard of. A queen would never open her nest to another queen without meeting her first."

I was silent a few moments, letting my weary brain process the ramifications. "A trap?"

"I don't think so. Mayte Zaniyah isn't known for political maneuvers. I think she wants to be your ally."

I wanted to see what a nest was like, and the chance to see how another queen ran her court would be fantastic. But… not now. I wanted *my* nest. My manor. First, I needed to rest. I wanted to go into my first possible kinship with another queen with a fresh mind, and preferably not with a hostile dragon in my Blood.

:*I'm not Blood,*: Levi growled in my mind.

Ignoring his words, I sent a wave of healing power through his simmering bond to heal the last of his injuries. I could take away the physical hurt with a thought—but there wasn't anything I could do about his hatred and rage. Not immediately.

He needed love. Steady, unfailing love. Like what I had with the rest of my Blood.

"Please tell Bianca that I'm honored by the invitation and will accept—but at a later date. I don't want to wait any longer." I snuggled into Rik's chest as he stood, cradling me against him. "Let's go home."

30

SHARA

I slept on the car ride back to the airport. I slept on the plane. I slept on Rik as he carried me to the car again for the winding drive into Eureka Springs. I was vaguely aware of arriving at my new home at dawn on Christmas morning. Enough to open my eyes and see the towers of my house. But I couldn't keep them open even to meet Winston or look around the guest house he directed us to. I was aware of low voices around me. Clean sheets, fluffy pillows, soft mattress. Heaven. Dr. Borcht checked my arm again, her murmured words too soft for me to make sense of. Though I sensed no urgency from anyone.

Rik tucked me against him, hot against my back, his arm a band of granite around me. Another Blood pressed closer.

Xin. His wolf touched me with his nose and darted off into the silent forest.

That left Daire, Guillaume, and Levi. Someone needed to watch him. I didn't wholly trust him yet.

:*He won't breathe without my knowledge, my queen.*: Guillaume whispered in my head. :*Rest well. Daire and I have first watch.*:

I woke once, when Guillaume traded places with Xin. I felt for Daire, and found his bond curled up on the floor by the door. Rik had banned him from my bed—but evidently not the room in which I slept. My brain still foggy with exhaustion, I lifted my head, worried that he'd be uncomfortable on the floor. He peeked at me from a mound of pillows and blankets and starting purring. :*Sleep, my queen. I'd sleep on a bed of nails to be close to you. I'm more than fine.*:

Xin ran the new property as a wolf, scenting for any predators or thralls that were close. Surprised, I felt Levi with him, walking through the woods, soaking in sunshine. I figured he'd be asleep somewhere after first watch.

:*I've had thousands of years to sleep.*:

His bond felt steadier in my head. Less frantic and angry was a good thing—but he also felt... bigger. More at home, more confident, and definitely more arrogant. Of all my Blood so far, he was going to be the biggest risk to the status quo. Right now, he didn't want to be at my side or in my bed. But eventually, he'd want to feed. He'd *need* to feed, and my other Blood weren't going to indulge him.

He'd have to come to me.

Which meant facing off against Rik. Because the king was eager to challenge my alpha.

I rolled toward Rik and burrowed against him, terrified and angry at myself, and yes, at Isis. Why did She send me after such a threat? Why couldn't life be easy for a change? Why did everything have to be turmoil and strife?

He made a low, rumbling sound like a distant earthquake and kissed my shoulder. "I'm not worried, my queen."

"If he hurts you, I'll never forgive myself."

Rik snorted and scratched me lightly with his fangs. "Have a little faith in your alpha."

"But he's thousands of years older." I tipped my head back, searching Rik's face. He smiled back, confident, eyes hard, ready to fight. No doubt in his mind at all. "Doesn't that make him stronger?"

He kissed my nose. "He'll realize the truth of it soon enough."

"What?" He wouldn't answer, and his bond gleamed hot and bright like a well-stoked forge. Confident. Hot. No doubt whatsoever. I rolled back over to look at Guillaume. "Do you know what he means?"

G inclined his head. "I do."

I waited, brow arched. "Well? Aren't you going to tell me?"

"Xin and I are both older than Rik. Arguably stronger in some ways, though not in brute strength. But he's still alpha."

"But you didn't want to challenge Rik. *He* will."

Guillaume gave one of his rare grins. "I can't help that

I'm smarter than he is."

I rolled my eyes. "What's that supposed to mean?"

"Go back to sleep," Rik whispered against my ear, tucking my back against his chest. "You need your rest so you can start building the nest."

Excitement surged through me, followed quickly by uneasiness. I didn't quite know what this nest thing involved. But I wanted to try. I wanted my own place. "How am I supposed to sleep if I'm worried about you?"

He bit my ear gently. "All will be well. I promise."

And yeah, his promise was enough. I closed my eyes and sank back into dreamless rest, wrapped in my Bloods' arms.

LEVIATHAN

Walking in weak winter sunshine, breathing fresh, crisp air, feeling the frozen earth beneath my feet, the promise of snowflakes on my face. So fucking priceless.

I'd forgotten the simple pleasures of being alive.

I wanted to hate her. I hated myself for savoring her blood and allowing her to bond me.

It would have been easier to die. I should have rejected her blood and allowed her to leave me there on the mountain that had been my prison for so long. I could have died with my rage burning bright. I could have died hating her, righteous in my belief that she was the same as all the other queens who'd tried to free me.

Only Shara Isador was not like other queens.

She'd freed me where all others had failed. And yeah, I

fucking hated her for it, or at least tried to stoke my rage against her. I didn't want to belong to her. I didn't want to need her.

But the fucking honest truth... Now I needed her more than anything I'd ever needed in my entire miserable existence.

Hope hurt. After endless millennia of despair, I dared hope again, and that glimmer of sunlight blinded and hurt with its brightness.

I dared to walk this earth again as a man. Not a beast.

Leviathan still crawled in my mind, twisting and snarling and raging at the gleaming moonlight bond she had looped around his neck. She'd freed me, the man, but imprisoned the beast with her magic. For the first time in my life, I couldn't shift. She'd locked the vicious dragon inside me with her blood. Where other Blood gained a beast when their queen's blood, I found myself looking back in the mirror.

A man. Lines around my eyes and mouth, a hint of gray at my temples, betraying my age and the trials I had endured. Fresh scars on my throat, a testament to how near death I had been, even me, surely one of the oldest Aima still walking this earth. I had forgotten what I looked like without scales and claws. I was taller than I remembered. Bigger. Though perhaps that was the queen's blood working its magic on me, because all her Blood were big and powerful. Especially the alpha.

I would have to deal with him, sooner than later.

Because I hungered. I burned with thirst, a weakness I

despised. I wanted nothing more than her blood. Her power. And fuck, yes, her body. My queen. Mine. At last.

I would have to go to her. Bend knee. Offer throat. Submit. While every muscle in my body screamed in denial.

Leviathan, king of the depths, was no beggar. He did not ask. He took. He killed. He raged.

Except I was not Leviathan now. I couldn't even manage one claw without my queen.

And oh, it galled. The loss of my beast stuck like a femur in my throat, even though that beast was what had kept me imprisoned for so long. I had everything I could possibly want: a new life, power, hope.

A new queen.

Which choked most of all.

I yearned to taste her again. Her blood, bright crystal on my tongue. Pure, sweet water after centuries of drought. Her passion like a hot, flickering flame on my skin.

It had been so long.

So fucking long.

And I was only a man now. A man who burned to touch the woman who had saved him.

It would be so much easier to hate her if she would command me to bare my throat on my knees, force me to feed her, and order me to her bed. Then I could fuel my rage and despise her like every other queen before her.

I wanted to hate her. I *needed* to hate her.

Because I didn't want to love her.

As the sun set, I felt her awaken. Excitement rose in her bond, mixed with nerves. She wanted to form a nest, but she'd never seen or lived in one to know how it was done or what it would feel like. Her nervous energy tugged on me like a leash, drawing me to her. To them. Her Blood could not bear to be out of her sight for long.

Even me. As much as that thought churned my stomach.

I wanted to feel her fangs in my throat again and remember the sensation of soaring through the night sky, piercing the clouds, impossibly high, only to fall in a death spiral toward the earth.

She'd saved me once. Would she be able to save me again? Would she care enough to try, or toss me aside like rubbish and leave me to rot as I deserved?

Three of her Blood glared at me as I approached, but the alpha only nodded once in acknowledgment. He didn't puff up his chest or growl or even block my approach. All things I expected.

He was young, though big and strong. He ought to be, since he was well-fed on our powerful young queen's blood. I didn't know his history—didn't care to—but I'd bend knee right here and beg for a taste of the honey between her thighs if he'd ever served a queen before. He wouldn't realize exactly how much power Shara Isador wielded.

:I know full well our queen is already mighty enough to rival the Triune, and she's still growing in power.:

I blinked, surprised that he'd spoken directly into my mind. I hadn't had his blood, nor he mine. So for him to touch me so easily…

Shara looked at me, her dark eyes shining with a midnight sky sparkling with million stars. Her bonds were so deep and strong that even her alpha could touch us all whether we'd shared blood or not. A sobering thought, not that I intended any secret mayhem. Yet.

The feline Blood snorted with disgust. "We all fully expect you to be plotting mayhem as we speak."

Correction. All her Blood could sense each other's thoughts. Even mine, the new one, who'd only tasted the queen once. She held my gaze, and I knew she was privy to my doubts. She'd heard me ranting and raving inside my own head, clinging to my hate, even while thirst burned like a white-hot flame in my gut.

Yet she said nothing to me as she turned away. "So, how do I do this, exactly?"

The alpha signaled one of the older Blood, the one who moved like a medieval knight. I would have had a very good time chomping on knights if I hadn't been locked away. I didn't bother hiding that thought, and the man's eyes narrowed, though he didn't grace me with a retort or direct look.

"Guillaume is going to walk you through it, since he's participated in establishing a new nest from scratch," the alpha said. "But it's basically like the salt circles you used when we first found you, only you use blood instead."

"Mine?"

"And ours," Guillaume said. "You're the power. We're the deterrent. The most important thing to remember is that whatever you start, we have to finish, or it's useless. If you make the circle too large, we may not be able to close it before one of us faints or needs to be fed. This first circle, I think we all should participate." He did give me a stern look then. I barely held back a smirk, though I'm sure he felt my disdain in the bond. "Then each time we walk the perimeter to guard your nest, we'll add blood to it. We'll constantly strengthen and expand your defenses. But this first time is crucial. This will be the heart of your nest, the tightest, safest, most secure part of your court."

"So it needs to be big… but not too big," she mused aloud, looking up at the main house. "I'm feeling better. Good, actually. How much blood do I actually need to put on the ground? A solid line? Or drops?"

"Drops are enough, but the more you do, the better, as long as you complete the circle."

She held her hand out and Guillaume made a blade appear in his hand like a magician. Yet the knight hesitated.

"I feel I should warn you about the… side effects."

"Yeah, I don't want any of us to faint."

He coughed, a slight smile curving his lips. "Indeed, my queen, but that's not what I meant. You know what your blood does to us."

"And what our blood does to you." The alpha's voice dropped an octave. "Plus, you'll be building power into the nest. A great deal of power."

"It's not uncommon to… uh…"

I started to laugh. I couldn't help it. The great Templar knight was blushing. "What the good knight is so reluctant to say is that a queen and her Blood usually establish the nest while nude. It makes the resulting orgy easier if there's no clothes to remove."

31

SHARA

Orgy? If he thought to shock me, he'd be sorely disappointed. At least my period was finally over. "How many humans are on the premises?"

"Frank and three humans are at the front gate," Xin answered immediately. "Winston's in his quarters in the main house. Gina left earlier in a car. No other human is within a three-mile radius."

I felt for Gina's bond. :*We need an hour undisturbed to set the nest. Can you call Winston and tell him not to look out the windows for a bit?*:

I didn't have to taste her blood to feel her laughter through our bond. She knew what a nest entailed.

With my human friends taken care of, I unbuttoned my jeans and started shimmying out of them.

Daire leaped into action like he was a competition stripper, though my other Blood were quick to get naked too. I didn't look at Levi. I didn't need to. His bond crackled and sparked, torn between surprise and lust. Frozen in place, he watched as I pulled my sweater over my head and tossed it in a pile.

"If you're not participating, could you go drag some blankets from the guest house so we don't have to fuck on the ground? Though ice and snow won't stop me once I get a taste of blood."

I felt Guillaume's concern in the bond, but he didn't say anything. He'd already said all my Blood should participate. The problem was that Leviathan didn't count himself as my Blood in any way, shape, or form. Not yet.

I didn't have to order Leviathan. I knew what he wanted. What he needed. And if I tried to command him... He'd gladly balk. He wanted me to give him a reason to hate and distrust me.

I sure as fuck wasn't going to cooperate in that regard. But my patience with him was limited. He had to let go of the past and start anew. Or he should have stayed in that motherfucking cave. I didn't send those words to him directly in the bond, but I made sure he felt what I was thinking.

Looking at my men, my hunger stirred. My nipples pebbled in the chilly December air and goose bumps raced down my arms. Though I wasn't cold exactly. Just...

exposed. My fangs started to descend, making my face throb. My stomach knotted and grumbled, ready to feast. In more ways than one.

Out of the corner of my eye, I saw Levi jerk his shirt over his head. I didn't look at him directly. I wouldn't give him the satisfaction. I didn't know all that he'd suffered yet, though hundreds or thousands of years locked away from the world would have driven anyone insane. I got it.

But I wasn't one to tip-toe around a man who wanted to be in my bed. Especially when I had four fearless, honorable, loyal men ahead of him. He could figure it out.

Or he could fucking sleep on the fucking floor.

I tried to gauge how far I wanted to pace out this circle. The heart of my nest had to include the main house, and the guest house, since that's where we'd stay for at least a few weeks while repairs were made. I was starting to regret picking out such a large house. I wasn't sure if I'd have enough blood left in my body to worry about any orgy.

"We'll help," Rik said at my side. "You don't have to walk it yourself. You just have to bleed. If you get woozy, I'll carry you."

Guillaume passed the knife around to each Blood first.

So much blood scenting the air. All five of them. Their blood glowed and sang to me, mesmerizing me like I'd stared into a fire too long. My fangs throbbed in time with my heartbeat.

Waiting to sink into one of them until I had the whole circle marked was going to be a pain in my ass.

Finally, Guillaume turned to me. I offered my left palm

and he cupped my hand in his. "I'm going to make a fairly deep cut. Squeeze your hand into a fist to control how much blood you drip onto the ground. You'll feel the power rising. That's a good thing, though it might seem like it'll never end. It will—once you close the circle. That's when all hell will break loose."

"The orgy." I wiggled my eyebrows, making him laugh. "I can't wait. Let's get to it."

He sliced me deeply enough I actually sucked in a breath at the pain. Fisting my hand like he said, I squeezed hard, applying pressure to the wound so that blood only seeped through my fingers.

The first drop of my blood hit the earth and the soft thud reverberated through my body like a gong. I'd bled plenty of times before, but I don't think I'd ever allowed my blood to drip onto the ground itself other than when I'd opened Leviathan's portal. Something wild and raw stirred deep in the earth. Mother Nature, Gaia, the earth goddess, the great matriarch of the Aima houses.

She felt her child's blood, no matter how thinned over the ages, and responded.

She accepted my sacrifice. In fact, She was hungry for more.

I walked quickly in an arc around the front of my house, trailing blood on the frozen ground. Each drop gleamed like rubies in the moonlight, sprinkled among the ice crystals and frosted grass. I glanced back, not surprised to see the red glow rising up from the ground. It looked like the tapestry in my head—only this was outside of myself. Power hummed and pulsed through me like a mighty generator coming online. Switches fired, flipping from dormant, to high speed ahead.

Switch. After switch. After switch.

I started to understand what Guillaume had meant. Power rose inside me—but it had nowhere to go. Nothing to do. Magic rose to a fevered pitch inside me, vibrated my bones, and screamed through my nerves. My hair crackled with static electricity around my head. If one of the guys touched me right now, I was afraid I'd blast him on his ass.

I walked faster from necessity. Half running now. I had to finish before I came apart at the seams. I stumbled over a low landscape wall and Rik grabbed my elbow to steady me. I heard him suck in his breath, his fingers going numb on my arm. But he didn't let go.

"More blood," Guillaume said on my other side, his voice tight with strain. "It's a little thin. Or slow down."

Fuck that shit. I wasn't slowing until I had my fangs buried in one of them. I worked my hand to get more blood flowing. My whole body throbbed with my heart beat, a heavy, steady thump that was driving me mad. I'm sure I looked like a lunatic, running naked around my own yard, my mouth gaped open with gigantic fangs protruded. I'd wished for fangs—but I should have been careful what I wished for. They grew even longer, poking through my own lip.

The taste of my blood in my mouth was a torment. I didn't want *my* blood. I wanted theirs. My hunger torched higher, searing my lungs like Leviathan had burst free and blasted my insides with fire.

I ran harder, dribbling blood from my mouth and my hand. Though I wasn't sure that my lip bled hard enough to help. The guest house was in sight. I could see the fiery glow of the finish line straight ahead like a wildfire roaring across the lawn.

A bird screeched in the night. What the fuck? Not an owl. It sounded like a crow.

Raven.

I jerked my gaze up as something black soared over the trees headed for us. Larger than any bird—but not as big as Leviathan. Rik roared, shifting to rock troll in a heart beat, the signal for my other Blood to leap to my defense. He shoved me behind him and Guillaume pressed me tight to Rik's broad granite-hard back.

"You have to finish!" Guillaume whispered urgently against my ear.

I could feel the strain in the line I'd laid already. It brightened, hovering on the edge of closing the circle… Or dissipating like fog in the night.

Xin and Daire pressed tight to my legs, silvery fur on one side, black stripes on the other.

Leviathan… or rather Levi, the man, stood alone. Forlorn, and yes, angry. He reached for his dragon. He strained to fill himself with scales and claws and wings.

But Leviathan the beast belonged to me now.

"I think it's Nevarre." I couldn't focus on the tapestry, not with magic pounding through my blood. I couldn't be sure, but I thought it was the man I'd dreamed about. The man I'd called as Blood, though he'd claimed it was too late for him.

I had to move. I had to close the circle.

Even if a dead druid raven was inside.

He dropped to the ground in front of us, a massive, black feathered bird.

"If you close it with him inside, and he's a thrall, you won't be able to keep him out unless you kill him," Guillaume said.

Fine. So be it. I'd kill him myself if he even thought about hurting someone inside my circle.

My home.

My nest.

I sprinted forward and closed the circle.

32

RIK

The circle snapped into place.

She threw her head back and screamed, lashing the heavens with her magic. Her hair blew wildly, power exploding out of her like fireworks. She stood in the center of a glowing nimbus, head back, arms outstretched, skin gleaming with magic, and I'd never seen anything more fucking gorgeous in my life.

Her magic called me. Like she'd tied a rope around my dick and jerked me toward her. All of us moved to her.

Even the new man. His long black hair gleamed in the moonlight like liquid ink. He didn't smell right, though. Ancient Celtic magic masked the truth.

This man was dead. Either a thrall... or something unnatural.

My first instinct was to pound him into a smear on the ground, but she'd dreamed this man. Like she'd dreamed the king. She must have need of him.

And what my queen needed, she received. Or I was no alpha.

:*Keep an eye on him,*: I told Xin and Daire. :*Guillaume and I will deal with Leviathan if he tries anything.*:

:*Understood, alpha,*: Xin replied. Then he blurred and disappeared. Through Shara's bond, I felt him closing on our new guest, though the man was too focused on our queen to realize death hovered at his side once more. If he tried to harm our queen, we would learn how well druid magic worked if he had no head.

I turned back to my queen.

Ribbons of blood ran down her forearm and droplets glittered on her chin, throat, and breasts like the finest, most expensive jewelry in the world. She opened her eyes, meeting my gaze, and my heart stopped. Waiting for her command.

She ran toward me, eyes glowing, fangs glistening in the night. She launched against me, but her fangs couldn't penetrate my rock troll's hide. Not unless she shifted to her cobra queen. :*Shift. Get inside me. I want my alpha first.*:

Normally my queen's wish was my command. But I didn't comply right away, no matter how hard my dick was. I widened my stance, holding my queen high on my body, and then I met Leviathan's gaze.

He burned. Thirst knifed through his gut like he'd swallowed half a dozen of Guillaume's blades. Desire blazed through him like wildfire.

But his pride kept him frozen in place.

Leviathan did not bend knee to any queen no matter how he burned for her.

I could forgive a great deal, especially mistakes made with love, like Daire's, when he'd worried for my safety in our cobra queen's coils. But Leviathan's greatest sin was his willingness to kill her to save himself. That I could not forgive. Not unless he made the realization that he would die, gladly, simply because she loved him.

I gently set her back down on the ground and crouched over her like a sprinter ready to surge at the first shot.

My challenge was clear. "Come, Leviathan. Try to take my queen from me. I'll rip your fucking head off."

He stepped closer, eyes blazing. "She won't let me have my beast. It's not a fair challenge."

"Unleash his beast, my queen, and I'll still rip his fucking head off."

She rolled over and rose to her knees beneath me. I hovered over her back, ready to leap over her and smash the fucker into the ground if he so much as thought about touching one hair on her precious head.

"I'll unleash your beast, Levi. But if you shift now, I'll never feed you again, let alone fuck you. Accept my alpha. Or get the fuck out. I don't really care."

"That's not the way this works."

Her spine stiffened, her bond ringing like drawn steel in my mind. "Oh really? Am I not your queen? Then I believe this is exactly the way it works. If you want your beast, you can have him. And you'll never touch me again."

"Because I'll kill your alpha?"

She snorted with disgust and turned back to me, ignoring the other man completely. "No. Because *he'll* kill *you*."

And that was the secret she had finally come to understand. My power came from *her*. Her love, trust, and magic.

I was alpha because she *willed* me to be alpha, and I could do no less than fight for and protect my queen. Because I loved her, and believed in her, and she in me, there was nothing that would make me doubt her power, or her right to be my queen. Let alone my ability to serve as her alpha simply because she willed it to be so.

She lifted the silver chains of moonlight she'd wrapped around the dragon living in Leviathan's bond, casting her magic aside. The dragon was free to go.

Staring at her, I went to my knees and allowed the rock troll to fade as she'd ordered, surrendering to her will. She wanted me. She'd have me. Even if Leviathan shifted and tried to tear me apart.

Climbing up my body, leaving bloody hand prints on my chest and shoulder, she took my cock inside her. I shifted back on my heels, seated deep inside her, and offered her my throat. I knew it made me vulnerable. I'd come as soon as she bit me, and a Blood was never as easy to kill as when in the throes of passion with his queen. I truly believed that was why queens took multiple Blood. So at least one Blood could stand guard while she blew another's mind.

She pressed against me, sinking fangs into my neck so deep. So exquisite. It was like being fucked in the throat. I roared with climax and she drank me down, gulping my blood like a woman dying of thirst. Maybe she was. Maybe we all were. Because I couldn't keep my fangs out of her, either, even though I knew she'd just bled a huge circle around her nest.

:G.:

Her bonds blazed higher, pulsing hot lava that seared my mind. Guillaume came to us, sitting back on his heels as I'd done, shoulder to shoulder with me, offering our queen what she wanted. Pressing her bleeding hand over his heart, she sank over his big cock with a groan and sank her fangs just as deeply into him. He couldn't hold back his desire. Not with our queen's fangs in his throat.

:Xin.:

He materialized beside her as if he'd been there, invisible, the entire time, though I knew that wasn't true. He'd guarded the new man well. I didn't have to look to ensure Daire had taken over that duty with Xin's absence. She took him inside her, smearing her blood on his chest, and when she sank her fangs into him, his wolf's howl reverberated through the night.

Guillaume recovered to take Daire's place guarding the new man when she called him. As was his nature, Daire invited her to take him flat on his back.

Still seated on his hips while he panted from the force of his release, she lifted her head from Daire's throat and said aloud, "Nevarre."

The new man came to her side. He went to his knees and bowed his head. "I'm sorry, my queen. Forgive me. I'm not worthy of your service. I have no blood to offer."

Her head tilted to the side as she studied him. Through our bond, I felt the absence of the man's heartbeat. He was dead, as she'd dreamed. Blood did not flow in his veins. Only druid magic sustained him.

Yet a dead man had never stopped the goddess of resurrection.

She cupped his cheek with her bleeding hand and tenderly pressed her mouth to his. He quivered, eyes flaring wide, as our queen sucked him down, draining him. Not of blood. But his magic.

When he didn't try to save himself, I knew him as true Blood. Even though his magic kept him alive, he gave it all to her without hesitation. He collapsed against her and Daire, a dead weight. Lifeless. The spark blown out of his eyes.

She smeared her blood on his lips. "Fly back to me, Nevarre. Your queen has need of you."

Invisible wings fluttered past my head, as if his soul came back to her call. His chest rose, his eyes focusing on her as she pressed her bleeding palm to his mouth. When she finally lifted her hand, his heart beat so loudly I could hear it. He laid back beside Daire and she crawled over to him, taking him inside her, sinking her fangs into his throat. Taking her fifth Blood.

Yes. I thought *fifth* very hard at Leviathan who stood watching our queen use us one after another, feasting on our blood, giving us hers. Guillaume and Xin knelt on either side of her. Holding her as she took her pleasure. Offering their mouths. Their hands. Their blood. Whatever our queen desired.

Mighty Leviathan, king of the depths, was beneath Shara Isador's notice and certainly not worthy of being counted as Blood, no matter that her blood fueled his strength and saved his miserable life.

Unless and until he deigned bare his throat for her, I would not count him as Blood.

Panting, she settled back on Nevarre's hips, arms looped around Guillaume and Xin. Daire curled around her front, nuzzling her breasts, though he made room for Nevarre when he recovered enough to join in stroking our queen. They kept her off the frozen ground, using their bodies to comfort her. To shield her. As a Blood should.

She still burned with need and thirst both. The circle was complete—though not in her Blood. But she didn't call Leviathan to her.

She called *me*.

SHARA

"Alpha."

One single word that meant so much.

I don't know why I had worried for Rik's safety. It was ridiculous, a moment of weakness, of doubting myself. Maybe part of Leviathan's beast had whispered those doubts into my head. Because one thing I knew for certain: I loved Rik.

I loved them all. And my love was enough to keep them all alive and well and safe. Love was enough. More than enough.

With love, I would bind them to me, strengthen them, and we would be invincible. With love, I would defeat my enemies.

And with love, I would take my king.

On his knees behind me, Rik wrapped his arms around me. He pushed into me, dick hard and big and ready to give me what I wanted. What I needed.

My Blood pressed close, all touching me. So many hands. Rik's big palms, granite tenderness. G's scarred, damaged hands. Xin's silent, deliberate touch, a wolf revealing himself to me, only me. Daire's playful flirt and tease, still feline even though he hadn't shifted. And now Nevarre, his long, elegant fingers reminding me of a musician plucking strings on a harp.

At that thought, music filled my head. Earth music. The sound of creation. The Mother nurturing Her plants, animals, and children. Living things growing, expanding, changing, dying, only to fuel another generation. Birds on the wing. Leaves rustling in a gentle breeze. Stars sprinkling diamonds across a black velvet canvas. Distant comets and planets spinning, singing the same endless tune.

Frosted grass cracked beneath his feet as he came to me. Still a man, though his dragon roared and rolled in his bond.

He fell to his knees, hard and graceless. Defeated. By

nothing but my steadfast determination to let him choose whether to accept the love I offered or not.

"My queen." He swallowed hard, his voice breaking. "The only boon I have left to offer you is my true name, Mehen. But if you wish to call me Levi I will answer your call without fail."

In his bond, the mighty, furious dragon stretched out his neck, braced for my sword to fall. Still and quiet at last. Surrendered. He fully expected to die.

I lifted my bleeding hand to his mouth and his eyes flared with pain. He had dared a small glimmer of hope, but had feared it was too late. He'd been hurt so many times. He'd fully expected to fall in his death spiral, and this time, I would allow him to crash on the rocks below.

"If you fall, I will always catch you."

"Why?" he ground out, his eyes blazing with emotion.

He needed to hear the words aloud. Only then would he truly believe.

I leaned toward him, my Blood moving with me, supporting me as one. "Because I love you."

And I sank my fangs into his throat.

33

SHARA

Only I could end up in a bloody orgy underneath the stars on Christmas Day.

I couldn't even begin to put into words exactly how okay I was with that.

"We should do this every year," Daire said, flashing his dimples at me. Somehow he'd wiggled around to get his head in my lap. His favorite spot.

"I couldn't agree more."

Headlights approached the house, driving up the long, winding drive from the main road. We all scrambled up like guilty teenagers before Gina could catch us naked as jaybirds on the front lawn. Too late. She yelled after us. "We're serving Christmas dinner in the main house in fifteen minutes!"

Daire and Xin raced to the guest house. I groaned. How were we all going to be presentable in fifteen fucking minutes? Wait, how did she even get through my circle?

I realized why before anyone could answer. Gina was mine. My blood lived inside her. Of course my nest would allow her in. I'd built the nest with Winston inside, so he could pass back and forth. Frank would be able to come through. What would happen if one of the other guards needed to approach me?

Rik swept me up into his arms. "They won't be able to cross until you allow it."

My two new Blood walked on either side of him. Guillaume brought up the rear.

"I guess we should make introductions," I said, blushing a little at the thought I'd been intimate with this new man and he didn't even know our names.

"No need, my queen," Nevarre replied cheerfully. "Daire, Xin, Mehen, Rik, and the legendary Guillaume de Payne. I gleaned their names from your bond easily enough."

Guillaume's gruff voice drew my gaze over Rik's shoulder. I'm pretty sure silver glinted in his hand, but I couldn't be sure. Where would he hide knives if we were all naked? "You've heard of me, then."

"Indeed."

"I wonder why we've not heard of any Nevarre?"

"Who was fucking dead?" Levi replied, an edge of his voice. Or rather Mehen. That was going to take some getting used to in my head.

"My tale is nowhere near as interesting as Leviathan,

king of the deep, let alone the headless knight, Desideria's executioner for hundreds of years."

Guillaume grunted. "You might have a point."

I called the crazy amount of blood we'd smeared all over each other and gave us all a quick dip in magic so we could get dressed. Daire helped me into a red velvet dress with a plunging neckline deep enough to bare several bites on my throat. I thought about bleeding enough to heal those bites, but I didn't *want* to make them disappear. I didn't care who saw them. I wasn't ashamed of what I was, and the people who were here knew exactly who they were sitting down to eat dinner with.

"Shara fucking Isador," Daire whispered, kissing my shoulder. "Our vampire queen, last daughter of Isis."

All the guys dressed up. Well, for those of us usually in jeans and a T-shirt, wearing khakis, sweaters, or button-down shirts was some fancy shit. I turned around and saw what Nevarre had put on and my tongue glued to the top of my mouth.

A kilt. A motherfucking kilt.

Daire sauntered over to him. "From her reaction, I think you need to give me one of those."

"Not on your fucking life."

By the time we started walking toward the main house, it'd started to snow, huge fat flakes that would make excellent snowmen. Or snowballs. And yeah, Daire had already thrown one at Rik's head. Of course he missed, because nobody would hit our alpha with a snowball and live to tell the tale.

Gina opened the door, dressed in a beautiful shimmering golden dress. "Shara, let me introduce you to Timothy Winston, your new butler."

He was the most dapper silver-haired gentleman I'd ever met, dressed in a checkered navy suit with a double row of buttons and red bowtie. He tapped the heels of his perfectly polished black dress shoes together and swept into a crisp bow over my hand. "Your Majesty, I'm delighted to make your acquaintance at last. I hope everything has been to your satisfaction."

"I—" I couldn't answer. I was too overwhelmed.

He'd somehow found the time to decorate for Christmas. A tall pine—root ball intact so we could plant it outside—stood in front of the staircase, glittering with decorations and lights. More fresh greenery and lights lined the grand staircase and the mantel above the fireplace, which housed a crackling fire. He led me into the next room—my formal dining room. The massive table I'd seen online was loaded with candles and fresh flowers and pine boughs and wine and food. Goddess, the food! A huge roast of some kind, a turkey, a ham… Several kinds of pie. Dishes I couldn't even identify but smelled incredible, making me literally drool.

They'd managed to find people to make this much fancy food, on Christmas Day, no less.

I would have burst into happy tears—but I was too fucking hungry to waste time crying. Though I did throw my arms around Gina and then kissed Winston's cheek. "It's incredible. Thank you so much. I never dreamed you'd be able to pull so much together on such short notice."

"Oh dear," Gina exclaimed. "Winston, we need another place setting. Our queen has called another Blood."

They scurried around the table, shifting a few things around and laying down another place setting.

Someone knocked on the door, and Winston immediately went to admit Frank. He hesitated, looking uncomfortable and stiff, like he counted himself as an employee, not my family. Even though he'd given up his old life to move with me.

"Frank!" I smiled, beyond pleased to see him. "Thanks for coming." I kissed his cheek too, and the gruff ex-soldier blushed.

Seated at the head of my table, with Rik to my right—naturally pressed tight with one big arm wrapped around my back—and Daire on my left, with the rest of my new family around me, it was all I could do not to cry. Everyone was laughing, talking, and eating. Nevarre regaled Guillaume and Frank with a crazy war story that had my stoic knight throwing his head back, roaring with laughter. Xin and Daire tore through dinner to see who could get to dessert first. Evidently Mehen highly approved of Winston's tailor and had requested an appointment.

Gina caught my gaze and smiled, lifting her wine glass. "A toast."

Everyone stopped talking and picked up their glasses.

"Merry Christmas to our queen, Shara Isador."

My Blood all stood, except Rik, tight to my side, and saluted with their glasses. "Long live our queen."

When Rik said *our*, he slid his right hand up my thigh

beneath my dress and kissed my shoulder. I shifted my legs apart, inviting him higher.

And he compiled. Gladly.

Merry fucking Christmas to me.

By the tenth toast of the evening, or morning, since it was almost dawn, we'd moved into the living room. Dark paneled walls reflected the Christmas lights and another cheery fire distracted from the water-stained ceiling that would need to be repaired. "Long live our queen."

Our queen. I saluted them with my glass and took a small sip of champagne that cost more than I'd made under the table all year cleaning hotel rooms. I'd seen the receipt lying on the kitchen counter. Thousands. Of dollars. On alcohol.

Just for this Christmas party. It still boggled my mind.

Watching my Bloods' antics, though, I'd pay a hundred times that amount if needed to keep the smiles on their faces. A thousand. Nevarre started to sing a bawdy tune—in gorgeous baritone—and I couldn't take my eyes off him. Though the kilt certainly contributed to my attraction as much as his singing.

A motherfucking kilt. Goddess. Every time I saw him, I had to stare.

I couldn't stop thinking about what was under that kilt.

I'd had a taste of him already when I closed the circle, but it had been too rushed. I'd been more concerned with making sure the king accepted me as his queen than sampling a new Blood.

"You have *two* new Blood." Mehen's low voice came from my right side. Though not too close. Not with Rik at my back.

My big alpha Blood cradled me between his thighs, my back pressed against his chest. His favorite place. *My* favorite place. He wrapped his huge arms around me, surrounding me with his heat and strength. His entire body was one gigantic muscle, ripped, hard, raw power at my fingertips.

I might have two new Blood, but we still didn't know either of them. Not really. I'd tasted their blood and yeah, I'd fucked Nevarre. I'd fucked all my Blood on the front lawn.

Except for Mehen. The one I'd trusted the least from the start.

Even now, Rik looked at him, eyes heavy with warning, his bond humming with intensity. He would welcome a reason to rip Mehen's head off with his bare hands.

I didn't turn my head to look at him. "Do I? Or are you still here under protest?"

He chuckled, a low rumbling growl like his dragon made —right before he'd planted his massive paw on my stomach and tried to drain me dry. "I can protest and still be Blood."

That last word came out a bit choked, as if his dragon had been feasting and got a bone stuck halfway down his throat. He didn't want to be my Blood, not really. But he'd adopted a fatalistic acceptance. It was too late. He was fucked. Trapped by a queen. Enslaved, in his mind. So he might as well enjoy the fucking. Even if he was still furious about the trap.

That he himself had set.

I stood and the room instantly fell silent, all eyes swinging to me. Gina and Winston both came to me, ready for their orders.

"Thank you for a wonderful, unforgettable evening, but I'm ready for bed."

Gina gave me a hug. "Of course, Shara. It was fantastic to have our first Christmas here with you."

Winston kissed both my cheeks. "Welcome home, Your Majesty. I'm so thrilled to be here with you at last. Are there any special meals you'd like to have when you awake?"

I couldn't imagine eating another bite at this point after we'd all gorged on the incredible feast they'd brought in for dinner. "Not really. Coffee, maybe some toast or something light. I'm usually not very hungry when I first wake up."

"We'll just play it by ear, then, until I'm familiar with your favorite foods. But please, if there's anything specific you'd like, don't hesitate to let me know."

"We live to serve," Gina said.

And they meant it.

We walked outside into a winter wonderland. It'd snowed five inches since we'd gone up to the big house for dinner.

Xin shifted to his ghostly silver wolf immediately. :*By your leave, my queen, I'll run the property and look for fresh tracks.*:

I nodded and he disappeared. Literally. His gift of invisibility worked whether he was a man or a wolf.

"I can check from the sky," Nevarre said.

"Good idea." At Rik's words, Nevarre leaped into the air and black feathers exploded out of him. With a throaty caw, he soared out over the forest toward the river. "Guillaume, Daire, guard close to the guest house."

All of them looked at the man walking on my right, their distrust written on their faces. Rik didn't say it explicitly, but he wanted them close enough to help protect me from Mehen if our lovemaking got out of control. I didn't think they'd be needed. Not because I trusted Mehen all that much…

But because I trusted Rik's ability to protect me implicitly.

A surge of heated lust mixed with pride in his bond. *:Even an alpha can be vulnerable when his queen has her fangs in him.:*

"I hate to admit he's right, but your alpha has a point." Mehen gave me a sardonic yet elegant shrug. His eyes glittered and his bond weighed heavy in my mind. His dragon was silent in the bond—but tense. Like he was hiding in his den, watching unsuspecting prey slowly coming near him. "I can't believe I'm actually saying this, but if you have any intentions at all of taking me to your bed, you should leash my beast now. I've never been able to keep from shifting when the dragon wants out to play. And he will want to play with you very badly indeed."

"Maybe Rik should fuck him into submission first."

Normally my cuddly purring warcat, Daire's words shocked me.

Even more, Guillaume grunted in agreement and Rik seemed to be considering it.

I sharpened my voice. "No one gets fucked into submission around here. Nothing happens to anyone against their will, especially in my bed."

Mehen didn't seemed bothered at all. In fact, he looked up and down my almost seven-foot tall alpha as if considering the possibility himself. "I'm game. It wouldn't be against my will."

"You can't be serious."

Staring at me with those dark emerald eyes, Mehen licked his lips and I had the distinct impression of his dragon crouched, ready to pounce. "Remember when you saved me? Even dying, I tried to lunge up to tear your throat out. He grabbed me by the neck and squeezed until I submitted to you. You didn't think that was hot?"

Rik's voice rumbled deeper, as if his rock troll stirred. "And when you had both Daire and me the first time. I restrained him for you so you could torment him at will. I know you thought that was hot. I sure as fuck did."

"Me too," Daire purred.

Eyes blazing with heat, Mehen took a step closer and Rik rumbled a warning, like he always did. But because of this discussion, I couldn't help but hear a sexual heat to that sound.

"Make your move and I'll fucking drill your ass into oblivion," Rik growled.

I gulped. And yeah, my fangs throbbed, my pussy ached, and my nipples rubbed against the velvet of my dress. I could all too easily imagine Rik and Mehen wrestling, fighting, fucking. While I watched.

And then I got to fuck them both.

But did they really want to do that? Or were they only willing because they thought I wanted it? I did, but not if anyone would regret it later.

"My punishment wasn't being chained up for thousands of years. It was being my *dragon* that whole time." Mehen said. "In case you didn't notice, no other dragons, male or female, were imprisoned with me. I've had all this time to dream of fucking again. Every single one of your Blood are welcome to take a turn at me. I want and need to fuck. I'll fuck anyone. I'll let anyone fuck me. Gladly. I'll even beg for it if you're dominant enough to make me. But your alpha would be best at least this first time, because after so long, I'm going to be… feisty."

Daire snickered. "That's one way to say horny as hell."

34

SHARA

"Leash my beast," Mehen growled, vibrating with tension. "Now. So I don't lose control before we even start."

I pictured his dragon in our bond, the snarling, hissing, fire-breathing monster that hated everything about me. Except my blood. He liked me bleeding, but that was about it. I looped my magic around his neck, binding him to my will.

The dragon's slitted emerald eyes, so like Mehen's, glared with malevolence, but he didn't fight me again. He knew who his queen was, even if he didn't like it.

Guillaume held the guest house door open for me, and the rest waited until I was inside before following. I'd been so out of it when we arrived, and then consumed with forming the nest, that I hadn't really looked around that much. The guest house only had three rooms: a great room with a mini kitchen, bathroom, and bedroom. The guys each had a bag of spare clothing against the wall, and Gina had arranged for some of my new clothes to be installed in the bedroom closet. Though when Rik and Daire had taken me shopping, I'd ended up with at least ten times as many clothes, from a single store. The master bedroom closet had better be gigantic if they kept up that level of shopping.

The sectional couch took up a lot of space, but hopefully the guys not with me would at least be comfortable.

"More than comfortable," Guillaume assured me, lifting my hand to his mouth. "If you need us, we'll be close, and even out here, one of us will stay awake."

I wasn't sure if he was afraid Mehen would be that dangerous, or if Ra would try to attack again. I hooked my arms around his neck and pressed against him. "I thought the nest was supposed to be impenetrable."

"It is, to an extent. But the moment you have people crossing the circle, even with your permission, it becomes a weakness. Carpenters and crews will have to cross the circle to work on the house. Deliveries will be made. New servants will be hired for the house. Any of them can become a weak point in your defense that allow a strike."

Daire pressed against my back, his rumbling purr vibrating through my body. "Good night, my queen. Sleep well."

I kissed Guillaume and then turned to Daire, kissing him too. My throat tightened but I didn't say anything. Rik had enough on his plate handling Mehen without either Daire or I nagging him about when he could return to my bed. I missed my cuddle buddy.

"I can cuddle," Mehen growled.

It made me laugh, though I don't think that's what he intended. Daire bumped noses with me, fully secure in his claim as best cuddler, even though he was currently banned.

"Trade off with Xin and Nevarre in six hours," Rik said, his voice rumbling deep bass. "If Mehen is capable of walking, he'll join you."

Daire laughed and plopped down on the couch. "Good luck, my friend."

"I am not your friend."

Sobered, I headed for the bedroom. Mehen was Blood—but he didn't fit in with the rest of my men. And he might never fit in completely. Tension simmered in my bonds, despite Daire's and Guillaume's efforts at keeping the mood light. I hadn't had Blood for long, but with just four of them, we'd had an easy camaraderie that I'd enjoyed. There hadn't been any jealousy or fights. It'd been easy to trade off between guard and bed duty. I didn't know Nevarre's personality yet, but he seemed much more personable than this growling, hissing Blood.

The bedroom was large enough for a king-sized bed and room to walk around easily enough, but with two large men glaring at each other, it felt like a tiny closet. I unzipped my dress, the sound loud in the room, and both males' gazes whipped toward me. I let the velvet slide down my body and puddle on the floor. I wore nothing underneath.

Mehen's eyes narrowed into slits and he couldn't take his eyes off me. Rik used that distraction to his advantage and stripped his clothes in record time while the other man just stared at me.

"Take your clothes off," I whispered gently, trying not to stir his volatile emotions too much. I wasn't sure who had lent him the clothes in the first place. He sure hadn't flown out of the cave in Venezuela with a suitcase. I didn't want him to feel like a beggar, or a burden, far from it. He needed his own things. They all did.

He jerked the gun-metal gray sweater over his head and threw it aside. "Daire's." He jerked the black jeans open and gingerly worked the denim past his straining erection and down his muscular thighs. "Guillaume's. I don't give a fuck about what clothes I have as long as you'll tell me to strip again. That's one order I'll never bitch about. Though none of your Blood compare to Winston's taste in clothing. If you ever go to London, I'll have a dozen suits made by his tailor."

"I'd like that." I ran my gaze over him. For him being so impossibly old, he didn't have nearly as many scars as Guillaume, but my knight had been tortured while imprisoned. They'd even cut off his head, but hadn't been able to kill him.

Mehen's skin gleamed like polished ebony, streaked with glittering dark and gold green tattoos across his shoulders, chest and arms. Actually, the marks looked more like scales, not tattoos. I'd have to touch them to be sure. He was just as impressive in the dick department as my other men, right up there in size with Guillaume. Not that I was surprised.

Overall, he was a muscled, powerful man who moved with lethal grace.

In fact, all six-plus-feet of lethal grace was suddenly moving in a blur toward me.

Rik slammed into him like a linebacker, tucking his shoulder, picking him up and tackling him on the bed.

Mehen roared and thrashed, but Rik had him in a headlock. Mehen bucked beneath him, fighting to get his weight off his back. He managed to roll my alpha over, but Rik slammed him back over on his stomach. Reaching behind him, Mehen clawed at his shoulder and head, but he couldn't throw my alpha's weight off, and without his beast, he couldn't actually injure Rik enough to make him let go. With a couple of hundred pounds of muscle pinning him to the mattress, he finally conceded with his low hiss.

Two gorgeous, powerful men in my bed. Angry. Mean. Fighting. Rik had the other man pinned, riding his back, his tree-trunk thighs gripping Mehen's hips.

Goddess. I almost had to wipe my chin. I definitely had to shut my mouth.

"All right, my queen." Boulders crashed and rolled in Rik's voice, but he didn't sound winded, or like he was straining at all to hold the other man down. "You may approach him now."

I stepped toward the bed and Mehen's muscles rippled, his body tensing beneath Rik's. He was biding his time, but Rik wasn't worried. In fact, his eyes smoldered, his bond lava hot. He was aroused by the fight. By the prospect of bringing this mighty dragon down to size a peg or two. Holding him down for me. Fucking him while I watched. Yeah. All of the above.

Climbing up onto the mattress as nonchalantly as I could manage, I fluffed the pillows and settled back against the headboard off to their left. I didn't draw my legs up or act like I was afraid in any way, shape, or form, because I wasn't. I wanted to see what Mehen would do.

What Rik would *allow* him to do.

Mehen's hand snaked out toward my thigh. Paused. Waiting to see what Rik would do. When my alpha didn't stop him, Mehen seized my leg and tugged me toward them, hugging my thigh against him. His mouth a hot brand on my skin. I felt the barest hint of fang and Rik clamped his arm harder on Mehen's throat, so his breathing became a wheeze.

"Our queen feeds first. Always. Unless she explicitly offers her blood to you."

Growling against my hip, Mehen pushed back against Rik, pulling on my thigh like he wanted me beneath him.

And yeah, I wanted that. Eventually.

I caught Rik's gaze and a slow, cocky smile curved his lips. "If you would be so kind as to lube him up with your blood, my queen, I'll break him in for you."

RIK

I loved watching my queen when she was aroused. So sensual, everything about her turned me on. The heat in her eyes. The way her pupils dilated, her nostrils flared, a flash of tongue on her lip. Better yet if she bared a little fang.

These were merely appetizers. Sometimes Shara went straight for the feast.

I half expected her to lunge up and sink her fangs into one of us. Hopefully him, because I was too eager to fuck the dragon to come so quickly.

I'd never fucked another Blood for dominance. Companionship, sure. Need, absolutely. Daire, my constant companion for years while we sought a queen, many times.

But never as the queen's alpha who needed to instill the hierarchy in her Blood. That my queen would take pleasure in it too was merely icing on the cake.

Mehen kept her thigh locked beneath his arm, his mouth on her hip. For now, I allowed it. She sat up, her eyes shining black pools, her fangs distended so much that she couldn't close her mouth. She bit the meaty part of her right palm, and the dragon shuddered beneath me. In her bond, I felt him large, dark, and furious, rising up from the depths, coming to the call of her blood.

Closing her fingers over her palm, she kept her hand level, pooling blood on her hand. Eyes heavy lidded, she reached between me and Mehen. I rose up a little, giving her plenty of room to play.

To torment.

But I sucked in my breath when she wrapped her bleeding palm around *my* dick. I'd been fully erect most of the night. How could I not be with my queen in my arms, reclining against me? But her blood, her touch, made my dick swell even more. She leaned in, her lips soft on mine, the brush of fangs making my own descend.

:*Do you have him?*: She asked, her words targeted to my bond alone.

:*Absolutely.*:

She pricked her luscious lips with her fangs and pressed her mouth more fully to mine.

Kissing my queen was always an exquisite experience. But a kiss flavored with her blood…

A deep, rumbling growl rolled from my chest. Hunger. Lust. Need. My fangs ached in time to my heart. No, her heart. I felt how fast her heart pounded in her chest.

Mehen exploded beneath me, desperate to taste her blood. Even though she hadn't offered it to him. Or maybe he just wanted her blood on his skin. Or he was tired of waiting for me to fuck him.

His bond said all the above.

He was strong. I'd give him that. Before I became Shara's alpha, he would have eaten my ass for lunch. But with my queen's blood pumping magic through me, he didn't have a chance. And he knew it.

He just liked the fight.

As much as I did.

Though it did piss me off that he interrupted my queen's kiss and I lost her touch on my dick.

I squeezed his throat harder, denying him air, and rode his body, letting him buck and fight beneath me. He threw his right elbow back, trying to crack me in the chin, but I turned my shoulder into the blow. It still felt like Guillaume's hell horse had kicked me.

"I guess he doesn't want any of your blood after all, my queen."

He stilled immediately. "That would be an incorrect assumption, alpha."

She slid her bleeding hand in between us, giving his ass cheek a good firm squeeze. "Where would you like my blood, dragon?"

"On every inch of me."

35

MEHEN

I'd had enough of this bullshit. I didn't mind torture to a point and I could stand a hell of a lot. Pain. Rough sex. Blood. Bring it the fuck on.

But don't bring my new queen so close, and let her bleed, and expect me to do nothing about it.

Finally, she touched *me* not him, dripping blood on my buttocks. Every drop exquisite torment. Every muscle in my body clenched hard, aching with need. Her blood sent my lust into a brutal spike. If the alpha hadn't already clamped most of my air off, I probably would have tried to fight him again.

"Is this what you wanted?" She whispered, a hint of wicked laughter in her voice that made my fangs and dick throb. I wasn't sure which was bigger at this point. If I tried to bite her, I'd probably cut her in two. Same if I tried to fuck her.

Which was exactly why Rik needed to take the edge off first.

Her blood dripped and smeared and heated my skin, giving his dick something to slide through. He started to push into me, taking his time. Probably trying to be considerate.

Fuck considerate. With a low growl, I pushed back against him, taking him deeper. Fuck. Yeah. I hurt with need. I burned, my muscles twitching, need hammering through me. I reared back as much as he allowed. I didn't need to breathe, not as much as I needed him deep inside me.

Shara trailed her bleeding hand up my side, over my ribs, my shoulder, down my arm. Leaving bloody fingerprints. Every drop burned like liquid fire dropped onto my flesh. Rik already had my head pinned against him, but I tried to throw my head back and roar anyway. My throat raw, tight, constricted by his unrelenting forearm clamped around my neck.

"They are scales," she said. "From a distance, they looked like tattoos."

"The hazard of living as Leviathan for centuries," I rasped out. "The dragon never completely sleeps now."

Rik slid to the hilt inside me, his weight grinding me into the mattress. Fuck. If I wasn't careful, I'd come just from having her touch my scales.

"That would be too easy," Rik rumbled against my ear.

Then he flipped us both to the side, away from our queen, rolling me on top of him. He locked his ankles above my knees and stretched me out flat on my back on top of him. He pulled my head back and thrust up into me, making me arch against him.

Belly. Exposed.

Dick. Exposed.

Did he know what that meant for a dragon to be on his back like this? So vulnerable? Open to anything his mate decided to do to him?

By the grim amusement slicing through his bond, he did. He did indeed.

"Torment him at will, my queen. I recommend biting him at least a dozen times."

She came closer, on her knees beside us. Barely close enough for me to get my fingertips on her thigh. But I could see her. Smell her. Both her heat and her blood. Her eyes gleamed like the night sky filled with a glowing full moon. She looked at my dick and licked her lips and I thought I would die. Literally. My heart stopped. I couldn't breathe as she leaned down. Her luscious lips inches from my dick. Closer.

"I've not had a dick in my mouth yet," she whispered.

Even Rik shuddered beneath me at the thought. I couldn't think of anything that would both turn on and terrify a Blood more than having his queen's fangs so close to his dick. Especially *her* gigantic fangs. I could heal from anything with her blood flowing through me, but none of us would care to have our junk bit off either.

She wrapped her bleeding palm around me and I gritted my teeth, fighting back the climax threatening to erupt. Her touch. The heat of her blood. I gouged my lips with my fangs, using the pain and blood to distract me. Her hair whispered over my groin. I'd never felt sweeter torture. Until she licked the tip of my cock and lightly scratched fang down my length.

With a ragged bellow, I came so hard I wouldn't have been surprised to find my come sprayed on the ceiling. Rik tightened his grip on me, squeezing my air off so that blackness threatened. I couldn't move anything other than my arms. I couldn't even squeeze her thigh or drag her on top of me. I would have too. I wanted to be inside her. Needed it like I needed to breathe.

As I quieted, Rik loosened his grip on my windpipe enough that I could draw in a few shallow breaths. He was still rock hard, a heavy weight inside me, pressing on nerves and muscles that kept me on the edge. It wouldn't be long before I was hard again. Maybe she would take me then.

He laughed softly against my ear. "Our queen is just getting started. She hasn't even fed yet. You think she's going to fuck you before she's slaked her thirst?"

Her tongue lapped at the head of my cock and I twitched, head to toe, like I had the black plague.

"You taste good. Almost as good as blood. There's power in semen too, isn't there?"

"All living fluid," I panted. "Has power. Some. More than others."

"Go carefully, my queen," Rik warned her. "It can be…"

Before he could finish the sentence, I felt the heat flare in her. Her simmering desire fanned hotter and she took my softened cock into her mouth. I felt the slide of her fangs on my flesh, nerves singing with tension. It should have made my balls try to crawl up inside me with terror, but instead, my dick stiffened. Answering her call as eagerly as if she offered me her blood.

She sat back a moment, licking her lips, her eyes closed, fangs glistening. "Addictive? Or just an aphrodisiac?"

"Sometimes both," Rik replied. "It's to a Blood's benefit to make sure his queen wants to taste him again. Blood feeds your power. Come feeds your desire."

"And both mixed together..." Her breath sighed out. "Brace yourself."

I wasn't sure why she warned me.

Until she sank her fangs high on my thigh, her face nearly in my groin.

Climax roared through me again, a compulsion I couldn't deny. I came so hard it hurt. My heart pounded from exertion, my head felt like it was going to explode, and I had a massive cramp in my thigh.

I'd come when she bit me before, but I thought it was only because it'd been so long. If her bite was orgasmic, and Rik told her to bite me a dozen times...

I groaned. And yeah, I arched up again, desperate for more.

She drank from me endlessly. I couldn't believe she could hold so much blood at once. Her power rose like a tsunami destined to obliterate the globe.

Before I was imprisoned, I'd seen plenty of queens, now infamous legends on the winds of time. Lilith. Medusa. Cleopatra. So powerful they were nearly goddesses themselves.

And young Shara Isador would rival their power.

Feeding on a powerful, old Aima like me required more than just a cast-iron belly and an alpha built like Hercules to hold me still long enough to get her fangs in me. She needed to have the stamina and reserves of her own to utilize that much power. The foundation and relays had to be strong enough to handle the load without short circuiting.

My queen's magic system was powerful enough to light up this entire backwards country. And what scared the shit out of me—she was still growing.

Every time she fed on me, she'd get even more powerful. They didn't come much older than me anymore. More powerful. The Triune queens would shit a brick when they realized the level of Blood this young queen had called.

She reared back, blood dripping down her chin, and I had never seen anything more beautiful. With a low moan, she climbed on top of me, straddling my groin, her desire rising to a fevered pitch.

But I couldn't satisfy her. Not after two climaxes minutes apart. A terrible feeling, to know her need, realize she burned, but I couldn't do anything about it.

:*Guillaume*.: she called through the bond.

I couldn't complain that she called another Blood, not when I'd already come twice. Though when the knight came to the edge of the bed and laughed, I'd have gleefully bitten *him* in half if I could have escaped our alpha.

"Now that's quite a predicament."

GUILLAUME

I didn't like Leviathan much and made no effort to conceal that fact. The man's arrogant saunter and sardonic comments set my teeth on edge. And then there was his fucking audacity to try and kill our queen to save his own hide.

That deplorable lack of honor I could not forgive.

Ironic, since I'd killed my first queen. But Shara was no Desideria.

So it was most gratifying to see the mighty dragon pinned like a bug by our alpha, and well used by our queen. Shara had already fed, so I knew full well why she'd called me. Her bond raged out of control with need. She didn't have to tell me to strip.

However, fully armed with my usual arsenal, it was going to take me more than a few minutes to remove all my knives.

I unbuttoned my cuffs and rolled back the sleeves to bare the wrist sheaths on each arm. I started to remove the smallest blade on my left arm, but a surge in her bond made me look up at her.

"Leave them. The leather straps and knives are hot."

I met Rik's gaze over the dragon's shoulder. I wouldn't care to have so many weapons near the bastard while we were in the throes of passion with our queen, though with my blood in her veins, she'd surely be as hard to kill with steel as the headless knight.

"Fuck, you're both idiots," Mehen growled out. "If I'm going to stick her with anything it'll be my dick. Not a knife. I don't need steel to kill her if that's my goal."

I still didn't like it, and neither did Rik.

Shara shifted on top of Mehen's uncooperative groin and groaned with frustration. "Please, G, I need you."

Fuck that shit. My queen should never have to beg. I yanked the shirt over my head without unbuttoning it and attacked my pants while toeing off my boots.

I climbed onto the bed and Rik unlocked his ankles to make room for me on top of both of their legs. She pressed back against me, her fingers settling on my forearms, pulling me close, stroking over the leather and steel strapped to my arms. The chest harness carried my larger blade and I'm sure it had to be uncomfortable against her back, but she didn't seem to mind. In fact, she leaned down toward Leviathan's waiting hands and lifted that hot, sweet pussy higher for me.

But I didn't like the dragon's hands rising eagerly toward her breasts. I slammed his wrists down to the mattress and leaned over her, using my weight to pin his arms flat.

He hissed at me.

I chuckled as I slid deep into our queen, making her moan. "How does it feel to be fucked by our alpha, while I fuck our queen on top of you?"

"Fucking amazing," he growled, arching up beneath her, trying to rub his belly against her breasts.

I sank to the hilt inside her and she quivered against me. Pressing my mouth to her ear, I whispered, "I think you should bite him again."

"Definitely," Rik replied, a hard glint in his eyes.

Mehen groaned. "At least let me get inside you first."

In your dreams, asshole. Though I didn't say it aloud. Instead, I shifted up to my feet to gain some leverage. Two sets of Blood thighs were too tall for me to do much thrusting from my knees. Plus, getting my weight off their legs gave Rik more leeway to push up into the dragon.

Using our queen's bond, it was easy to time our thrusts. Rik shoved up when I drove deep, just like the third man wasn't even there. Exactly what we wanted him to think about. He had no part in our queen's pleasure, other than giving her blood as often as she wanted it. He was her food. Her donor. We were her dicks. We gave her pleasure. We met her need.

I felt her climax rising through her bond and drove deeper, harder. I knew full well what she liked now. I knew how much she could take. And I knew that she'd want my bite when her pleasure broke.

Her breath caught and her head fell back against my shoulder, her neck curved to the side in invitation. I sank my fangs into her throat and she cried out, digging her fingers into Mehen's chest. Her pleasure spiked through our bonds. Rik bent his knees, bracing his feet to drive up harder into the man on top of him. Mehen groaned as our alpha came inside him.

I fought back my own release despite her blood filling my mouth. Hot, spiced silk and velvet, spun sugar and decadent wine, swirling on my tongue.

"Give me some," Mehen rasped, his eyes burning pits of lust. "One taste of your blood and I'll be rock hard again. Bite me as many times as you want as long as I'm inside you."

Holding his gaze, I clamped my mouth tighter on her throat, refusing to let a single drop escape. It was her choice. If she told me to give him some, I would. Even if I thought he hadn't earned the right yet.

She leaned down toward him and I moved with her, keeping my mouth locked on her throat. Her power flowed into me, lighting up my nerves like a circuit board. Even now, she managed to heal me a little more. Soothing scars, both inside and out while hardening my gift even more. I seriously doubted if anyone would be able to injure me with steel at all now, though her fangs had no problem penetrating me.

He leaned up since Rik had loosened his grip a bit, eyes blazing with thirst and lust both, but she ducked and sank her fangs into his pectoral.

He bellowed, thrashing beneath us, coming hard with nothing left in his balls. Dry spurts shook his big body. Blood dripped down his chin and throat where he'd gnashed his own lips.

She lifted her head, dribbling blood on his chest. "Hold his head."

"Gladly," Rik replied, tightening his forearm on the man's throat again, and wrapping his other hand around his forehead to hold him steady.

She slowly crawled up Mehen's body, licking blood from his skin. Which gave me plenty of time to shift forward with her, using her movement to slowly slide and thrust inside her. She licked his blood from his chin up to his lips.

He tried to lean up, whether to kiss her or bite her, I couldn't say. But Rik squeezed his big palm and tightened his forearm, ready to pop the bastard's head off with an easy snap.

"So mean," she whispered against his lips, drinking from him even as she kissed him. "So angry."

"My queen." The fight bled out of him. He quit struggling against Rik's grip and softened his mouth, opening his lips for her instead of trying to inhale her. "*Please.*"

I wasn't sure which touched her the most: that he finally called her my queen without an edge in his tone that said he wanted to kill her, or the fact that he pleaded for her rather than demanded. Or both. Regardless, she lifted her head, bared her fangs, and sank them into my forearm rather than him.

With a roar, I plunged deep inside her, shaking, her fangs pushing me over the edge. I shuddered against her, spurt after spurt rocking through me. And yeah, I lost my punctures on her throat.

I expected him to surge up and take my place at her

throat, but he didn't move. His emerald eyes flashed like chipped ice, locked on the twin ribbons of blood trailing down her throat.

But he didn't take what she hadn't offered to him.

Even I had to admit that was impressive. Maybe Mehen was finally starting to trust her. Or more likely, he'd simply come too many times to get his damned brain to work.

"All right, my dragon. Show me what you're made of."

SHARA

He lurched up and locked his mouth to Guillaume's bite, sucking hard enough to make my throat ache. But it was a good hurt that tightened my lower body too. I half expected him to flip me over on my back in an aggressive roll, but he didn't haul me into position, even though I felt his hardened cock beneath me.

Maybe I'd put a dent in his desire by biting him so many times. Or maybe he was finally settling into his role. Not that I even knew what that was exactly.

Rik sat up, still underneath us all. But he didn't seemed bothered by the fact. At all.

In fact, he wrapped his palm around Mehen's dick and

squeezed him hard enough the man's breath caught on a moan. Touch. What he craved, even though he might be too proud to admit it.

"Is this what you want next, my queen?"

I wrapped one arm around Mehen's neck and the other around Rik's shoulder, keeping them both close so that the dragon was sandwiched between us. "Yes."

Guillaume's hands settled on my hips and he lifted me up over the tip of Mehen's dick and let me slide slowly down over him.

:*Hold me too,*: I said through the bond.

Pressing against my back, he wrapped his arms around the three of us.

Every inch of Mehen touched somebody. He relaxed against us, supported in our arms. His head fell back against Rik's shoulder and he panted softly, eyes closed, soaking us in.

"So long," he said hoarsely, his voice cracking on what might have been a sob.

I nuzzled into his neck, breathing in his dragon scent, mixed with Rik's hot iron and Guillaume's horse. Just smelling them made me tighten on his dick. But he already came several times, painfully hard. I didn't want to damage him…

He snorted and tipped his hips up against me, giving a little stir and friction inside me. "As if that would even be possible. No Blood ever complained that his queen used him for too much sex."

I leaned back, seating him deeper. "I didn't think you were Blood."

He shrugged, his eyes flashing. "I don't know if a king can ever be Blood, not really. Let alone me. I had a lifetime of independence and then centuries of imprisonment where I could do nothing but simmer with my rage."

His gaze dropped to my throat, his fangs adding a lisp to his words. I felt his hunger, but more, a desperate need to pierce me. To bury his fangs in me as deeply as his dick. He wanted to be inside me as much as possible.

I tipped my head to the side, offering the other side of my throat that Guillaume hadn't marked.

Waiting a moment, Mehen gave a wary look at the knight behind me, his back tensing as if my alpha might thump him if he made his move. "I do know one thing."

"Yeah?"

He sank his fangs into my throat, making me arch against him. :*I'm yours.*:

Gasping, I jerked between him and Guillaume. It felt like a live wire connected his fangs and his dick, pulsing and sparking with power. A positive and negative charge that met and exploded inside me. I'd never felt anything quite like it. He felt bigger, wider, his fangs impossibly long. In moments, I came again, but the current didn't relent.

In fact, my pleasure made that connection surge even higher. My muscles quivered and I cried out again. Unable to stop the climax pounding through me.

Guillaume's arms squeezed me hard and he locked his

mouth back over his marks. Rik growled and sealed his mouth over mine. Our bonds flowed hotter, winding through my mind like rivers of flaming oil.

We were going to come again.

Even Daire, who wasn't in the room. I felt him on the couch, quivering with me, panting through my desire. Worried for Xin and Nevarre, I touched their bonds and found them both on the verge with me. Shifted back to human form, Xin leaned against a pine, gasping for breath, and Nevarre had a hand braced by the other Blood's head, leaning against Xin. Needing touch.

The same as Mehen.

The same as me.

All my Blood, even though they weren't touching me, were going to come.

I had a feeling that I wouldn't be able to stop coming as long as Mehen was inside me. The easiest way to make him finish…

I sank my fangs into his shoulder.

He thrashed against me, unable to move much with Rik and Guillaume squeezing us so tightly together. He let out a muffled roar against my throat, unwilling to miss a single drop of my blood. His hips jerked beneath me, lifting us both up off Rik's thighs, but finally the brutal pleasure loop broke and his softened cock slipped out of me.

Tumbled down into a heap, we all lay tangled together, a quivering mass of exhausted muscles. Distantly, I felt Xin and Nevarre leaning against each other, holding each other up until they caught their breath.

Daire was by himself.

:Not for long,: Rik said in our bond, and then I felt him call, *:Daire.:*

He must have already been sneaking in because barely a second went by and he launched up onto the mattress with us.

On top of me, naturally, because with three other massive Blood in bed, there wasn't a spare spot for another body.

Daire being Daire, he managed to scoot and worm his way beneath and around me so that I wasn't squished at all, just wrapped in smoking hot flesh. His hair slid down over my cheek and he started up a rumbling purr that vibrated his chest against me.

"Fuck," Mehen said in a disgusted voice at my ear. "Does he do that all night?"

"Usually," Daire replied cheerfully.

My head was on Rik's chest, his arm curved around my back, his hand on my stomach. Mehen had his head on Rik too. Daire had wedged himself in partially between Guillaume and Rik, but my knight's thigh was tossed over mine, his groin hot against my thigh.

"Can you all sleep like this?"

"Of course," they all replied except for Mehen, who said, "Fuck, no. But no Blood is going to waste time sleeping when he's in his queen's bed."

Guillaume grunted. "The snake has a point."

"Dragon," Mehen retorted.

Daire purred louder.

Smiling, I closed my eyes, enveloped by my Blood.

Keep reading for a preview of QUEEN TAKES QUEEN. Be sure to sign up for Joely's newsletter to find out when it's available or pre-order today!

QUEEN TAKES QUEEN

SHARA

Lounging in bed was a luxury I'd been denied most of my adult life. When you're on the run, afraid for your life, the last thing you want to do is close your eyes. Let alone drop your guard enough to actually sleep soundly and deep. Sleeping made me vulnerable, and alone, I couldn't afford to be vulnerable. I couldn't relax one minute without worrying I'd end up dead.

That fear was long gone now. I could lie in bed all hours of the day or night and sleep without a single worry. I didn't have to keep one eye on the door, or strain my ears to hear a whisper in the hallway. Because I would never be alone again, not with my Blood by my side.

Before I opened my eyes, I liked to touch each of my six Blood bonds one by one, locating their position. Partly to know who was in bed with me, but also so they would each feel me touch their bond. They'd know I was awake and well, and I'd know *they* were well.

Of course as my alpha and my biggest, baddest Blood, Rik probably knew I was awake before I realized it, but I always felt for him first, even though I knew he'd be right there beside me.

Until he wasn't.

He isn't here.

I jerked upright, my heart pounding. "Rik?"

He hollered from the bathroom. "In here, my queen. Sorry, I didn't meant to worry you."

"Even alphas need to take a leak now and then," Xin said beside me.

Whew. My heart still pounded, but I lay back down beside him and curled into his side. Even in his human form, Xin smelled like a wolf. Well, that didn't come anywhere close to a good description. He smelled like a wolf, paused in a clearing in the middle of an ancient forest beneath a full moon on a cold winter's night, with frost and snow crystallized on his fur.

Touching him felt so strange with that image in my head, because his skin was so hot and smooth. I ran my palms over his chest and shoulders, enjoying the play of muscle and sinew beneath his skin. He was one of my leaner Blood, but no less powerful or strong as the others. As my second-oldest Blood—born in 712 AD—he had endured centuries upon centuries of a cold, untouchable service to his queen. To say he was starved for touch was the understatement of the year. All my Blood were starved to a point, but he and Mehen, my oldest Blood, who'd been imprisoned as the mighty dragon, Leviathan, definitely felt the need most severely.

I pressed closer to Xin, tangling my legs with his and sliding one hand around to his back. My eyes drifted shut and I relaxed into his embrace, just enjoying the feeling of companionship.

Okay, I was starved for touch too.

"Tell me something about you," Xin whispered against my forehead, stroking my back. "Something no one else knows. Something good."

It would be impossible for me to tell him a secret when my Blood bonds tied our hearts and minds together. They usually knew what I was thinking before I realized myself. But he would at least be the first to hear the words.

Silent a few moments, I tried to think of something not just good, but special. "It's funny, but when you're a kid, you think that your life is normal and everyone else is weird, you know? So I thought everybody had terrible nightmares and saw red glaring eyes outside their windows. I thought everyone was scared of the dark because of the monsters. So when I talked about it at school, I got labeled 'special' pretty quickly. After a few years, Mom took me out of public school and I stayed home with her. Dad was gone by then, but she really tried hard to make things normal and safe for me. Fun, even. But I didn't have any friends, and as much as I loved her, I was still lonely, even before she died."

He made a low sound against my skin. "I said something good, my queen."

"I'm getting there, I promise! So I didn't have a lot of friends, and I hung out mostly with Mom. But all through my life, little things happened that made me feel like I wasn't alone. That I was watched over. Like I had a guardian angel. Maybe I'd find a flower on the porch, something tropical and hot pink, when we didn't have anything like it growing on our street. Or a really pretty red leaf in the middle of winter, pressed to the windshield of the car. Or I'd smell something sweet and soothing at night when I was scared, and I'd close my eyes, and it'd feel like someone was there, watching over me. I didn't know then who it was, but now… I think it was my real mother. Even though she was dead and I had no idea of her existence, she was always with me."

I didn't bother saying her name. Thanks to a geas Esetta Isador had placed upon all Aima, no one living could say or remember her name. I didn't have that problem, since I'd technically died the first time I came into my power when Rik and Daire found me just a few miles from here.

My throat ached and my eyes burned, but with happy tears. "Even though she knew I had no idea that she even existed, she still made sure I felt her presence. That's pretty special."

Mom would always be Mom, the woman who raised me, who died to keep me safe, even though she was technically my aunt. But now I had Esetta, too. I had her words she'd written to me. Even if no one else could remember her name, I would always remember.

Thank you, Esetta.

Something soft brushed my cheek like a feather—though I didn't see or sense anything.

"Thank you, my queen," Xin whispered.

He didn't tighten his grip or press against me, but something tugged on my sixth sense in the bond. I sank deeper into his bond, now used to the gray fog that seemed to surround him. Each of my Blood's bonds felt different in my head, and Xin had always been distant. Not that he tried to deliberately hide from me, not at all. His gift of invisibility wrapped his bond and made him harder for me to sense. His former queen hadn't wanted any of her Bloods' emotions to leak into her head, and so he'd learned a long time ago to keep his emotions tightly under wrap. When I first met him, I'd had to jump off a metaphorical skyscraper to find his true self. It was easier now, but I still had to reach to feel him.

Raw need raged through him so fiercely it made my breath catch on a soft gasp. I already knew he was starved for affection, but this… A gnawing black hole ate through his bond. He needed my blood. He needed to fuck. Preferably at the same time. More, though, he burned to be alone with me. To have me to himself. Like this. Just me and him in bed together. Even if only for a few minutes.

He'd never had that. None of my Blood had me alone, except maybe Rik. And even then… How often was I completely alone with even him? With six men all dedicated to protecting me and seeing to my every want and need, it was usually crowded around me.

Especially in my bed.

"Xin. Why didn't you tell me?"

The corner of his eyes crinkled slightly but otherwise his face remained smooth. "Tell you what, my queen?"

Again, he wasn't trying to hide or obscure anything. He honestly didn't know. He was so far removed from his own emotions that he had no idea what I sensed. It was his nature to remain controlled, hidden in plain slight, without complaint or request or reaction. He was a blade. A weapon I sent to kill my enemies. My food when I wanted it. He had no expectations other than I use his particularly deadly talents.

And that damned near broke my heart. Because he was so much more to me than that. They all were.

I cupped his nape and rolled over onto my back, drawing him toward me. On his elbow, he looked down at me, more curious than anything. Still waiting for my command. He wouldn't act. Not of his own volition.

So be it.

I threaded my fingers in his hair and gave a little teasing tug. "Rik's going to take a walk while you fuck me."

XIN

Her words did not make sense. I stared at her, afraid to breathe or move a single muscle until I understood. A queen never sent her alpha away. An alpha never left his queen's side. That Rik trusted me to guard her long enough to hit the bathroom was already a boon.

A Blood was lucky to have even three minutes alone with his queen in a lifetime.

To have her alone...

Her blood *and* her body...

It was unheard of.

My last queen had never allowed me to touch even her hand. Her Blood did not feed from her directly. Even among her full court, my physical interactions had been limited to feeding from my sibs. Sexual need was a weakness.

Something I'd cut out of myself a very long time ago.

At least so I'd thought.

"You cannot," I finally said, each word cutting my throat like broken glass. "Rik would not allow it."

Eyes smoldering, she smiled slowly, each incremental curve of her lips an invitation to insanity. Soft, full lips. The delicate tip of her tongue. The flash of white fang descending. "Oh really? I'm your queen. I decide who's in my bed. And this queen hungers."

"Take every drop of blood in my body, my queen."

Her lashes fluttered down over her gleaming eyes. "I want more than your blood."

I swallowed hard. "I will give you anything. Anything you ask. Anything at all."

She didn't elaborate, which made my nerves tighten like a drum. She had a need. I must meet it. Whatever it was. That's what Blood did. My alpha would expect no less than I give her exactly what she needed. Even better if I could offer it before she must ask.

But a Blood did not initiate sex with his queen, especially *without* her alpha.

Her hand stroked down my chest, her fingers trailing over each ridge and hollow. My abdominal muscles quivered with her advance. A tiny crack in my control.

The chilled silence of my gift filled my head like impenetrable fog. Still. Calm. Silent. If Rik happened to look at the bed, he wouldn't be able to see me here with our queen, unless he used her bond to locate me. An unfortunate side effect. I didn't want to hide—but I had to maintain my ability to serve. I could do nothing about the erection, but I wouldn't make a sound or demand or request. Never.

"No," she whispered against my lips as her hand closed around my cock. "Look at me."

I hadn't realized I'd closed my eyes. Stupid. Another weakness I couldn't afford. I couldn't shut my eyes when my queen's life was in my hands. When I focused on her face, she tugged me firmly by my cock, pulling me on top of her, her thighs opening to cradle me against her.

Shit. Fuck. Another quiver slipped through the stillness, a twitch that slithered down my spine and made my hips move, dragging my dick through her grip. Wholly involuntary. Wholly unacceptable.

I pierced my bottom lip with my fangs, letting blood fill my mouth. The small pain distracted me enough so that I didn't move again. Even when she wiggled beneath me, sliding into position to take me inside her.

Her thighs came up around my waist and I was almost lost. Almost undone. A crumbled wreck.

In my mind, I fled to an abandoned temple at the top of the mountain near my birthplace, wrapped in fog and lost in time. I went there as a child, my safe and secret place that no one knew of but me. I ran up the treacherous slopes, my lungs burning, thighs aching, and pushed open the tattered woven mat that served as a door.

And found Shara lying on silken cushions, pulling me to her like a ceaseless tide.

"I want your emotion," she whispered against my mouth. Licking my lips. Demanding I give her the blood she must have smelled, even though I carefully kept any from dripping on her. "I want you open to me. Not locked away, lost in silent fog. I want you here, eye to eye, even if it's raw and ugly. Share your mind and heart with me."

"I cannot," I whispered, my voice breaking with the overwhelming failure. I would give her anything. My life. My blood. But I couldn't give her my emotions. I didn't know how. And even if I did figure out how to unlock that door after centuries...

I feared it would leave me broken. Unusable. Could her best blade serve as a killer if I became crippled with emotion?

I couldn't think. Not with her muscles tightening on my dick. Her mouth on mine, teasing my lips apart so she could taste my blood.

"Show me," she whispered, her words a caress that my starved body soaked up like a sponge. "Show me everything.

I want it. I need it. I want to know you, Xin. I want to *see* you. All of you."

See me.

See me huddled in the corner of my hiding place, hugging my knees to my chest with arms too scrawny, legs like sticks, my back a mass of welts. I learned early not to cry or protest or react in any way. A Blood never asked for mercy or complained at cruelty, and I was born to be Blood. While human children would have been learning to read and write, I killed my first thrall. When other human boys my age would have been thinking about girls, I was tested by the best and most powerful alphas within a week's ride of my home court.

They'd sniffed me. Bit me. Tasted my blood. Watched me fight against the other potential Blood candidates.

But Wu Tien's alpha woke me in the dead of night and took me through the court to stand outside a dark house.

"A threat to my queen sleeps within. She wants this threat dead but no one must see or hear you. If you're successful, she'll call you as Blood."

Most people probably would have asked how many were inside and which one was the target. Which one I should kill.

But not me.

The alpha had chosen his words carefully. If no one must see or hear me…

They would not live to tell the tale.

I had done my duty. Beautifully quick, silent and deadly. Though I had cried without sound when I killed the youngest. A girl, younger than me. Her eyes had opened a moment before my steel bit into her throat, pupils flaring with terror though she didn't cry out. I had felt something in her. Something that called to what I was becoming.

A fledgling queen. Calling a fledgling Blood. Calling me.

I had always wondered what would have become of me if I'd refused Wu Tien's order that night. If I had answered the still, quiet call I felt in that child. Before I slit her throat as my new queen ordered. Though I killed many queens through the centuries, I never felt that call again.

Until Shara Isador pulled me to her side in Kansas City, Missouri only days ago. Would I have killed her on Wu Tien's command? Would I have been able to look down at her sleeping beside Rik and slit her throat?

My gift would have made it possible. Rik would never have seen me. While his queen died in his arms. *Our* queen. Mine.

Her eyes swam with tears. "How many did you kill that night?"

Ice spread through my veins, freezing my marrow, slowing my heartbeat to a ponderous, uneven gait. I couldn't have moved a finger to defend her or myself. "Five. The target was Wu Tien's eight-year-old niece who would be queen one day."

"How old were you?"

"Twelve."

Her eyes flared, her emotions slicing me like the knight's deadly blades. Surprise. Horror. Shock. "You killed at twelve years old?"

"No. I killed much earlier. But I was Blooded that very night. All the Wu queens took Blood early in life. It made us easier to train how best to serve."

"My father was killed when I was six years old. If I had the knowledge of how to kill the monsters, I would have slaughtered them all that night. Without hesitation."

Ice spread through my body, brutal cold that cut through my lungs and encased my heart. It didn't matter. I didn't need to breathe. "If I had known of your need, I would have killed them for you. Your parents would still be here with you today."

"I have a need now," she whispered against my lips.

So cold. I couldn't understand why her lips didn't freeze to mine. Why she still found my blood to taste, rather than a frozen river in my veins. "Yes, my queen. Whatever it is. Yes."

She tightened her grip on me. Her fingers squeezed my neck, holding me close. One hand slid down my back, gripping my ass, pulling me in harder. Her thighs hugged me. Her mouth on mine. Heaven. The most exquisite torture.

Her hips undulated in a slow roll against me, her fingers digging into me. Pulling me. Demanding. Something. Her lips were hard on mine. Her tongue slid into my mouth, risking my fangs. I couldn't make them retract and I didn't know why. I'd never bitten my queen until Shara. My fangs throbbed, extending even longer, vicious icicles that would tear her tongue and shred her lips. I would hurt her. Wound her. And not even mean it.

Rik would have my head on a plate if I hurt one hair on her head. I would serve it to him myself.

She groaned, a soft aching sound that cracked something inside me. She needed. My queen. Mine. I fisted my hands in the bedding and ground harder against her. If I could not give her everything she desired, I would at least give her pleasure. She drank blood from my lips, but I drank her cries and sighs and moans, muffled only by my own mouth. More beautiful music I had never heard in my life. I wanted more of it. More cries. Louder.

The crack widened inside me, slicing me to ribbons.

"Yes," she groaned against my lips.

Blood. Her blood. I didn't know if she punctured her lip, or if I did, but I could taste her on my tongue.

Ice shattered. Splintered. Jagged and sharp. I heard a guttural cry, a raw, ragged growl.

That rattled *my* chest.

I had made that sound. Me. The silent, invisible killer.

"I want to hear you, Xin." She arched beneath me, her head rolling back, her throat bared. "Please. Show me. Tell me without words how much you love me. I want to hear it."

My name on her lips. Her throat offered to me. With a plea.

I thrust deep, every muscle straining on a groan that hurt my vocal chords. Again. The headboard thudded against the wall with the force of my thrusts. I tried to draw back, spare her, but she'd have none of that. She kept saying my name. Aloud. Her eyes locked on me.

Seeing me.

Calling me.

My wolf snarled, my spine bulging with the effort of keeping him contained. Claws burst from my hands and I shredded the sheets. Better to destroy the bed than damage my queen. Though her nails raked down my spine and dug into my buttocks, urging me deeper, harder. Her words a whip.

"Yes, yes, Xin, please. Show me everything. Let me in."

I was afraid I would hurt her—but I was the one who cracked open, broken in a million pieces.

All the kills I'd made over centuries in Wu Tien's name. Enough blood to fill an ocean. Wasted. Lives destroyed. Entire bloodlines lost forever.

So much regret.

When I had become a killer who lived only for the hunt?

Emptiness. A million lifetimes lived alone—while surrounded by people. Unseen, unheard, untouched, unneeded. Until my queen pointed at me, and her alpha whispered a name in my head. A target. My prey to hunt.

Never my queen herself though. She'd never touched my bond, my mind, my body. Let alone my heart.

No wonder I lived for the kill. It was all I'd ever had.

I tried to find the boy I'd been. The boy who'd fled to the forgotten temple on the mountain. But that child had died long ago. I'd never known my mother or father. As customary in those times, I'd been taken from my home at age three and raised among the other candidates. I'd shown early promise. They'd seen the wolf in me. The predator who would kill and kill and kill.

Shara tightened around me, her pleasure rising in our bond. Shining like beacon in the dead of night, a star bright enough to dim the noonday sun. I didn't want her to see the centuries stretched out like a graveyard with all the tombstones I'd wrought with my own hands.

How could she love a killer like me? She would turn away. Exile me. I deserved it.

She sank her fangs into my chest and I roared with release. I jammed my dick deep into her. So deep. I wanted to disappear. Into her. Forever. Grunting with effort, I rutted on her like a mad beast, unable to stop coming. I sank my fangs into her throat and drank her pleasure directly from her vein.

In a vast, ancient forest, her scent floated through hoary, twisted trees heavy with vines and moss. A hint of laughter on the breeze. A challenge. My wolf darted after her into the shadows. Silent. Deadly. Hungry.

But cold no more.

RIK

Evidently not even alphas were above jealousy.

Forehead braced against the bathroom door, I fought my need to be with my queen. She needed this time alone with Xin. With each of us.

She needed. I provided.

Even if that meant I was not the one holding her now.

I'd never seen a queen like Shara before. She loved each of us. Really and truly loved us. She wanted to touch us. All of us. She wanted to sleep with us, make love, sleep again, feed, dance, party, eat, laugh, everything. I loved it. I loved her. I loved them.

All of them. I wanted their happiness as much as I wanted hers. But I'd sworn my life to fulfilling *her* every need. Not theirs.

It would be easier if she didn't love us each so much. Easier for me. Not easier for her.

Xin was right. The more I loved her, and the more she loved me, the more I wanted to be alone with her too. A selfish need, and something I must guard against to ensure my queen received everything she wanted and more. My jealousy would only hurt her, and it would be too easy as alpha to drive them away from her.

I'd seen it happen many times before. Alphas had to be close to their queen at all times, yes. Alphas gained the most power from their queen, they fed her the most, and fed *from* her the most. They needed to be the strongest because they were the last line in her defense.

But that power easily went to an alpha's head. Power to choose who to send on guard duty. Who to allow into her bed. Who would be allowed to feed her first. Ultimately the queen had final say, absolutely. But it was an alpha's job to keep her Blood in line and deal with any discipline and hierarchy issues without drawing it to her attention.

The larger her court, the easier it would be for these kinds of abuses. And it was abuse in my mind, a huge abuse of power. My queen would be stronger because all of her Blood were strong. Because we all fed from her nearly daily. We all shared in her pleasure and her magic openly. She was well-fed and terrifyingly strong.

Which made us all a nightmare for anyone who even thought to harm her.

I would ensure each of her Blood had time with her alone, as Xin did now. They needed it. She needed it.

I lifted my head, sensing the change in her bond. The subtle tug on me that signaled she wanted me with her. I opened the door and paused at the side of the bed.

Xin lay sprawled on top of her, still panting, unable to move. She'd used him well and hard, breaking through the reserve that had been ingrained in him from his former queen at such an early age. Not an easy feat.

But my queen was up for any challenge.

I hid nothing from her. She felt how hard it had been for me to stay in the bathroom while she fucked another man. Even a man I'd shared her bed with several times before. It was different when it was just him. When I had to stand there and feel her pleasure in our bond and know I had no part in giving it to her.

She met my gaze and held out her hand. :*Thank you,*: she said softly, touching only my bond. :*You're an incredible alpha and I love you more everyday.*:

I settled into bed beside her and lifted her hand to my mouth, pressing a kiss to her palm. :*You're an incredible queen and I love you more than life itself.*:

"Sorry." Xin lifted his head a little, sweat dripping down

his forehead, but quickly dropped his face back against Shara's throat. "Alpha."

I draped an arm over his back and pulled them both into my embrace. "No need for apologies, Xin. You gave our queen exactly what she asked for. You'll never hear me discipline you for that."

"You may change your mind," he panted. "If I'm no use to you now."

"What are you talking about?" Shara's voice sharpened. "Why would you no longer be of use to us?"

Xin shifted off to her other side, but didn't withdraw completely. "No offense, my queen, but you broke me."

He didn't mean to upset or hurt her, but I felt the surge of heartache in her bond and I very nearly thumped him on the head for it. "I give you a boon and you're a dickhead about it."

He blinked, which in Daire or Mehen would have been a very vocal, very loud retort. "I am?"

"You are," I said agreeably.

"I've only ever been a killer. A silent, deadly, and most importantly, emotionless, blade." He ducked his head. "I don't know that I can assassinate your targets now, my queen, if I can't find that stillness again."

She cupped his chin and tugged his face back up to hers. Leaning in close, she glared at him, her bond a fierce, white-hot blade of ice. "I would rather have you here, looking at me, talking to me, letting me see into your heart, than ever have an assassin. Even if you never kill again."

"What if your goddess meant for you to send me after

Marne Ceresa or Keisha Skye?" Xin asked softly, regret clogging his words. "And now, I'm unable to kill them? What then, my queen?"

She sat up, tossing her hair back off her shoulders. Her face hard as marble, her neck long and graceful, breasts jutting proudly, blood trickling down her throat.

My queen. My goddess. "Then I'll fucking kill them myself."

Pre-order QUEEN TAKES QUEEN

ABOUT THE AUTHOR

Joely Sue Burkhart has always loved heroes who hide behind a mask, the darker and more dangerous the better. Whether cool, sophisticated billionaire, brutal bloodthirsty assassin, or simply a man tortured by his own needs, they all wear masks to protect themselves. Once they finally give you a peek into the passionate, twisted secrets they're hiding, they always fall hard and fast. Dare to look beneath the mask with delicious BDSM in a wide variety of genres with Joely on her website, www.joelysueburkhart.com.

If you have Kindle Unlimited, you can read all her indie books for free!

Wondering what's next? Sign up for her newsletter and receive exclusive free content.

ALSO BY JOELY SUE BURKHART

Their Vampire Queen, reverse harem vampire romance

Free in Kindle Unlimited

QUEEN TAKES KNIGHTS

QUEEN TAKES KING

QUEEN TAKES QUEEN

Zombie Category Romance, paranormal romance

Free in Kindle Unlimited

THE ZOMBIE BILLIONAIRE'S VIRGIN WITCH

THE MUMMY'S CAPTIVE WITCH

Blood & Shadows, erotic fantasy

The Shanhasson Trilogy and Prologue

Free in Kindle Unlimited

THE HORSE MASTER OF SHANHASSON

THE ROSE OF SHANHASSON

THE ROAD TO SHANHASSON

RETURN TO SHANHASSON

Keldari Fire

SURVIVE MY FIRE

THE FIRE WITHIN

Mythomorphoses, Paranormal/SF Romance

Free in Kindle Unlimited

BEAUTIFUL DEATH

The Connaghers, contemporary erotic romance

Free in Kindle Unlimited

LETTERS TO AN ENGLISH PROFESSOR

DEAR SIR, I'M YOURS

HURT ME SO GOOD

YOURS TO TAKE

NEVER LET YOU DOWN

MINE TO BREAK

Billionaires in Bondage, contemporary erotic romance

(re-releasing in 2017 from Entangled Publishing)

THE BILLIONAIRE SUBMISSIVE

THE BILLIONAIRE'S INK MISTRESS

THE BILLIONAIRE'S CHRISTMAS BARGAIN

The Wellspring Chronicles, erotic fantasy

Free in Kindle Unlimited

NIGHTGAZER

A Killer Need, Erotic Romantic Suspense

ONE CUT DEEPER

TWO CUTS DARKER

THREE CUTS DEADER

A Jane Austen Space Opera, SF/Steampunk erotic romance

LADY WYRE'S REGRET, free read prequel

LADY DOCTOR WYRE

HER GRACE'S STABLE

LORD REGRET'S PRICE

Historical Fantasy Erotica

GOLDEN

The Maya Bloodgates, paranormal romance

BLOODGATE, free read prequel

THE BLOODGATE GUARDIAN

THE BLOODGATE WARRIOR

Printed in Great Britain
by Amazon